Praise for *The Frog King*

"Probably the funniest young-guy-in-New-York novel since *Bright Lights, Big City*."
   —**Bret Easton Ellis**

"The literary invention, metaphorical pizzazz, and sheer cleverness of the prose and wordplay in *The Frog King* is astonishing."
   —***The Wall Street Journal***

"One of the more appealing literary narrators to surface recently . . . Davies has created a clever tale that delivers moments of simple beauty."
   —***Chicago Tribune***

"Truly hilarious and so much more—*totally* original and yet classic, romantic, and real. With his first book, Davies has become one of my all-time favorite authors. And since I can't kiss Harry—hard to believe he's just a character in a book—I'll kiss the book instead."
   —**Jennifer Belle**

"In his sly, slippery way, Davies picks apart language and puts it back together, offering us a tell-all exposé of the publishing industry. . . . Davies's story is as touching and hilarious as Nick Hornby's *High Fidelity*, as heartfelt and ironic as Dave Eggers's *A Heartbreaking Work of Staggering Genius*. [And] unlike Eggers, Davies delivers right to the last page."
   —***The Baltimore Sun***

"Harry Driscoll is a young man on his own in New York. He is touching, funny, often maddening beyond belief, but I rooted for him all the way. *The Frog King* is quite an extraordinary first novel."
   —**Dominick Dunne**

"Adam Davies has a delicious command of the English language. He coins so many phrases in *The Frog King*, he should probably start his own currency. . . . Kiss this frog. You won't be sorry."
   —*St. Petersburg Times*

"Wildly funny and original, Adam Davies perfectly recalls the crazy days of being young and daring and clueless about love and life and work. *The Frog King* is a captivating joyride from the very first page."
   —**Laura Zigman**

"*The Frog King* takes the coming-of-age-of-a-young-writer-living-and-self-destructing-in-New-York genre to its highest level. It's so funny, timely, and smart that the fact that it's really a love story sneaks up on you, till it's too late and you're really sucked into the tragicomic romance. Broken hearts, lives in ruins, and a little bit of redemption—what's not to love?"
   —*New City Chicago*

"Harry is an incurable know-it-all, part Holden Caulfield, part Alexander Portnoy. . . . Harry and Evie have a high-octane office banter, like Rosalind Russell and Cary Grant in *His Girl Friday*. [This] roller-coaster story is charm itself."
   —*New York Newsday*

"A frisky coming-of-age novel sure to have reviewers reaching for *Bright Lights, Big City* analogies and *High Fidelity* comparisons."
   —*Entertainment Weekly*

Also by Adam Davies

The Frog King

Goodbye Lemon

Adam Davies

Riverhead Books

New York

THE BERKLEY PUBLISHING GROUP
Published by the Penguin Group
Penguin Group (USA) Inc.
375 Hudson Street, New York, New York 10014, USA
Penguin Group (Canada), 90 Eglinton Avenue East, Suite 700, Toronto, Ontario
M4P 2Y3, Canada (a division of Pearson Penguin Canada Inc.)
Penguin Books Ltd., 80 Strand, London WC2R 0RL, England
Penguin Ireland, 25 St. Stephen's Green, Dublin 2, Ireland (a division of Penguin Books
Ltd.)
Penguin Group (Australia), 250 Camberwell Road, Camberwell, Victoria 3124, Australia
(a division of Pearson Australia Group Pty. Ltd.)
Penguin Books India Pvt. Ltd., 11 Community Centre, Panchsheel Park, New Delhi—
110 017, India
Penguin Group (NZ), cnr Airborne and Rosedale Roads, Albany, Auckland 1310, New
Zealand (a division of Pearson New Zealand Ltd.)
Penguin Books (South Africa) (Pty.) Ltd., 24 Sturdee Avenue, Rosebank, Johannesburg
2196, South Africa

Penguin Books Ltd., Registered Offices: 80 Strand, London WC2R 0RL, England

This is a work of fiction. Names, characters, places, and incidents either are the product
of the author's imagination or are used fictitiously, and any resemblance to actual per-
sons, living or dead, business establishments, events, or locales is entirely coincidental.
The publisher does not have any control over and does not assume any responsibility for
author or third-party websites or their content.

First Riverhead trade paperback edition: August 2006

Library of Congress Cataloging-in-Publication Data

Davies, Adam.
    Goodbye lemon / Adam Davies.
        p.   cm.
    ISBN: 1-59448-071-0
    1. Fathers and sons—Fiction.   2. Domestic fiction.   I. Title.
PS3604.A953 G66   2006
813'.6—dc22   2006040949

PRINTED IN THE UNITED STATES OF AMERICA

10   9   8   7   6   5   4   3   2   1

For my father, Michael J. Davies

Dead bodies have their dead body language.
It says nothing.

—Martin Amis

Prologue: Theories of Dexter

His eyes were brown. His mouth was round. His fingers and toes were small and trinketlike. His skin was nearly transparent; you could see delicate blue veins at his temples and in his wrists and this inspired either an impulse to cruelty or the wild urge to protect him. His hair was curly. Our mother cut it herself, and she kept it long. With its ringlets, and her irregular technique with scissors, he looked like a sad little prince. He always seemed profoundly melancholy and reluctant at the same time, as if he knew there were something urgently required of him that he simply could not provide, and that because of his deficiency the people around him would suffer.

Dexter liked to draw stars on his wrists in permanent markers. He had strong feelings about uncapped tubes of toothpaste and made regular nighttime rounds to assure they were intact. If he was nervous he would chew on the topmost button of his shirt, which made it look like he had a drooling problem. When I was in another part of the house and he wanted to play with me, he would always call out, "Where is the Jack Attack?" and I'd come running.

His favorite show was *Mutual of Omaha's Wild Kingdom* but whenever the predation segment came on—the scene of the cheetah tripping up the baby gazelle before cutting dramatically to commercial—he would run crying from the room. He would wait just on the other side of the door, his head in his hands, his eyes clenched shut, and beg us to tell him when that part was over so that he could come back in. Press would always tell him it was safe before it really was and every time when Dex would return to see the cheetah dragging the beautiful, broken, velvety gazelle up a tree by its neck he would flee the room wailing. It happened this way every Sunday night. Without fail Dex believed that Press was telling the truth, and every time when Press fooled him he seemed astonished and crestfallen. Press won't say it now, but he thought Dex was a sucker. I think Dex just wanted to trust his big brother.

He wanted to believe that his family wouldn't let him down.

He was terrified of birds and moths. He loathed the sound of zippers and would do a madcap, leprechauny jig of disgust when Pressman would zip his coat up and down over and over just to torture him. He loved books, though, and could tell you everything you ever wanted to know about mushrooms and pneumatics and reptiles. "Herpetology," he would say proudly, out of nowhere, as if he had just discovered a cure for cancer. "Herpetology is the branch of zoology dealing with reptiles and amphibians. Herpetology. Herpetologist. Herp-e-to-*logic-al*." Cooking thrilled him; he would stand, petrified with wonder, as the packet of powdered cheese turned white pasta coils into yellow macaroni as my mother mixed them together in a pan. And he valued his personal space. In the backseat of our old pea-green Volvo he would always separate himself from me or Press by lowering the armrest. He loved us but he was afraid of us, too. He required a protective membrane around him to function in the world, and Pressman and I, his own brothers, weren't always allowed in.

Only six years old and already he was beginning to distrust his family.

It was as if he had intuited that one day soon he would be sucked under the waves of Lake George and no one would be there to pull him back up.

But I could be wrong.

Maybe his eyes were hazel, like mine. And his mouth was lopsided and smirk-prone. His fingers and toes were not trinketlike at all but long and flexible, brachiatory, made for climbing hazardous branches and throwing curveballs. His skin was tanned and pulled taut over compact muscles. He could roller-skate like the wind. His hair was straight but jagged because even though our mother made him sit on the stool and endure her haircuts, he would, five minutes later, administer his own finishing touches with dull safety scissors. This gave him the appearance of a frantic muppet, but he didn't care; he wanted control over his own world and shrugged off the punishment he always incurred. He was braver than any of us, even Pressman.

He wasn't a timid, empathetic, bookwormy brother. He was a proud, unbeaten brother. He was incisive, kinetic, pioneering, action-heroic.

But he was also kind. He smiled funny for photographs. His eyebrows would arch wildly, his eyes bulging as if he were in shock, and his face would be split by a maniacal, open-mouthed smile. The number of visible teeth was an infallible index of happiness, he thought, so he tried to give you all thirty-two at once. It looked like he was trying too hard, though, like he wanted to reassure you that it meant a lot to him that you were taking his picture. He wanted you to see how grateful he was so that you would feel good about it. I can still see him clearly in my imagination, that brittle smile creasing his face, eyes popping clownishly out of their sockets, willing you to be happy.

He didn't have time for books but he loved sports radio and prided himself on knowing all the baseball players that the other kids didn't know. Rolling naturally from his mouth came names like Honus Wagner, Tris Speaker, James "Cool Papa" Bell, and if someone tried to argue that George Brett was better, Dex would smite them with an unimaginable barrage of stats and figures. And then, as his vanquished adversary stood there stunned and mute at the verbal thrashing he had received, Dex would wrap his arm around him chummily and say, "Ah, maybe you're right. George Brett is pretty awesome."

If he had lived I think he would have been a do-gooder talk show host or a lobbyist for lost causes or a guidance counselor for at-risk youth. Something that required a lot of fast-talking, but also conviction and love.

But this could be wrong, too.

Maybe his eyes were blue, like my mother's. And you never saw his fingers because he kept his hands in his pockets all the time. And his skin was nondescript. And his hair was Nordic blond like Pressman's, or black like our father's, or inexplicably coded for baldness like mine. And he didn't watch TV, period, or ever listen to the radio and had no opinion on sports or snakes or photographs or predation or mac-and-cheese or zippers. He didn't chew buttons. He was not the invigilator of uncapped toothpaste. He never invited me to play by calling out to me, "Where is the Jack Attack?" and I never came running.

Maybe he wasn't great at sports but wasn't terrible either. Maybe he liked normal kid things and was afraid of all the normal kid-scary stuff. Maybe he thought Pressman was aces but didn't like me because—even though I was only one year younger—I was still too little to be much fun. Maybe he tried but failed to love our mother, just like Press and I did. Maybe he was afraid of our father, too, and deep down inside his heart somewhere he knew that one day he would drift out too far into Lake George when our father was supposed to be watching him—not drinking—and that no one would be there to save him.

Maybe he felt it coming.

Maybe he was shocked. He couldn't believe it was happening, even at the last moment, when he felt his beloved orange flip-flops sucked off of his feet. That last sensation might have felt heavy, like being pressed under a mattress. It might have been epiphanic, like finally getting a joke you never understood. Maybe it felt like being airborne. Or like forgiveness.

Sometimes I think he wanted it to happen. Maybe he felt alone and unloved and wanted someone to notice him in the most dramatic way: a rescue. How luxurious it would be, he could have thought, to have your father's powerful hands snatch you from deadly water, pull you up and return you to the shore where your family is waiting for you. Then they would recognize how valuable you are.

You wouldn't be ignored after that.

Every day you would be loved the way you deserve.

But I don't know. I don't know any of it. I can't remember what my brother Dexter looked like. I can't remember his odor. I can't remember what he loved or what he hated. I can't remember how it happened that day in August at Lake George. I was barely five years old, too young to have a clear memory of it, and no one would ever tell me about it. I wasn't there when he waded into the water. I wasn't there when his head went under. I wasn't there when our father struggled back to shore without Dex in his hands and with scotch on his breath.

I don't know any of this, and it breaks my heart.

What else can I do but try to write him back to life?

Part One

Welcome to the Suicide Palace

You are going to hurt yourself.

This is what Hahva tells me as I push into the darkness of my father's garage. With each step closer to the door I have not opened in fifteen years I feel myself contract into something smaller and smaller. I have tried everything to remain calm—I have endured nine waves of urgency in the car; I have been covertly breathing five-on-sixty for the last hour—but nothing can help. On the trip up from Georgia I kept telling myself that things are different now. I'm an adult. I haven't dreamed of Dexter in years. I have two degrees, even if one comes with an asterisk. And I am loved by Hahva Finn. But still I feel it happening, my body constricting in on itself like a desiccated sponge. It is a curious feeling. It is the feeling of becoming my old worst self once again.

"You're going to hurt yourself," she says again when I crash into something else unseen.

"What the . . . a ramp? Did I just trip over a ramp?"

"Like I said."

"Shh. You're going to wake them up."

It's crazy, but panic flutters in my chest at the prospect of waking up my father. It's ridiculous in the first place that I should be afraid of seeing him after nearly fifteen years, but last week my father suffered what the doctors described as a "catastrophic" stroke. The pons area in his brain, they said, was obliterated. He now has something they call locked-in syndrome. He has no muscle movement at all, my mother said in her phone call last week, but he has full cognitive function. He can see everything, hear everything, understand everything, but can't move a muscle—his fully functional mind is locked inside the prison of his paralyzed body.

If he can't even speak, then why is my sadness for him so overwhelmed by dread at the prospect of actually being in the same room with him? It's stupid, but maybe not that surprising: when Hahva finds the switch and floods the garage with fluorescent light, I am nearly terrified by what I see. Everything is exactly as I remember it: immaculate, with an unappeasable majesty. There are spare saddles hanging from the walls, brass-filigreed bootjacks with no mud on them, and shovels whose faces are dressed in blanched, bound Invincible roses. It can't be normal to be scared by shovels and saddles and flowers, can it?

"Jesus," I say. "Look at this. Three locks. It's like fucking *House and Garden* meets *Good Times* out here."

"Don't they have a key?"

"Yep. And there it is. Same place it was fifteen years ago. Under a mat. And this one key opens all of them. How utterly charming yet simultaneously totally undermining the whole point of having forty-four locks . . . They work. Drat. It's not too late to turn back, you know."

"Sorry bub."

I inhale hard and savor the pain of yet another dire wave of urgency. It is my tenth wave, a personal record, and it gives me a pleasurable sensation of getting things done. When I push the door open it makes a sound that is like someone shucking corn and I have to protect myself by thinking in lists. This time it's: 61 Promethium, 62 Samarium, 63 Europium, 64 Gadolinium . . .

"What did you say?" Hahva asks.

"Nothing," I say. "Here we are."

"I can hardly believe it."

65 Terbium, 66 Dysprosium, 67 Holmium, 68 Erbium . . .

"The Tennant family seat," I am finally able to say. "Home sweet home. Scene of the crime. Cradle of western loathing."

"Oh my gosh!" Hahva exclaims, flitting through the kitchen and around the furniture of the living room. She is experiencing the rooms, it occurs to me, the way certain insects experience a new environment: instinctively, with frenzy, by touching everything. Her skin—a complexity of browns and pinks: part nut, part peach—grows candent with fascination.

To me returning home with Hahva is the cause of complicated shame. I don't want her to think that I am like my parents. But another part of me is apprehensive about how they will treat Hahva. In high school we had an exchange student from Portugal staying with us (she lasted four weeks before she fled back to her country) and my mother said, "Inez, this is a re-frig-er-a-tor. Americans use it to keep their food cold so that it lasts longer." And she referred to Alma, our "domestic," as Jamaican, even though she was from Orange, New Jersey. It fills me with dread when I think of how they will treat Hahva's Celto-Sicilian-Israeli heritage and upbringing in the slummy urban South. Will they try to show her how the garbage disposal works? Will they augment meticulous speech—"Hahva, this is a sal-ad-fork"—with hand signals? Offer her pickled pigs' feet? Show her how to make fire and demonstrate the usefulness of the wheel?

Why did I let Hahva talk me into coming here? I don't understand why she wanted to come anyway. Why does she want
to know the worst parts of me?

"Oh Jack, it's just as I imagined it."

"That's disappointing."

"It's so . . ."

"George Stubbsy?" I say. "*Rob Reportie?*"

"Unlike you."

"I appreciate that. Thank you."

"My God. It's true," she says, picking up a photograph
from the mantel. "My boyfriend does have a past. Photo-
graphic evidence."

"I believe what you are seeing there is incontrovertible
and quite damning proof of—what is the clinical term?—a
childhood."

"Where is it that you posed for photos with such rugged
abandon?" she asks. "A camp perhaps?"

"A music camp, as I recall."

"I didn't know you were musical."

"I am full of secrets."

Hahva lets me inspect the photo. I slide the backing out to
see if the letter from Juilliard is still there. It is not. I feel incredible relief even though the audition was twenty years ago. It's
been years—hasn't it?—since I've thought about that day. Still, I
can't help wondering what happened to the letter. Lost? Committed to the Pain Box? Perhaps my father found it and threw it
away? The Tennants have a bad way with letters, after all.

"And look at this. Who's the boy in this picture?"

My heart quavers for a moment when I think it could be
Dexter, but when Hahva holds up the photo I see it is just
some kid from the neighborhood. I should have known better
than to panic. I wasn't just robbed of my brother's life; I was

robbed of his memory. Years ago my parents disposed of the photos, all his toys, his clothes, his books—everything, everything—and no one ever spoke a word about him. I wasn't allowed to know the first thing about him. There is no evidence he ever existed, no surviving artifacts, no legends, no anecdotes, nothing. I long for the day someone will say, "God, that reminds me of the time Dexter nearly burned down the house," or, "Do you remember how Dexter used to do that thing with the oranges and the Ping-Pong paddle?" or, "Dexter would laugh out loud right now if he could see you with that gorilla. Man alive." But no one ever does. And no one ever answered my questions.

My brother was simply erased—expunged, deleted, ghosted.

So it's a relief I recognize the kid in the photo, because if I ever see a photo of a kid who might be Dex there is a good chance I'll get teary. He is, for me, no one and everyone. He's nowhere and everywhere. It makes me jumpy. Especially when I am half-dying to know every possible thing about my lost brother while I am simultaneously half-crazy never to hear his name again.

Figure that one out, Tennant.

"Bobby Martilotta. Pressman's friend. He used to put sparklers down my pants."

"Little barbarian. I bet he's in the big house now, don't you?"

"Beats me. I'm fifteen years behind on the local news."

"I can't believe you haven't been back even once."

"I've been busy."

"And you've really never had any contact with your father since then?"

"Not one syllable."

"What could have been so terrible? I know we're supposed

to have a gag order on the subject of your family, but . . ." She allows a delicate beat. A half-hold.

What can I say to this? That my father broke my dream of being a concert pianist? That he ruined Pressman's life? That he is the reason Dex never saw his seventh birthday?

69 Thulium, 70 Ytterbium, 71 Lutetium, 72 Hafnium . . .

"That's right," I say, trying to sound casual. "You've violated one of the principal conditions of this visit. You must be punished."

"I want to know—"

"I've never kissed a girl on this sofa," I say. "I grew up with this sofa. But not once have I made my move on it. It is a sofa tragically devoid of moves. As far as I can remember no female glute other than dear *maman*'s has ever adorned this fabric. That doesn't seem right, does it?"

"Fifteen years, Jack. What could have—"

I pull Hahva down to me. "Lonely sofa, your time has come!"

"Jack, cut it out. I'm being serious. What did your father do that was so terrible?"

"He secreted Nazi officers out of Germany after the war."

"Jack."

"Ask a stupid question."

"This is important. We're at the house now. You can't just not tell me anything."

"Shh. You'll wake them up. And if we wake them up, there's a good chance they'll come down, and if they come down there's a near certainty we'll have to talk to them, and if we talk to them we may end up having to act civil."

"Well," she says, giving up. "We don't have to worry about being nice until at least tomorrow. They left us a note."

"Hardly *they* . . ."

" 'Make yourselves at home. Press and I are at the hospital with your father. We'll be back late. Help yourself to the refrigerator. Your room is made up. See you tomorrow.' "

"Thank God."

"O.K. I'll try to back off the big personal questions," Hahva says, nearing sarcasm. "But I could at least get some details, couldn't I? Just so I can know how to operate when I meet them?"

"You want factoids?"

"After twelve hours of freakish silence in the car I think I deserve one."

"I was concentrating on the road," I say. "Safetyness is next to godliness."

"Jack."

Her complaint isn't even true. Before we left Georgia I gave Hahva a family tree, which is more than I ever thought I would.

Mother, I told her. Adair Tennant, née Witherspoon. Born 1949 Brookline, Massachusetts. Fluttered fritillary-like through cloisters of Hollins until netted by Marine officer and aspiring honcho from Annapolis by the name of Colonel Guilford Tennant. (And that's *full bird* Colonel to you, Private.)

Father born in 1944 in New Haven, Connecticut. Son of somebody or other. As far as I know he emerged from the womb wearing dress blues and barking orders to the nurses. Age sixteen he won the Maryland state Golden Gloves, cruiserweight division. Had a summer job at a slaughterhouse. The rest of my knowledge, I told her, is just a resume. Education: BS, United States Naval Academy, Phi Beta Kappa, summa cum laude, political science. MBA, Chicago, graduating fourth in class. JD, Georgetown University. Work experience: the Corps, Fleet, BankOne, Cloudsplitter Jets.

Then there is the eldest brother, Pressman Montcalm

Tennant. "Press" to everyone but my mother. Thirty-seven years old. Started drinking at nine. Owned a beautiful 1972 BMW Toaster Tank motorcycle on which he would take me for rides. Physically powerful, he was a boxer, too, and heavily favored in the Maryland Golden Gloves before he had to drop out because of getting arrested for trying to steal a random-orbital sander from a construction site.

Omitted from the biography was the big mystery about Press: that he escaped the house, but, for reasons I've never understood, came back again. Out of high school he got a scholarship to this incredible college in northern California—he was totally free; he needed never come back—but he didn't make it through the first term. He didn't even make it two weeks. He never told me why. He just called me from the airport and asked for a ride. When he got back to the house he went to the basement and started drinking.

"A factoid," I say to Hahva. "A factoid. Let me think. Shit. I haven't been here in so long I don't know if I can think of anything interesting. How about a wager instead? I bet you that every single bottle in the trash is alcohol. My mother doesn't touch the stuff—I have no memory of her ever taking a sip of alcohol—but Press and my father are like liquor vampires. It's the one thing they have in common."

I lead Hahva into the kitchen, pull out the trash can from under the sink, and, sure enough, a carnival of clinking bottles erupts. "Scotch, scotch, vodka, scotch. Oops. Orange juice. Well, no one's perfect."

"But you've never even had one single drink since you were twenty-two."

I think: not entirely true, Your Honor.

"Exactly. You have discovered the very quintessence of the Plan."

"The Great Plan . . ."

"Go ahead and laugh," I say. "It's why I'm alive today."

"Your father is a captain of industry—"

"Colonel, technically."

"And you become an academic. Your father doesn't like music, you have season tickets to the symphony that you can't afford. Your father drinks—"

"Every day at six o'clock sharp."

"And you don't touch the stuff."

"It's like Opposite Day. Only it's Opposite Whole Life."

"That sounds awfully exhausting. Did you ever just talk to your father about it?"

Please, God, I think. Let's not start this.

"Talk? Are you kidding me?"

"How do you think he'd feel if he knew you told him you had devoted your life to being the opposite of him in every conceivable way?"

"He doesn't listen to anything. His ears are vestigial. They're just for show."

"Well, I guess now you have an opportunity to find out if that's true."

"What I have, Hahva, what I have is an opportunity to ask you to quit it, please, about opportunities. Just because he can't talk doesn't mean he's going to listen."

"Then why are you here, if you really don't want to try to talk to him?"

"Look," I say, feeling a flare of anger ignite in my chest. "I'm not here to make nice-nice. I'm not here for some talky talky huggy huggy so so sorry. I'm here because you asked me."

"But what about—"

It is hard enough to see Hahva pollinating the room, but I really can't stand the probing.

"Let's just drop it, O.K.?"

Now: more than a beat. A long beat. A full pause.

"That sounds like something your father would say."

"What?" I say.

"Isn't that his trick? Never saying anything?"

I know what she is doing and I don't like it. Sometimes her social worker reflex confuses me with one of her cases. She tries, in these moments, to improve me. And I hate it. No one likes it when another person tries to shrink them out, but what makes it so unbearable to me is the pseudoscience that she employs. I don't understand it. How can someone whose daily life depends so heavily on clinical precision believe in things like the Ennea-gram, the semimystical system of classifying personalities into nine archetypes? The Three Vital Doshas. The chakras, whatever that is. They are. Whichever. She is also always encouraging me to take certain herb-ridden medications and pursue therapeutic action that involves things like rune stones or seaweed con-sumption or Papua New Guinean tribal dancing or something.

So I know what she's thinking right now: that this trip is not so much a chance to help my father as it is a chance to im-prove myself. And she wants to be a part of it.

"Look," I say. "It's late. We're tired. We're stressed. We're not our best selves. Let's just get some sleep, O.K.? How does that sound? Why don't you take one of these suitcases up and I'll join you in a second. Last door on the left."

"Sir yes sir."

"What's that supposed to mean?"

"I'm sorry, I was under the impression I was being dis-missed."

"Oh Christ."

"One of these days you're going to have to communicate with another human being, you know."

"What are you talking about? All we do is talk. Ticky ticky ticky ticky talk talk talk." I am not sure what I mean by this but it is too late. It is already out.

"But not about *this*. Not about your family. Not about your father. God, Jack, can't you see why I hate it? I feel like you're not letting me in the club. I feel like you've locked me out of the house, our own house for Christ's sake."

"That's a ridiculous metaphor. We just got in the house."

"Jack."

"Sorry, I don't want to speak about my father, O.K., nosey nose?" This is probably a mistake. Probably I should have held back on this one. Hahva does not appreciate being called nosey. Every time I have used that term, it has met with poor results. Once, in extremis, I even called her a "snoop," and things got real unfriendly awful fast.

Quickly I try to get out something propitiatory about her shoulders but she cuts me off with, "I give up." Hahva whirls, surging toward a grand exit, then immobilizes. She takes a few deliberate breaths—I can't help wondering if she learned this from me—then squares her shoulders and swans, chin high, up the stairs, dragging all the light in the room after her.

Scoreboard

House: 1

Me: 0

Audition

In the silence of the room I stare down the Bösendorfer. Nine feet six inches of individually hitched Imperial concert grand with ninety-seven keys, nine black ivorine extras on the lower register for the heavy artillery. The good thing about the Viennese behemoth is that it has the clarity of the lighter Europeans while somehow retaining plenty of gravity and plenty of boldness. Good for Beethoven, good for Clementi. And the projection is remarkable. The bad thing, though, is that with the solid spruce soundboard every mistake is clarion. There's nowhere to hide with the Bösendorfer. The relationship with this piano is the most unambiguous of any I have ever played. You are either its master or are mastered by it. But somehow, even as a kid, I had a strange affinity for the Bösendorfer. It was the piano of choice for Liszt. It was the only piano that he was never able to destroy.

All those years ago, I felt, while sitting at my piano, that the notes were communicating with Dex, and he was telling me that nothing would destroy me, either.

But when I sit down at the bench now it produces a confusing sensation of wariness. It is unclear how we are to receive each other. It feels like an awkward first romantic encounter; what is called for is some darkness. I turn off the lights and then, in the enervated air of my father's house, I sit on the bench, flip up the fallboard, and run my fingers over the surface of the keys. This is a motion I have not made since I was a teenager. The upweight is surprisingly strong, almost like a froward dance partner trying to backlead. Closing the lid and being careful not to stroke too hard so Hahva can hear I run some scales on the damper. It feels good. It's remarkable how little speed I have lost. My cadence is light and precise and deliberate. The action of the piano is as clean as it was fifteen years ago, which is astonishing. The nine extra notes make it almost impossible to tune, yet it feels as if it has been tuned, regulated, and voiced in the last six months. No loose hammers, no verdigris, no moths have been at the felt or cotton. The humidifier below even reads an exact fifty-five degrees. It is perfection, not a semitone off.

Someone's been loving you, Bösendorfer.

I pick out a tune that Press liked to hear me play when our parents were not home, something balletic and *liscio*. But who wrote it? This is my gift and my flaw. I could not read musical notation, but I could hear a tune once or twice and sit down and play it without error. Christof told my parents that I was a curious case. "The boy does not learn music. He is incapable of it. It is as if he was born knowing it already and only needs to hear it played to be reminded. His imitative talent is remarkable. Whether he can produce art is a question best answered by another teacher. But until he is ready for that day I will teach him."

How many times did I envision that audition? I pretend I'm in New York now, in front of the judges, playing Beethoven's *Pathétique* Sonata, one of the few pieces I can remember. It is pure impulse; there is no thought to my fingerwork at all. Each key is like a bird I know by name. It is exhilarating. Then it happens. It always happens. I miss a vital crossover in the first movement in *allegro*. The words spring to mind with painful clarity: Permission to start again, judges? I backtrack a few frames and try again. Again I blow the crossover. And again. My ruined finger just can't span the gap. This is what the doctor at Hopkins termed, with euphemistic understatement, "inappropriate compensatory action." Violently I cock a doughy fist above my head but freeze before savaging the keys. Instead I intone bitterly to myself, "Thank you, thank you. You're a wonderful audience. It is a real pleasure to play for you tonight at the Suicide Palace."

'Night 'Night

I have lied already. There is one artifact that proves Dex was alive—a pair of orange flip-flops. And I remember how I got them.

That night at Lake George, hours after my father shambled ashore, shirtless and empty-handed and smelling of scotch, I sat on the dock staring out over the water, waiting for something to happen. The machinery of retrieval was fired up by then; there was action everywhere. The driveway was filled with state and county vehicles and bustling men in uniform asking questions and clicking pens, and the water was covered in boats with brilliant lights dragging nets along the bottom of the lake, but I felt that I had a power that they didn't have. Dex loved me, I knew, and would want to come back if he saw me waiting so patiently.

He never surfaced—it took nearly eighteen hours for the

crew to discover his body on the far side of the lake, as if, even in his last moments, he wanted to get as far away from his family as possible—but before Press came out to retrieve me I was given a gift. A pair of orange flip-flops, Dex's favorites, the last things he touched, washed up against the pilings of the dock, within reach. Before they could drift away from me I stretched down—to the surface of the same water that took my brother, I thought—and saved them. It was as if Dex wanted to leave me something to remember him by. I have had them ever since.

No one knew it then, and no one knows it now.

The left is interred in the Pain Box, still buried by the dilapidated kiln in the woods behind the house, and the right I always keep between my mattress and box spring. I have observed this ritual for as long as I can remember. It started that night at the lake. One of them I put into a box—later formally ratified as the Pain Box, it would eventually also contain a bottle of brag, the label from my Everlast punching bag, a 9mm Colt 1911 beavertail—and the other one I put under my mattress every night, as if there existed a dead-brother fairy who could return Dex to me if I was vigilant, if I told no one what I was doing, and if I loved him hard enough.

Tonight, when I nestle the tear-toughened flip-flop in between the mattress and box spring, at the house I swore I'd never come back to, I feel the usual wave of love and grief for Dex, but also a renewed hatred for my father. It seems obscene to me that I have come back to help care for him now.

How did I let this happen?

Three Days Earlier: The Ark

Nowadays it's women-only at the Ark. Until Zoli P. we allowed men at the shelter, but then she started hanging around late-night with Devin, a dually diagnosed 1013 with suicidal ideation, and next thing you know she was begging off chore duty and sporting Lycra pants with expandable waistbands. She miscarried three weeks later in the laundry room while folding his darks. Zoli P. was fourteen; he was twelve. So now it's just women past the yellow line.

And me, of course. But I don't count as a man to the residents because I have no record. "Where you serve time?" was the first question Miss D asked me when we met. When I told her I hadn't she squinted doubtfully at me. "How many times you been divorced?" was her next question. "And how many kids you got?" she also asked. "That you know of?"

"Do you always start conversations this way?" I asked her.

"Only with men," she said.

Another reason I don't count as a man at the Ark is because they all know that this is not my real job, that by day I teach freshman comp at the university. When this bit of gossip started getting spread around I was terrified that they would start calling me Professor. This happened at my last night job, at the fish house. That was why I finally quit. Every time I heard those three syllables I cringed. I felt like a fake when someone called me Professor. For I am not a professor. I am only an instructor. I didn't finish the degree; I bailed out—was thrown overboard, thanks to the handiwork of Jordana Mochnik—with a master's. A terminal degree, as they say. And now it looks like it will be "Class, this is your friend the semicolon" for the rest of my career.

Most days I question my employment. It's not easy at the Ark. The women here are bungled and betrayed, abandoned, victims of wrong direction, hopeless, lifeless, loveless. They have broken teeth and skin that is raw and abraded, sharp as gills. They work at the insect lab, the Waffle House, the blood bank, the chicken plant. Gail is here because of alcohol. Fern is here because of man trouble. Miss D, who is forty-four but looks sixty-four, is here because when she was in the hospital for two days her son cleaned out their joint bank account and sold off everything in the house of value, including what remained of her clothes, and all the doorknobs, exterior and interior. She came home from the hospital and found that all she had left were the clothes on her back. Even the carpet, plumbing, and wiring had been stripped for scrap. Sometimes at the Ark when the community phone rings she will still run and snatch it up and cry beseechingly into the receiver, "Dukie? Dukie? Is that you? I love you, honey, please come home!"

And then there's Rodney, who, as a resident's child, is the only other male allowed at the Ark. He has it tough. His Risperdal-popping mother is, as Hahva likes to say, "DSM-eligible." She spouts gospel at people as if it were an accusation and thinks everyone is out to get her all the time, even when we are clearly trying to help. For example, she has a bad habit of urinating on their mattresses. When confronted about this she says she wants to make sure that no one gets their "jelly pads" on them. Why does she think someone is going to come into her room and steal their mattresses? I don't know. That's

Hahva's area, not mine. If you ask for my diagnosis it is that she was made crazy by heartbreak.

You'll do anything from heartbreak.

Hahva is the shelter's caseworker but unlike the other social workers she doesn't shrink out the kids. She says what they need is not analysis but love. And as Rodney is only eight, and likes to dance—the stridulation of his waxies fills the hallways well after lights-out if I'm night staff—she instead likes to give him the James Brown treatment.

"Get up offa that thing," I will hear her grind out from her office. "And dance till you feel better. Get up offa that thing."

"And try to relieve the pressure!" Rodney will finish.

"Get up offa that thing!" they will roar in unison. They will go on about keeping it on the good foot, getting over before going under, Rodney not taking no mess, soul power. Sometimes they'll pull me out of the night staff office and make me dance with them, pointing out my errors of footwork and rhythm. They enjoy the spectacle. I enjoy it myself.

"I'm only a social worker," Hahva will say, clutching her chest, her skin dewy with sweat. "But wherever possible I do like to make it funky."

I like these moments with Rodney and Hahva. I also like the mornings at the Ark. Every day I am awakened by the sandpapery sound of Miss D shuffling in her worn-out slippers across the tiles to the kitchen to make coffee. It will be so dark in the room that even as she passes my cot I can't see her. But I can hear her heavy, asthmatic breathing and a few low dieseling Lord Lords. There will be a fraction of light slicing into the room as she opens the freezer to get the coffee and crunching noises as she spoons out the grounds into the filter. Then the spitting sound of percolation and the bitter smell of burned donation coffee fill the room. Miss D then shuffles past me again and out onto the back porch, where she will light up and sit in silence until Gail gets up and teeters into the kitchen for a coffee and joins us on the porch. Miss D and Gail will smoke Virginia Slims and I won't write them up. Instead I'll read the sports page. Go Dawgs, I'll say because I know they like to hear it. But a lot of the time we don't even look at each other. We just sit there together in silence as apparitions of mist rise up from the grass and the prehistoric smell of Georgia fills our noses. Together like this the three of us will watch the morning take hold as one by one the other residents get up and stagger into the kitchen, where they start making sounds: the clicking of the stove ignition, the tinny chafe of the toaster, the rustling of newspaper, the popping of jam jars, the suction as the refrigerator door opens and closes, the semiaudible high-frequency wail of the ancient TV playing Rodney's cartoons on mute—life sounds.

I love these routines. They give me a feeling that I haven't had since Leon Flanders—revered mentor and idol, dissertation advisor, beloved father figure, inquisitor—betrayed me back in New York: the feeling that I am in a family.

But there are plenty of bad times at the Ark. There are savage fights over Saran Wrap and computer time. Gail's daughter got pregnant and the father likes to come around and break windows, the idiot, until she agrees to see him. As night staff it's my job to dispense, or deny, cab vouchers; assign strikes for undone chores or misbehavior; collect all the residents' wages or HOPWA money and make deposits into an account they cannot access; liaise with police. I've had to separate two residents attacking each other with a pizza slicer and a toy crane, and have the scar on my palm to prove it. I've midwifed residents through DTs and broken water and incarcerated off-spring. I've evicted two pregnant women and had to watch them walk into the night toward destinations unknown even to them, gravid and limping and friendless.

Why do I do this to myself? Why do I even work here? I only get minimum. And there are plenty of other part-time jobs I could have taken. It isn't easy working amid the wreckage. But every time I start thinking this way I tell myself:

Rodney

Whenever I look at him I think of Dex. Maybe Dex would also like James Brown. Maybe he would also find keeping it on the good foot/getting on up/soul power both revitalizing and cathartic. Maybe he would run around late at night like Rodney and refuse, sometimes for an hour, to come down from the top bunk.

Is this realistic? I don't know. But I do know that Rodney is also just a kid. He also has a family that doesn't help the situation. He also needs someone to be there.

It isn't too late for Rodney.

Versus 1.1: From the Ark to the Apartment

It is at the Ark one night—after lights-out, with the residents all checked in and Rodney talked down from the upper bunk—when I get the phone call from my mother. Hahva is immediately agog at the prospect of the parental contact. She doesn't know that my mother always calls this time of year with the same pitch. Your father misses you, she will say. He is just too proud to say it. He doesn't understand what happened between you. You're his son. He's getting older. He's changed. Pressman would like to see you, too. Do it for me.

My mother also always wants to know what I think of the letters my father has written me. The letters, I always reply, are addressed in your handwriting, Mom.

I am proud to say they have been thrown away unread, all thirteen of them.

"Forget it," I say. "I'm not answering it. It's not important."

"Well, why would she be calling you so late on a Friday night?"

"She probably heard of some revolutionary new bathroom cleaner that works on both tile *and* linoleum surfaces."

"It's got to be important if she is calling on Friday night."

When I finally submit, pick up the phone, and find out the reason for the call, I try to be steadfast about not going. Hahva is mortified that I will not go home to assist with the care of my father, and so we have at it. Boy do we ever. The argument endures through the night, breakfast at Five Star Day, and back at my apartment, a scabby unfinished attic with ceilings slanting so steeply you could impale your skull on the exposed nail points if you walk too close to the walls. Hahva sits clutching a pillow to herself on the scrofulous love seat, expecting reason.

"I can't take the time off work," is my weakling opening gambit.

"Bullshit. Term is ending."

"There's summer term."

"In three years you have never once been selected for summer term."

This hurts, and it indicates an unnerving resolve on Hahva's part. She knows this is a sensitive subject, my continually getting passed over for vital summer work, and how painful it is to me that my name—in every lexicon of every dialect in every tongue of the academic world at large—is mud. Mud Tennant.

"Maybe I got selected this term. Did you ever think of that?"

"Did you get selected?"

This I decide to leave unanswered.

"But you can't take time off work," I say.

"Wrong again. I have plenty of days saved up. Two weeks' worth, in fact."

"The Ark would sink without you."

"Our interns can cover while I'm gone."

"Then we should use those days to go on vacation."

"Excuse me?"

Uh-oh. I have inadvertently invoked one of our recurrent domestic themes: no real adult romantic time together. We have never been on a vacation together, not even an overnighter to Tybee Island. Sometimes we go to the beach but we never have—which is code meaning that Jack Tennant, former child of privilege, product of decades of private education, one-time first-classer, never has—the money to stay overnight.

"Oh really? Unless you know any places that take wampum I think we might be screwed on that particular score, as I am only two years into paying off twenty years' worth of MSW payments and you are about to be unemployed for three months."

"We have no way of getting there."

"Are you serious right now?"

"I am."

"Your father is the president of a private jet company, jackass. You can fly anywhere you want on earth for free."

This is true. The Colonel—Treetop in the officers' lounge, but Colonel Tennant to you, Private—left the Corps for the corporation and is now the COO of Cloudsplitter, the third largest private jet company in North America. This means that I get free transportation on any Imperial-class jet to and from any airfield on earth if only I ask my father to call in the clearance code number.

Familiar words: if only.

This access to free travel complicates our vacation arguments. What is more important, Hahva wants to know, asking one lousy question of my father—a question, in fact, that would probably help normalize relations—or securing the means to have a romantic getaway with the woman you love? This is a fair question, and it pains me.

It is too late now for wishes, but man: would that I had that fateful night in grad school in New York to live over. Would that Leon Flanders believed me. That he would even return my calls. Maybe then, even after the fallout, I would have my PhD. Maybe then my usual summer job wouldn't be distributing phone books and selling dog food door-to-door. Maybe then I wouldn't have to deal with overhearing this undergrad Kantist madman we call the Philosoraptor say to my friend McGurk in the hallway, "Is it true what I hear about Tennant and New York? If it is, then damn. Tennant couldn't get hired as an assistant prof at East Wyoming State Technical Community Vocational Junior College, could he? He couldn't get a job teaching pigs to shit. Fucking A."

"You know my policy on asking for anything from my father."

"Do I ever."

"There you go, then."

"We can drive."

"My Omni won't make it and you won't let me in your car."

"I'll clean out my car."

"You'll what?"

"Extraordinary measures are necessary right now, Jack."

"Why?"

"Don't be a jackass. Your father just had a stroke."

"So?"

"Your mom said he's not responding to anything. He's in some sort of coma or something. The only thing he can move is his eye. He can blink it or something."

"And . . ."

"They think he might die, Jack. What will you do if you don't get to see your father before he dies?"

For a long moment I say nothing. I do nothing. I am stunned; it had never occurred to me that he might actually die. It just didn't seem possible.

"There is no good reason for you not to go home for a while to help your father," Hahva persists.

"There is a perfectly good reason, for your information."

Three Perfectly Good Reasons

There are, in fact, three perfectly good reasons.

1. I swore I would never go back and I am a bit of a madman about keeping my word.

2. *a*) My brother is there. *b*) My mother is there. *c*) My father is there.

3. Big plans are cooking. I am in the process of secretly trying to sell the Omni. Blue Book says $1,375 but I figure I can get at least $1,500 for it because I remember the lessons Coen taught me. And I will need every penny I get for a down payment on the ring I have already selected at Lux, Bond & Green. (A beauty: a premium-cut round .54-carat VS2 that the Lux, Bond guy said was a "J" color quality, which is supposed to mean that its color contains hints of yellow and brown, but I can't see them. To me it is pure white light.) And since I only live two miles from campus I figure I don't really need a car. I have already bought a swayback hybrid at J & J Flea Market on 441 and a special biking poncho with retroreflective piping. That way I can use a bike pretty much every day of the year in Georgia. It will suck a little bit, but who cares. Hahva will have a ring and with the savings I've put aside from the Ark and some help from Wachovia I should be able to afford a ceremony at the botanical gardens and seven complete days at Tybee Island next summer. The place I've checked out doesn't

have a view of the ocean, but still: it will be a legitimate honeymoon. Adult romantic time alone together. And if I leave Georgia now I will not be able to handle the secret sale of my car that will make all this possible.

Versus 1.2

"And what is this good reason?"

"Nothing. Forget it."

Unable to bear the force of her reason and moral goodness I retreat to the bathroom. At the sink I splash water on my face, inspect the follicles in the front, which seem to be abandoning ship despite the scrupulous application of tonics that allegedly aid microcirculation, and stare myself down.

She's right. I know she's right.

So why does it feel like defeat?

Sheepishly, I rejoin Hahva. Lying in bed, our bodies jigsawing under the starwork of exposed nails while the rain detonates against the tin roofing and insects keen in trees outside the window, I concede. My finger aching, I lean over her body, inhaling her odor of seaweed and earth, and say, "O.K. Two weeks tops. And I'm not asking for Cloudsplitter clearance. We'll take your car up this weekend. But I'm driving, O.K.? You don't get anywhere near the wheel, Mad Max."

Hahva

I have amassed a small archive of information that is vital to my relationship with Hahva. Her whole life is circumscribed by mysterious predilections and arcane rules, without knowledge of which you can give up any hope of maintaining peaceable relations. They include:

Do not shrug at her.

Do not whistle in the house.

Do not approach her frontally while she is sitting down.

Do not fail to recognize her voice instantaneously on the phone.

Do not ever use the word "exotic" as a descriptor of her appearance.

Do not criticize her driving. For example, it would be inadvisable when asked if you would like to be relieved while driving on a long road trip to your parents' house in Maryland to say, "No thank you. Even though I am tired I would prefer to keep driving, for with you at the wheel it is too Bo Dukey for comfort."

Appended to this rule is the rider, "Also do not criticize/make reference to/establish visual contact with the interior of her car or its contents." This one isn't hard to obey. Who wants to look? It's atrocious in there. In the past her car has been filled with items including, but not limited to, empty containers of laundry detergent, ravaged copies of health and lifestyle magazines, knots of clothes both dirty and clean, games she meant to donate to the shelter, scattered plastic playing pieces from same, candy wrappers, mugs with her MSW program's insignia stenciled on them, cracked jewel cases, the detritus of crushed fortune cookies and tortilla chips and Lunchables, balls of soiled napkins compressed like white dwarfs into the densest possible mass, a subsoil of shifting powdered kitty litter and comminuted dog food—dry only, thank goodness—in the footwells, empty cans of tuna fish and the discarded jagged discs of metal they produce, unopened cassette tapes dating, I am pretty sure, to the late eighties (including, I remember vividly, Falco and T'Pau), a number of petrified ancient Weetabix sarcophagi both jumbo and mini, rattling cans of Ensure, color-coded dumbbells, dynamometers, a DSM-IV as well as less, ahem, *clinical* books on personality typing, packages of yarn from an abandoned project on knitting in order to reduce gift-giving expenses, a fugitive raisin here and there, crushed flat or tumor-swollen with spilled water, sticky lesions of corn syrup from soda drinks and health food bars glossing up the dashboard and door pockets, and an army of wispy plastic grocery bags that spinnaker treacherously around the cabin when Hahva drives with the windows down.

Burgers and sandwiches must be wrapped in a modest bonnet of paper before consumption. (Because of leakage? I asked. Because of the risk of meat detritus? No, she tsk-tsked, because that is simply what one does, obviously.)

She will not drink hot liquids out of glass containers, as it induces the feeling that her teeth might crack.

Her mother's favorite reprimand: You're going to hell in gasoline bloomers.

Only white towels will dry her body. Sleep will only occur in white linens. Anything else, she says, can change your personality. ("Hey," she said. "It's not my rule. It's Katharine Hepburn's. And if it's good enough for Kate it's good enough for me. She was a steadfast lady.")

She loves having her hands bitten on the knife-edges, the section of flesh that extends from the pinky to the wrist. In karate this is known as *shuto*. In palmistry, the Mount of Mars. For best results you should insert one knife-edge into your mouth, clench carefully but firmly down, and hold for a minimum of thirty seconds, during which time Hahva's eyes will roll sharklike back into her head with pleasure. Then you must repeat with the other hand to avoid inducing in her an uncomfortable feeling of being "lopsided."

I am proud to say that I am currently the only person with clearance to do this.

Another clearance I am proud of: exclusive knowledge of her X-ing.

When Hahva was little she got this big-deal scholarship to train at this big-time ballet academy in DC. For three months every summer she stayed with her mother at a fleabag motel and bussed to the school mornings and nights. All the girls had to wear the traditional stuff—black leotards and pink tights—and if anyone ever made a mistake the mistress would put a big white X on them in chalk so that their mothers would know that they had been bad. It was like something out of a Victorian shame novel. The other girls—rich girls—made fun of her cheap shoes and hand-me-downs. They mocked her accent. One time a girl, discovering that Hahva's mother worked as an usher at the theater to make extra money, tipped her a bus pass.

But the worst thing was the X-ing. The mistress always singled Hahva out for punishment. She gave her an X when she took a wrong step. She gave her an X when another girl tripped her and she started crying. And she gave her an X whenever Hahva spoke an accent-tainted word in class. "We are ballerinas," the mistress would say of Hahva's Southern inflection, "not barbarians. Enunciate clearly or remain silent."

Then Hahva would slink to the bus stop feeling the chalky letter burning her chest.

Her mother never totally believed Hahva when she told her how unfair it was. Her mother thought maybe Hahva was goofing off, squandering the hard-earned money they had saved up. Her mother, in a dark moment, even said that Hahva was ashamed that she worked as an usher when other parents were sitting in the seats in their designer clothes. She implied even that Hahva wished she had another, wealthier family.

After that summer Hahva gave up ballet permanently.

When necessary to apologize for an act of jackassery (such as inadvertently leaving the bristles of her toothbrush turned away from the lightbulb in the bathroom, therefore promoting the rapid growth of "spores") it is appropriate to inquire about her shoulders. "How are the shoulders?" you should say. "I think they look bigger. Have you been carbo-loading, by chance?" This is advisable because Hahva is very touchy about her physique, her shoulders especially. Growing up she was very thin and was subject to all the usual taunts. Don't worry, her parents told her, you'll grow out of it soon. But she went through junior high, high school, college, and grad school without even growing out of a pair of shoes. So two years ago she started a grueling exercise regimen, a sutra of sweat and push, and now her body is laced with long striated muscles. But still she has not managed to increase her size. Still she wears a zero. Still clients will inquire if she is anorexic even though she conscientiously consumes three thousand calories a day. Still it rankles as it did when she was a sexless twelve-year-old and classmates asked her if she were a boy. And by far her leanest body parts are her shoulders. O for shoulder bulk! she thinks. O for shoulder brawn! Where can one sign up for a lumberjack camp?

Chief among her passions, however, is full disclosure. She is a sucker for the truth. You should see her at the shelter. When Gail's daughter's boyfriend comes around breaking windows like a fool everyone else calls the cops but Hahva just sits him down, puts a reassuring hand on his forearm, and asks him questions about his home life. "What is your father like?" she says. "Do you talk to him?" With me she is the same. She can't even stand it when I'm reading a book and laugh at something funny. "What is it? What is it?" she'll cry out, running over and burrowing her head into the pages. "What's going on? What part is it? Have I read that part, too?"

Imagine if she found out I have been hiding Dex from the world—and her—all these years.

Etymology

Her name, in Hebrew, means "love," but to me it is a sonic expression of a slow, vulnerary embrace. "Haaaaaaaaaah" goes the first arm, drawing you in. "Vaaaaaaaaaaa" goes the other arm, pulling you close, pinning you in, making the miseries of your life abate, your memories blur.

Windows Open

The first time I kissed Hahva was in the parking lot of the Ark, after hours, when the residents were all asleep. We were standing under a cone of sputtering canary light from the streetlamp, listening to the rataplan of the rain coming down on the hot asphalt. The burned-cabbage smell of the chicken plant was vivid and heavy, awash in my nose. Some kids rattled past, drinking from paper bags while pushing each other in a grocery cart. When they wrecked in the gutter the liquor they spewed out of their mouths looked like a spray of diamonds.

When I kissed Hahva at that moment I felt hundreds of windows fly open inside my heart. It made me wish that I had never kissed anyone else.

Me

I have a hard time considering my incipient baldness anything but a type of moral punishment. It smacks of gene justice, poor planning, left-out-ism, improbity. As a child I had hair that gave no intimation of going AWOL—lush and curly—but now, as an adult, it has thinned and attained a mad scientist appearance that I hope, on good days, looks cavalier and rakish.

People say I look like a fattish John McEnroe. Or a middle-aged Kathleen Turner.

I have definite tastes. I prefer analog to digital. I like the effect of having applied lotion but detest its application: the flatulent pump, the viscosity in the webbing of your fingers, the meniscus-scab of dried lotion that you must first remove from the tap. I enjoy and excel at puzzles. I hate punning barbershops (Hair 'Em Scare 'Em or Shear Genius) and cafés (Ground Zero or Bean Town) and headlines ("Bulls Horn in on Championship"). I observed with an outsider's pain the proto-romance of dodgeball between boys and girls on the playground. I wore mittens into high school, into college, into adulthood. Most days, even during the hot summer months, I wear thick-soled boots for a little extra verticality.

Turnstiles make me feel important.

It gives me a semierotic frisson to smite recalcitrant coin-operated machinery.

At Turnbull Academy I sought out foreign exchange students and tried to befriend them. I understood their loneliness.

I love—I mean I go gaga for—any mandarin: oranges, clementines, dancys, satsumas, ponkans, you name it. They are my vice, my comfort food, my refuge, and, I might add, an excellent source of follicle-building and shine-conducive vitamin C.

I am the preferred interrogee of people on sidewalks in need of direction.

I have exquisite drive-through manners and often tip.

I hate it when singers say "fie-*uh*" instead of "fire."

I also hate it when people make "pianist" sound like "penis." I am not a penis.

When McGurk lets me borrow his car I hold the keyless entry remote high above my head at point-blank range, as if the radio waves might spill out groundward in the manner of water from a cup. It looks like a salute, I've been told.

Hahva watches TV in bed on her stomach, arms in front of her, head up, Sphynx-like, but I cannot do this for more than a minute. I'm inflexible, as she will attest.

The worst job I've ever had—with the possible exception of my current one—was chloroforming a baby tiger. It was part of a petting zoo at the Towson Town Center. For five bucks you could pet him but for twenty you could get a Polaroid with him on your lap. The baby tiger was small, the size of a terrier, but he was still equipped with serious teeth and claws and it was my job to give him this special hug with a chloroform-dipped rag. It was supposed to look as if the hug were merely reassuring, as if I were wishing him bon voyage, and if a customer saw the rag pressed to his mouth I was to say that the little fella had a runny nose; he's not used to life outside the canebrake. But what the hug really did was put him into a nonviolent daze for thirty seconds or so—long enough to get him situated safely on the kid's lap and snap the pic. That poor tiger lived eight hours a day in a constant narcotic stupor. His eyes were always glassy and he had a hard time controlling his slobber and he fell down a lot. Kids thought it was because he was a baby and was still figuring out how to walk. Sometimes when it was bad I'd have to employ a cover story.

"He loves you so much he's delirious with joy!" I'd say, and the kids would squeal and stamp their tiny feet while their parents nodded sagely as if they expected it all along.

The tiger's real name was Arai but my mouth-breather boss, Fishman, called him Keith Richards and I never had the guts to say anything. By the end of the day, when the mall was closed and we were doing the money, Arai couldn't even stand up on his own. I would set him right-side-up inside his port-a-cub and he would fall down like a drunken sailor. "I don't care if you have to staple Keith Richards to the bars, just get that tiger standing," Fishman would say. "No one's paying a dime to pet a dying tiger."

I shouldn't have done it. I should have made a stand. But by then I was spending three nights a week at the airport watching people reunite under the Arrivals/Departures sign and I needed shuttle money, so I would lean Arai up against the bars of his cage and do my best to act natural. It broke my heart.

In high school I cultivated the ability to eat without switching the fork from my left hand, postcut, to my right hand. I did this because I had heard that it was the European style and thought that chicks would dig it. I spent many lunch periods eating with my fork in my left hand while staring meaningfully at Karina Thiergartner.

I am a real liability at sad movies. Death scenes make me angry and unsympathetic. When a beloved dies and the protagonist mourns, thinking of all their special times together, I never get tearful and tender. I get bitter and sneery. I think: Greedy jerks. You have your memories. They are beautiful. They will sustain you for the rest of your life. How would you feel if you couldn't remember your loved one, no matter how hard you tried, no matter how many stories you invented?

How would *that* make you feel, Tom Hanks?

I carry a copy of a key to a 1969 Jaguar E-Type on me at all times.

I am apt to alert a stranger to errant food particles or unzipped zippers.

My brother used to make reservations at restaurants under

the name Roy G. Biv and I thought it was the funniest thing I'd ever heard.

Once I heard that to be in love was to find someone inexhaustible, and I believe it.

Favorite epitaph: "I told you I was sick."

Least favorite band name: the Yam Teddies.

Hottest childhood crush: Suzy Chapstick.

Recipient of first kiss: Karina Thiergartner.

Most taught poem: "The Arrival of the Bee Box" by Sylvia Plath.

Most read line: "They can die, I need feed them nothing, I am the owner."

Lifelong dream: to be like my father.

Lifelong dread: to be like my father.

Hahva Meets the Mother

This morning, back in the dormitorial anonymity of my childhood bedroom in rural Maryland, while committing my shameful hair-fluffing ritual, I think for the thousandth time that perhaps the day has come to shave my head. How did this happen to me? I am only thirty-three years old. I should be touring the countryside top-down in Italian convertibles at injudicious rates of speed and swimming recklessly in salt water, shaking my head vigorously and discharging photogenic sprays of prisming water when I emerge athletically from the surf. In the classroom I should be able to clutch my head in histrionic vexation when students flail over the serial comma or the semicolon's relationship with the conjunctive adverb. I should lather, rinse, and repeat with abandon and feel free to comb or brush or blow-dry willy-nilly.

But I do not. Instead I adhere zealously to a set of rules regarding hair preparation and guidelines for activities. When anyone tries to touch my hair I recoil and can't help making angry squinting expressions. Preparation for appearances in public are exhausting. The hair must be completely dry before exposure to any external influences such as wind, ultraviolet light, or, God forbid, headwear. The drying process is arduous. The first phase involves surgically precise towel-fluffing followed by blow-drying on the fan setting only. Then I rewet the thinnish forehead parts and fluff and dry again separately to potentiate the visual merging of the wispy front with the thicker areas in back. When I'm finally ready to pull on a shirt it happens with fantastic delicacy, easing my head through the collar as if it were a flaming hoop at the circus.

Today the process isn't going so great. I make a few more exasperated attempts to tame the cumulostatic of the front but it just makes it worse.

"You look fine," Hahva says from the bedroom.

"Easy for you to say. There aren't too many Celto-Sicilian-Israeli genes that carry baldness."

"You're not bald, Jack."

"O.K. Balding."

"You're not balding, either."

"I look like a frightened koala."

"You don't look like a frightened koala. You look like a handsome devil."

"Koala," I say miserably.

"Jack, you are not going bald. No one but you can see the

thinning part you're talking about. And even if it were thinning, you'd need a telescope to see it. Honest."

"Really?" I say, mainly to appease her.

"Really. And if you play your cards right, that lonely sofa might see some action later. Now. Are you ready?"

"O.K.," I say, avoiding the mirror.

As we descend the stairs—I can't help succumbing to the impotent, sock-padded tiptoe—it registers that I should warn Hahva about my mother's mania for cleanliness. Hahva, at first, thinks I am going overboard, and I can only convince her by instancing some specifications.

The doormat is a thirty-two-inch diameter mud-busting slab made of heavy-duty coco coir fibers that is replaced every three months or after ten foxhunts, whichever comes first. To avoid any messy stray needles and sap over the holidays we had not a regulation Christmas tree but a lighted faux ficus that arrived in the mail every year already encased in a white plastic liner and a durable genuine clayette uni-pot for easy disposal. The rugs in the entryway are power-loomed in Belgium of SynSylk polymers, which are colorfast, permanently antistatic, mothproof, and pill resistant. Take-out menus are archived in the Take-Out-Tote covered in a wipe-clean plastic laminate that resides, under penalty of thin-lipped rage, in the second drawer by the phone. Only industrial-grade precision-balanced ceramic knives cut Tennant tomatoes, lest bruising occur. Salads are not tossed by hand but with oversized clear acrylic tossers to avoid flyaway lettuce and bacteria. Once a month the clothes dryer gets a good vent cleaning with the extractor brush. Mouthwash does not sit on the counter in its own barbaric packaging that is, as we all know, so prone to unsightly peeling and flaking; rather, it is housed in a stylish white retro dispenser with nozzle and matching porcelain cups. In the garage hang netted bags stuffed with nontoxic volcanic granules that absorb any trace of indelicate odors.

"How do you know all that stuff?"

"I lived here for almost two decades." Then, after a moment, "Hey, you see a theme here? Around here it's regular alcohol and rubbing alcohol. Drinks and cleaners."

In fact, our family crest of arms should reflect this: dexter chief, an almost empty bottle of scotch; sinister base, a container of Formula 409, *en spray*. Our *cri de guerre*? A prolonged silence.

"Weird," she says.

In the kitchen the coast is mercifully clear. Except for the inane susurrus of the programmable climate control system there are no noises. The air is parched and pharmaceutical. In the daylight you can see that the appointments are as lush as I remember—many an *objet d'equinne*—but everything is astringent and unopened. The rooms are eaten with an emptiness so vast it has its own acoustical properties.

But the peace doesn't last long.

"Hey," Hahva says. "Do you hear that? Is there incoming?"

I do hear it. There is incoming. Quickly I pour us some fortifactory coffee and make some unexemplary motions of self-preening, preparing myself for maternal contact. Hahva does the same, rubbing herself nervously down, fluffing her hair and then flattening it, flattening it and then fluffing it. The room around us becomes thick and ghosted, the insensate fruit on the counter just waiting. Then Hahva thrusts her left hand at me, which I bite, then her right, which I also bite. We are as ready as we will get. Footsteps click metronomically down the staircase and then there she is, my permafrosted mother.

A voice that sounds like thumbtacks falling on glass says, "Hello, Jackson."

With the exception of the slotted area between her nose and chin, my mother's face is entirely uncreased when she speaks. Then she moves to embrace me. It is an awkward gesture, like the way you might hug a Christmas tree: arms wide, face turned aside, making contact only with hands that pat in an upward motion like ground control personnel telling a plane to come on in, come on in. Even with this slight contact I can perceive my mother's popcornish lightness, as if her bones were hollow. Fifty-seven years old and still a blade.

I feel something contract hotly in my stomach, unclench, then go cold. This is my mother.

"Mom," I say, careful to see if the diminutive ruffles her. "This is Hahva Finn. Hahva, this is my mother, Adair."

My mother appears to be regarding Hahva with judicial scrutiny, measuring her as if she were some kind of postulant. This is not good. My mother is especially unpleasant with my girlfriends. I haven't let her meet a girlfriend of mine since I was sixteen, when she called Karina Thiergartner rustic and stiff-necked. "I'm just saying that she's a little rustic and, well, stiff-necked for you, dear. Her father is what, a tradesman? I'm sure that she's nice in her own little way but really, Jackson, remember who you are." My mother is always attaching "little" to things. At Karina: "It's nice to meet your little girlfriend." In a card to celebrate the reception of my ignominious—my terminal—MA: "Congratulations on getting your little degree, honey!" Through the latticework of the closet door to me, hunched up in the dirty clothes hamper, clasping my broken finger and sobbing: "I'm sorry about your little audition, dear. There will be other ones."

And Hahva, I can tell, is evaluating my mother with her

semiclinical acumen. Is my mother an Individualist with Loyalist subinfluences? A Kapha/Vata? For a moment I fear that Hahva might try to hug her—she is an inveterate hugger—but she does not. She merely extends her hand and my mother, with galactic slowness, like a starship approaching a space station for docking purposes, moves toward it and takes it in her own hand.

I fight back a desiccant fear swelling in my throat. I have— or used to have—an authoritative mediumistic ability to predict when my mother is about to do something cruel. Now seems like such a time and so I gnash my molars and think of ways I could smite my mother if I had to: crumple and besmirch the fox-motif guest hand towels in the downstairs half-bath; advertise a rummage sale at our address; cover her SL with psychedelic bumper stickers espousing peace and leftist political ideologies; send her a package in the mail with an anonymous note constructed from cut-outs of magazine headlines—YoUR SoN LiVES HeRe—and paste it on a photo of a bedroom at the Ark.

No, I must stop thinking like this. I discipline myself with another quiz. Emperor, I think madly. Antiquarian, grand eagle, double elephant, colombier, atlas . . .

Before I can think of more Hahva says, "It's nice to meet you, Mrs. Tennant. I'm very sorry to be meeting you under these circumstances, though."

"Thank you. We are all very concerned about Guilford." When she says this her voice is devoid of any emotion except, perhaps, bafflement. She might be speaking of a toaster that inexplicably stopped toasting.

"It's good to see you, Jackson," she says.

"Same here," I say, concentrating on my expression.

"And I know your father is going to be happy to see you. It means the world."

This one I cannot lie about. I change the subject.
"Where's Press?"

Hahva Meets the Brother

From downstairs comes an explosion of noise that sounds like a violent symphony of eggbeaters. This signal causes my mother to extract from the cabinet a canister of Oust air cleaner, which I happen to know is preferable to Lysol for air freshening, as Lysol is intended for surface disinfection and aromating and does not maintain its molecular integrity in air like Oust. A basso profundo voice echoes up the stairway. My brother is singing a spiritual.

Hahva gives me a look. She is struggling to figure out the poverty of grief.

"Nobody knows," the voice sings, "the brain cellicide I've seen. Nobody knows but Seagram's . . ." Then the door opens and my brother appears, attired in only a dirty T-shirt and boxers worn enough to show pink through the fibers, clasping a mug in one hand and making fending-off gestures with the other. "Hey, would somebody please turn down the volume on that sun? And lay off the bongos, Ricky. No one wants to merengue at this hour. It's indecent."

If Pressman apprehends any of us he gives no indication. He lurches by in a miasma of stale cigar smoke and halitosis. My mother trails his footsteps to the cabinet, spraying bursts of Oust after him. As Press upends a bottle of Worcestershire sauce over his mug—already containing a copper liquid, I see—my mother gives the fumarole of the basement stairway a few hits before forcing the door closed. This whole transaction occurs wordlessly and has the refined air of a ritual.

After a long drink my brother, refreshed, says, "Ah, house-guests. I fear I'm underdressed. Forgive me. It's you, I see. The improdigal son. You may remember me, your elder sibling. They call me Pressman. And you must be Hahva. It's nice to have an increase in the womenfolk around here." Pressman then gives Hahva a hug that involves his pelvis, downs a shot of Worcestershire, and judders. "So," he says. "You must all be wondering why I gathered you all here today. One of you is . . . a *murderer*."

"You look as well as ever," I say to him, although it is not true. My brother's face is either voided or very well guarded. Is it alive and secret or is it just dead?

"Excellent fettle, yes. Thank you, little brother." Press gives me a hard, nail-driving slap in the shoulder. This produces a familiar sensation. When we were kids Press would hit me hard on the head every night before we went to sleep. It was part of a regimen he observed to make sure I did not grow taller than he was. It worked. I'm 5'10" in Doc Martens with inserts and two pairs of socks with perfect posture. He's 6'3" barefoot and slumping.

And his hair looks good. It is preposterously luxurious and grabbable. It is sculpted and thick, tousled in a way that makes it look like the cresting waves of a blond banana cream pie. Just looking at it makes my scalp constrict over my skull. I can almost feel my pores opening up and jettisoning strands of hair.

"This is Hahva," I say.

"Hi," she says.

"Hahvapopodopodopoulos. Glad to meet you."

This must be an offshoot of my brother's enthusiam for hypocorism. He was always inventing idiotic nicknames for people. Hellenifying surnames is a new one to me, but I remember that countless ex-girlfriends of his have endured names such as Snacky, Ferrethead, Bob (for Big Old Butt), George McGillicutty, Sprouts, Izzo, Ribeye Jones. Friends were called Glands, Shanghai, Bonzi, Earlobe, Dr. Schmulevitz. I answered to Fliptop and Bungalow Brain and Digdug, but when he was being tender—when I had done something right—he would call me Lt. Boscovich.

"Thanks for the lift, Lt. Boscovich," he said when I picked him up at the airport and didn't ask him any questions about California. "You're a good soldier, Bosco."

Suddenly my heart loses altitude when I remember that he had a nickname for Dex, too: Lemon.

"I don't want to talk about Lemon," he would always tell me when I was drunk enough to ask him. "I told you never to say that name, didn't I?"

He had. And he meant it. He meant it so much, he would never even explain where the name came from.

"What?" Hahva says, confused.

"Hahvapopodopodopoulos," he repeats with exaggerated patience, stressing each syllable, as if talking to a child. "Or do you prefer Hahvaphilophilious? Hahvadorutrephales? Hahvapapandrea—"

"That's quite enough, Pressman," my mother says.

"Oh. Quite right, quite right. Very poor taste. You must forgive me. I'm not myself at the moment. We are all very *concerned* about Guilford," he says in a pitch-perfect mimic of my mother's own line. "And I know your father is going to be happy to see you. It means the world."

"So," I say. "Is there a plan? Isn't he due home today?"

"The nurse should be bringing your father home any minute now."

Hahva, I know, is wondering why no one in the family is driving him home.

"Nurse?" Press says, expanding.

"The therapist. Your father needs a lot of rehabilitation—exercise and so on—if he is ever going to regain any movement."

Press clears his throat. "I thought those chances were pretty much, well, scotched, ha ha. I thought that's what 'locked in' means."

"No one knows how much he might recover. And it is the only way they would let us take him home."

"Really?" he says with interest.

Hahva issues me a private look of bafflement.

"Aren't you looking forward to seeing him, Jackson?" my mother says.

Then my gut clenches up. Wheels crunch on the gravel in the drive. We all hear it. Doors open and close. There is squeaking on the ramp and the scraping of a key in the lock. I try to say something polite but my mouth fills with dirt.

My father is on the other side of the door.

What I Could Tell Hahva 1.1:
The Barbasol Incident

If I could tell Hahva something about my past, perhaps I would start here:

"There's only one explanation. You are a bastard."

This is how Press used to taunt me. Press always had the long muscles, the straight-backed spring-loaded potential for violence that our father has. He also had the fast hate juice, the tight-corded grip strength that suggests certain choke talents, the cut-crystal celebrity of Guilford Tennant. But I had none of this and when Press used to question my provenance, I believed it.

I was never strong; my chest has always been lean and spatulate. My molars are planed from years of nocturnal gritting. The follicle situation has caused me to see the whole world in terms of the Hairs and the Hair Nots. People who have full heads of hair at thirty-three simultaneously sicken and intimidate me, yet I seem to have nothing but contempt and pity for others who are going bald.

The only physical feature of my father's that I share is the sharp Tennant cowcatcher jaw.

As a kid I was so confused—simultaneously hateful and emulous. How I loathed my father, how I longed to be like him. When I was being cross-examined by the Disciplinary Committee in grad school some of my father's fortitude would have served me well. When he was a cadet at the Academy and was being initiated under duress by the officers, my father gritted his teeth until a molar cracked while the men around him cried out. Even his nickname, Treetop, was inspired by virile action. On training missions he would regularly fly his A-4 so close to the treeline that branches would be ripped off and explode into the atmosphere. It is probably one of the great sadnesses of his life that he didn't get to serve in combat. Probably my father fantasized about getting captured so he could get tortured and try to crack another molar while smiling pleasantly at his enemies and saying nothing.

That's how he would like to go out: with a triumphant silence.

Boxing was one of the great sore points with me. My father

was a boxer at the Academy and fought his entire first year with a broken rib that prevented him from ever throwing an uppercut. His record in four years was tarnished by only one loss, when he fought southpaw, with his right hand tied behind his back, on a dare. The victor in that bout was the sergeant instructor, who had already lost three matches to my father. When he graduated and went into business the Academy would periodically call him in for special training sessions. Once, in eighth grade, I took the bus to Annapolis so I could spy on the class. I didn't last long, though. My father was leading a drill on how to make yourself a small target, how to bunch the shoulders and sink the head on the neck so the chin is protected. He had the cadets on the focus mitts with partners throwing jabs, shirtless with their faces covered in shaving cream. "I want those shoulders up!" he screamed, his own shoulder frosted in Barbasol from the demonstration. "Jaws down! Loose! Bird-wing that chin! If I don't see white on that shoulder it's going to be the *shinai*!"

What exquisite jealousy: all those men, getting such passionate attention from my father. In that first minute of spying I had seen my father utter more syllables to these men—men he had never met before—than he had deigned to give me all week. Sniveling and heartbroken, I limped out of the compound alone.

I was desperate to be one of those cadets: admired and approved of, a suitable object of acknowledgment, ratified by blood. I thought, Why won't he scream at me? Why won't he hit me with the *shinai*? What do I have to do to get him to slather me in shaving cream? Would he love me if I had a broken rib and played Handel right through it?

One day, in tenth grade, I screwed up the courage to force the issue. After school I hanged my father's ninety-pound

Everlast from a tree in plain view of the study, stripped my shirt off, worked up a thick, peachfuzz-busting lather, and had at it. From the backyard I could see my father at his desk, watching. My father had a blur for a jab. It had no preamble, no telegraph, no warning. There was no twitch in the shoulder before it was thrown. He didn't sink his weight. It came back twice as fast as it went out. I tried so hard to duplicate everything I had learned from watching him, but I had never actually hit anything before and could tell that I was sluggish and awkward. My jab had a lot of useless motion. The elbow dropped and kicked out as the punch fired. It looped pointlessly from my shoulder—easy to bob under, I knew. My pelvis was uninvolved—I had heard my father scream at the cadets, "Your fists are your bullets but this is your gun!" as his hips pivoted the punch home. But still that day I fired off jabs as long as I could under the hammering Baltimore sun, trying to replicate the impeccable violence of my father. I jabbed that bag until I was nauseated and my legs burned and I could feel each individual abdominal muscle strain. Finally, when it became clear my father wasn't going to come out, I unlaced the gloves—my father's gloves, heartbreakingly redolent with the yeasty odor of his fists—and went back into the house to make a spectacle of myself.

Adult Jack thinks: what I want to know is, how can you see your son standing before you slathered in shaving cream, sweating, with knuckles bloodied from savaging an unbroken heavy bag and not say anything?

What could young Jack do? He provided the assist.

"Phew," I said at last, wiping my forehead with knuckles facing out so my father could see the evidence. "Just getting a few rounds in. Working on the jab today. Had to lay off early, though. Ran out of shaving cream. Wow."

"You're making a mess on the floor," my father said, handing me a paper towel. "Clean that off before your mother gets home."

What I Could Tell Hahva 1.2: Act the Lion

Or perhaps I would tell her this.

I do not have opinions. What I have had from childhood—to the deep disappointment of my father—is a profound sense of empathy.

When I was six my parents took me to a neurologist because they thought I had a cerebral impairment. What aroused concern was that after school I would sit for hours at a bus stop and just stare at people in a daze. Why? It wasn't until two decades later that I finally comprehended why watching people walking by was so fascinating. What I couldn't articulate about watching strangers, what I was searching for in the intense scrutiny of the codes of their faces, was an answer to the big question I haven't been able to stop asking since Dex drowned:

Are you being loved the way you deserve?

It is because of this question that I still can't resist other people. In middle school I would pack a lunch and take the shuttle to the airport and camp out at the Arrivals/Departures sign to watch men and women run into each others' arms, reunited. Nowadays I am often late to class because I get caught on the benches outside the English department on the quad, staring at students. Lots of days I don't even want to be their professor. (Adjunct, adjunct, I must remind himself. Let's be honest.) Forget comma splices. Who cares about the role of the subjunctive. And so what if your antecedent is unclear? What I want to tell them is never mind. Let's talk survival. Let's talk loss. Let's talk heartbreak.

I don't even want to teach them, I think. I want to save them. I want to be their shepherd.

Or, more accurately: their lifeguard.

* * *

When I was younger I wanted to be more like Press. He was defiant. His mechanism was to drink openly, fail classes, get in fights. He cultivated a sidebar of small-time crime. His bedroom was rife with stolen Blaupunkts and radar detectors. He bought a rusted International Scout that he used to cart off supplies and tools looted from construction sites to sell privately at cut-rate prices. Once he got stabbed in the shoulder with a screwdriver when he tried to sell a guy his own reciprocating saw.

Cool, I thought. The only thing I have is a callus on my pinky from trying to out-Liszt Liszt.

And Press was so incisive. He dealt with the world by reflexes. He was brilliant and arrogant, consistently contemptuous of his teachers, and his grades suffered accordingly. But his standardized aptitude test scores were off the chart—he even challenged a question and succeeded in having it revoked; he was right and ETS was wrong—and with his essay he won a scholarship to the university on the West Coast. Then it happened: the phone call from BWI, the silent ride back from the airport, the unstopperable drinking. The next week Press found an efficiency in the Canton canning district and took a job as a motorcycle escort for funeral processions. He didn't last long, though; he was fired for stopping the procession at a liquor store on the way to the cemetery. The ensuing jobs weren't much better. Graveyard-shift clerk at a twenty-four-hour photocopy café. Laundry room tech at a Towson public swimming pool. Forklift operator in an east Baltimore appliance warehouse. Anything where he didn't have to deal with other human beings. He drifted in an eroding orbit from job to job and sofa to sofa until he found himself back at the house in Huntfield and touched down in the basement. How did this happen to Press? What became of him?

And why did he come back from California in the first place?

It should have been me. I should have been the one who got stuck in that house. I was not strong like Press. I was always so afraid. In high school I had to read *Henderson the Rain King*, in which a rich American travels to Africa in a fit of spiritual desperation and meets a tribal king who treats him with his own kind of therapy, which involves, mainly, cultivating a friendship with a lion. At first the American is terrified in the presence of the lion and can scarcely control himself. But the king counsels him to "act the lion," to be as the lion is—as strong and fearless and noble. Finally the desperate American is able to overcome his fear and the lion loves him for it. They become friends.

How I wanted to act the lion. How I wanted to be like Press. O to feel truckish! To enjoy huge inertia, to be malevolent and strong and dauntless, spontaneous in speech, an issuer of comebacks and rebuttals, a fuck-off artist, coiled. To be dangerous and unpredictable, capable of surprising acts of menace or gentleness. "Maybe he'll nurse injured baby chickadees back to health. Maybe he'll vandalize public statuary with Quikrete. Who knows?"

But I was not this way. I was frightened, the hair scared right off my scalp, Press said, stricken with the follicle fear.

And so my skills were different. I cultivated an extensive tantra of self-control.

I held my breath. Breathe for five seconds, hold for sixty; breathe for ten, hold for ninety; breathe for fifteen, hold for one twenty. All external forces are out of my control, I thought, but I will be the overlord of my pneumatics.

I memorized the order of all the presidents and quizzed myself silently. When I became too familiar with them I would order the First Ladies, by chronology, then by party, by astrological sign, by hairdo.

Shortly I graduated from the alphabetical order of U.S. state capitals to those of foreign countries. Chişinău, I'd think. Ulaanbaatar, Maputo, Windhoek. When this ceased to challenge I would mentally recite which territories bordered which, changing compass direction. East to west: Komodo and Rinca, Lombok, Bali. North to south: Komodo and Rinca, Sulawesi, Kalimantan.

Prime numbers, Oscar winners, Kentucky Derby jockeys, state birds, hunger strikes. My energy turned inward on itself. When it was dinnertime and the Tennants were once again congregated at the table in eerie battlefield silence, I would clench up and mumble to myself, "Kitty Eisenhower." When I approached the vital crossover in *allegro* that I always screwed up, I'd chant, "Zapotec, Zia, Zimshian, Zuni." Late at night, lovingly tucking the orange flip-flop under my mattress, I'd whisper, "Budapest" or "patella" or "boron."

As a teenager, after I cracked my tooth on the barrel of the 9mm Colt 1911 beavertail in an experiment with parasuicide, I would run my tongue silently across the chipped incisor until I recovered some clarity.

These strategies helped me endure the punishing silences—I thought: I can take this and I will show you nothing back—but they also did something else for me. My kid self thought, If I can do these things, then my father, so uninterested in me since Dex died, will rediscover me. He will admire my steely resolve and understated strength. He will see my mastery of self and put his fighter's hand on my head and say, "I've trained a lot of cadets, boy, and I've never seen a pain threshold/hunger tolerance/knowledge of esoterica like yours in my life. You did good, son."

They were mental rosaries, in a way.

Possibly this is also what Dex prayed for when he went into the water: notice me.

As I grew older, however, the point of these exercises changed. Instead of praying my father would be impressed, I thought to myself: if I can do all these things my family will never be able to touch me again.

What I Could Tell Hahva 1.3: My Ruined Finger

Or I could tell her how my finger got broken and how it foiled all hope I ever had of being a pianist. It's a quickie, easy as ABC.

A. One night at thirteen, drunk, miserable, pining for Dex, I screwed up the courage to confront my father about him. When I uttered his name, just that one syllable, my father—driver of hard bargains, taker of no guff, enemy of topmost tree branches everywhere—applied the full g-force of his rage charisma on me. It was nighttime, I should note, so my father had been drinking since six o'clock sharp, and in the billiards room we drunkenly squared off. We actually stood, opposed each other, circling. I was in over my head, terrified, but also a little proud of myself.

B. A direct order for silence was issued, processed, disobeyed. An accusation was levied and emphasized by the faceward wagging of a demonstrative pointer finger. "It was your fault," I may have said. "You were supposed to be watching him." Shame, shame went my pointer in his face, fingering him for the tragedy.

C. Suddenly I discovered my index finger vised in a powerful boxer's grip. The speed of it all was astonishing. It happened so fast I almost didn't realize it had happened until after I heard the noise that has haunted me ever since: the sound of someone shucking corn. Partially a sudden rip—*rrrrrrriiiiip*—partially a bark. That is what a broken finger sounds like. It's possible—possible—that he just meant to get the digit out of his personal space. He certainly wasn't going to be arraigned by his weakling youngest offspring, after all. Sir no sir. So maybe he didn't mean to break it. Perhaps it was just a reflex against insubordination. Against defying orders. I've thought about it. But I can't be sure: we never spoke of it again.

Permission to Start Again?

Three weeks later I had my audition. I stepped onstage in front of the finest music teachers in the world, rolled up my sleeves, sat down on the bench, and flubbed it.

"Permission to start again, judges?"

They let me try a few times but I couldn't get past the first movement in *allegro*. The judges were polite about it but the snickering backstage was audible. There was an uncomfortable moment when my mother, Press, and I had to walk past the other hopefuls limbering up in the hallway. A suety kid whose face was stuccoed with acne chortled with his friends and made gestures that mocked my crossover. "Dur, dur," he said, making the spastic gesture, "I am the epileptic pianist." As Press walked past he punched him savagely in the chest. The kid collapsed to the ground, making lugubrious off-key accordion noises.

In that moment I loved Press intensely.

Another Idea

Or, if I were brave enough, I could tell her about The Night. How hot it was, how humid, and how the nighttime air was rich with the odor of pine needles and mushrooms and fresh water. How the trees felt ancient and the dark water was both romantic and menacing, how you couldn't stop looking at it move. How the fireflies were starting to come out, making it look like all the stars in the galaxy were bobbing around us.

Press and I were playing an adrenalized game we had made up that we called Ambush. One of us would dress up in a white sheet, carry a flashlight, and crash around through the woods while whistling or singing loudly. The other one dressed in dark clothes and stalked him. The point was to make the ambushee easily detectable so that the other one could scare him as severely possible. It was an excruciating game. When Press got close to me, he'd crouch like a cat, then pounce, crying, "Ambush!" It felt real; you were being attacked. You would sprint like mad through the trees and underbrush for about a hundred screaming feet and then, when you tired out and fell on the ground, your brother would roll down with you and laugh like crazy.

Dex hated the game and refused to play it with us. He was supposed to be inside watching TV with our father. Mother had gone into town for shopping and it was our father's turn to watch us. Dex stayed in; because Press was old enough, I was allowed to go outside and play. I was the ambushee, but was tired of being found so easily, so I decided to hide down by the dock. Turn the tables, maybe. It took me a few minutes to shed the white sheet, tuck it under the dock, and nestle into the bushes. Then I heard a noise coming from the open water.

See, the truth is I did see it happen. I am just too scared to admit it. Because it proves that I am worthless. And a coward. He wasn't that far out yet. I could have pulled him back in. I know I was only five years old, but I could have at least tried. I could have done *something*.

I might have saved him.

Instead of swimming out after Dex I ran to get my father. But not at first. At first, and for reasons I still don't understand, I was transfixed. I have never told anybody this. In those first moments—when I should have been sprinting to the house to get help or diving off the dock to attempt a rescue—all I could do was watch Dex struggle. His head went under suddenly, as if something had pulled him down, and then abruptly it popped back up. His arms were churning in the water but weren't making much noise. He didn't scream. I could only hear the froth of the water and a gagging noise as he choked. It looked at first like maybe he was just playing. Faking. But he wasn't. It felt unreal. I was angry with him. I was desperate for him to be playing.

I was just so scared.

I kept hoping Press would leap out of the shadows and cry, "Ambush!"

I wanted him to do the saving for me. Because I couldn't do it. I wanted out.

My bare feet felt glued to the dock. My ears went deaf with static, then silent, then roaring again. I teetered out over the water, then stumbled backward and finally sprinted into the house, lodging splinters in my feet. When I got there I couldn't open the screen door. My fingers didn't work. I burned the skin off my hands trying to claw through the screen before I could communicate to our father, reeking of alcohol, what was happening.

But I'm not even sure if *this* is true. Maybe I just stood there, paralyzed and useless, crying as my six-year-old brother drowned. Maybe there was no Ambush, no sheet around the piling, no screen door. It could be. I can't tell what's real. The only reason I know the orange flip-flops are real is because I still have them. They are the one artifact I am allowed to have, and they are my most private, treasured secret. They are a message to me from my brother Dex.

Remember me, they say. Don't forget I loved you. It wasn't your fault.

I wish I could believe them.

But

I want to tell Hahva. I do. I want to tell her the awful, irreducible truth. "I had a brother," I could say. "He drowned. I couldn't save him. He was only six years old."

But I can't. It seems just as important to tell her about the pine needles or the splinters or some fucking flip-flops as it is to tell her about how Dex died. And I want to get it right. It's important. If it was windy. If I was barefoot. If fireflies were even out at all. What the water smelled like. What the nets dragging the mud looked like. Which one of the emergency workers tried to comfort me by letting me play with the CB in his car.

If I can't get it right why tell it at all?

Meanwhile, Back at the Suicide Palace: Reinsertion

A thick-jointed woman rolls a wheelchair through the door and the air in the kitchen parches. The windows craze. Something hot and acid beetles in my stomach. Pulsating images of my youth flash upon my retinas: the shaving cream, the beavertail, the finger, two orange flip-flops washing against the pilings of the dock at Lake George.

All because of the crumpled wad of a life-form in the corner.

"So you're Jackson," the woman says. "Nice to meet you." Her handshake is forthright and vigorous—Midwestern—and her speech is tight with optimism. Her voice has the squeaking quality of two pieces of Styrofoam rubbing together. She gives us all a no-nonsense look through the thick lenses of her enormous Swifty Lazars.

"Jack," I say.

"Bessie Wickwire. Bess will do. And . . ."

"Hahva."

"Hahva, Bess. O.K. I'm going to be helping with Gil."

Press, holding in one hand a mug of fuming liquid, offers Bess a ragged smile. "Pressman Montcalm Tennant. Capricorn. I like long twilight walks on the beach, Old Bushmills, and Django Reinhardt records."

"Good to meet you, Pressman," she says, giving him nothing.

"Good handshake. Do you work out?"

I notice my mother noticing the tracks the wheelchair is making on the white tiles. She is calculating the amount of Swiffering this will require.

"It's good you're all here," Bess says, ignoring my brother. "Gil is going to need all your help if this reinsertion is going to work. It took some doing to move him from the subacute care unit but with all these helping hands and the Lord's blessing—"

"Hallelujah!" Press blurts.

"—it will all work out. Jack, I'm especially glad to see you here. We've got a lot of work ahead of us. The good news, though, is that Gil has already made super-duper progress. Haven't you, Gil?"

"Both super and duper," Press says under his breath. "Gold star gold star gold star."

"That's right, Gilly. Adair, Press, you know all this already but I want to explain for Jack and Hahva. What happened to Gil is a very rare form of stroke in the pons area of the brain. Strokes are fairly common—there are about seven hundred thousand in the U.S. every year—but a stroke in this area of the brain stem is extremely unusual. And destructive. What would normally be a minor stroke—say about the size of a dime—is completely debilitative in the pons. Sixty percent of people who stroke in this area die immediately." To my father she says, "So it's a good thing you're made out of Kevlar, isn't it, Colonel?"

I have never seen anyone act this way with my father. She is being schoolmarmish and patronizing but I also detect genuine affection. It is either sickening or exhilarating.

"The pons area controls pretty much everything from the nose down. Breathing, kidney function, bowels, the perceptual systems, body temp, you name it. When this kind of stroke happens it's called locked-in syndrome. The locked-in can hear and smell and taste and feel everything but cannot articulate. They are fully intellectually and perceptively intact but have no speech and no significant communicant movement."

"And the stroke was how bad?" Hahva can't help asking.

"It was a serious stroke," she says diplomatically.

" 'Nuked' is what the emergency room doc said," Press offers.

"So he's . . . locked in?" Hahva asks, kneeling down next to my father and putting her hand on his forearm. This is something a lot of case managers do at the shelter. Touching the forearm is neutral and reassuring, but I don't have this power. I'm not a toucher.

"That's right. To what degree we can't be sure yet. What I can tell you is that he is very confused and frightened and lonely. He can't describe his pain or fear to anyone. In his mind he is his old self but his body won't respond." As she speaks Bess circles my father's wheelchair, looking at him as often as she looks at us. She stands to the left of the wheelchair, to the right, over by the sink, by the fox-headed vessel on the mantel.

"Um, would you like the bathroom?" Press offers.

"Although in locked-in syndrome the eyes often retain some activity it is almost always only vertical, and this move-ment is often impaired, as it is in Gil's case. See for yourself." While everyone else bends forward to examine my father I fo-cus on the spot directly above his head on the refrigerator. "See how his one open eye is bobbing up and down? He is strug-gling to normalize the movement, sort of like a TV set strug-gling with vertical hold. This vertical action is promising; it's the lateral movement that is problematic. By walking around Gil you force him to try to track you. This is important. The more we work Gil now the better. The chances of improvement diminish day by day."

"The emergency room doc said that if he wasn't moving or talking within three days that he never would again," Press says.

Bess goes deeply silent for a moment, during which time it is hard to discern her attitude. It may be rage. Then she says, "Yes, that is the current conventional medical thought. Most neurologists believe this. Fortunately I'm not a neurologist, and I subscribe to a different theory. 'For I, the Lord your God, will hold your right hand, saying to you, "Fear not, I will help you." ' Isaiah 41:13."

"What theory is this?" Press says. "Pray-real-hardism?"

"Neuroplasticity. What most neurosurgeons don't like to talk about—mainly because they don't understand it, can't quantify it—is the brain's ability to remap itself. Although this area of Gil's brain has been destroyed it is possible that it can find a way to reroute signals. For this we need two things: active intervention and repetition. That's why it's so important to have you all here. I can only help Gil so many times a day. His regimen will have to be very disciplined." From over by the mudroom—nearly out of comfortable verbal range—Bess says to my father, "Welcome to boot camp, honey!"

"So you think he really has a chance of improving?" Hahva says, flashing at my father a gigawatt of hope and encouragement.

"He's already improved. He has improved his respiratory autonomy. No more machine, and it seems the trachs are getting smaller by the day, doesn't it, Gil? At first he had wild body temp swings, from way down at 90 degrees to a fever-high 106, if you can believe it. But now that's stabilizing. And he has increasing control of one eye and as of yesterday he has some very promising movement in a finger. Show 'em, Gil."

My father's eye starts flickering inside the socket in frantic, rapid-fire movements and then he makes a barely perceptible motion with his right index finger.

"Bravo! Isn't that great?" My father's chin, I now see, is candied in a thick, honeyish drool. "Whoopsie daisy. You've got a little something there, Gil. Allow me."

As Bess delicately wipes my father's chin Press says, "Is he going to be doing that kind of thing a lot?"

"His body's control center has been destroyed, Press. You'd better get used to this. You're going to need to take care of all sorts of things. Gil can't even control his bowels or bladder. I know this is embarrassing for you, Gil, but that's where we're at. No point in being coy. Just have to soldier through it."

"So you're some kind of locked-in syndrome specialist?" Press asks.

"There are no experts. It's too rare. There is almost no clinical research on it. There wasn't even any mention of locked-in syndrome in any medical publications until World War II. We can only guess how many locked-in patients—fully cognitively aware, remember—were given up as comatose in hospitals. Imagine it. You go to sleep on a night just like any other and then you wake up a week later paralyzed in a strange bed surrounded by people you've never seen before. They don't talk to you. They don't pay you any attention, in fact, except maybe to drain urine and bowel output and turn you over once or twice. Your family comes to visit and they have conversations about you over your frozen body, thinking you can't hear." Bess shakes her head. "We'll never know how many people this happened to."

A polyphonic tunelet rings out through the room.

"Ah. The manual laboriat," Press announces. "And right on time. The last segment of society from which you expect the element of surprise."

"Let them in, Press," my mother says. "We're converting the billiards room into a bedroom, Jack. Your father won't make it up the stairs. You boys will just be in the way while the workmen set it up," she says, looking meaningfully at Press, whose mouth is fizzing with alcohol. "Jack, why don't you show Hahva around and later Pressman can take you out for dinner? Everything should be settled by then."

"And why not?" he says, extending a hand, into which my mother places a few crisply folded bills.

On her way out, Hahva pulls Bess aside. "How many people usually survive locked-in syndrome?"

"That I know of? Technically?" Bess asks, the joints in her jaw clenching. "None."

Hahva Gets a Crumb, Or: The E-Type and Me

The grounds resuscitate my hatred. It is all the same, a time capsule of landscaped anguish. Here the stone-flushed garden. There the wartlike deposits of excrement from lesser ruminants. Here the fat country insects that jerk and marionette in the air over the manicured countersunk croquet pitch. There the polished nickel sconces with articulating arms. Here the many patinated bronze urns organized in patterns identical to those in the Sun King's garden. There, along the fence, the Invincible roses, thrilled with their own nerves. They are vivid; they are unknowable; they are coveted by my parents.

These are my places. To everyone else they are beautiful. Hahva inhales at the sight of them. O the flora. O the fauna. It's like something out of a magazine, she says. It's like something from a movie. So why are they so terrible to me? Why do I want to farm the croquet pitch with Press's Scout? Why do I want to uproot the Invincibles? Why do I want to run off the horses?

"You have to watch where you step, don't you?" Hahva says as she *jetés* over a mound of steaming nuggets. "What does your dad feed these sheep? Metamucil? Or is it the goats? I can imagine goats being very . . . productive."

"It's the foxes, I think."

I lack even the most basic evidentiary farmyard knowledge and have no idea what animal has produced this pellet-filled copropolis, but it seems important to tell Hahva that it is the foxes so she will not grieve over the hunts: local foxes, alive and defecating well, thank you.

"God. I just cannot imagine living here. It is like the set of a soap opera or something."

"It has a certain quality, I suppose."

"I feel like you should have a butler running around and, well . . ."

"Butling?"

"Right."

Hahva has a seizure of wonder and delight at the mutinous beauty of it all.

"Don't you have a special place or something you want to show me, Jack? Oh, that sounded dumb, but you know what I mean. Didn't you have a clubhouse or a hidden fort or a special place or something? I mean, this is where you grew up. Is one of those horses your horse? Show me. I want to see. Just a crumb."

Immediately, against my will, I think of the Pain Box. It is only a few hundred feet away, through the trees. Imagining it even at this distance produces a mulchy feeling of dread. Barbasol is in there. The beavertail—loaded with hollowpoints, I'm pretty sure—is in there. The left flip-flop is in there. I can't tell her about that. But maybe I can tell her something.

"You want to see something?"

For a moment Hahva is not sure what to make of this offer.

"Really?"

"Come on."

In the barn I pull the cover off of the E-Type. It is a powerful, nearly totemic gesture; it feels as if I am removing the sheet from the corpse of a loved one to identify the body. I avert my eyes until the car is fully revealed. Then I stand back and briefly, there in the barn, with the disconsolate lowing of the cows outside and the barn flies making static in the corners, Hahva disappears and it is just the two of us again—the E-Type and me.

"There it is," I say at last. "A 1969 Jaguar XKE Roadster. Pearlescent Cornish Grey paint with magnolia hide piped in mulberry. Two hundred sixty-five base horsepower—monstrous for a European of the age—with four-wheel servo disc assist brakes and four-wheel independent suspension. High-tech. And it's a Series II, before they got the bulky bumpers and before they were asphyxiated by the Series III's emissions reductions. It's got a synchromesh gearbox, so you can downshift into first while still rolling without dropping the tranny. And note that it has the chrome-pressed wheels, not the sissy spokes that you see so much of. It's practically a one-hundred-point car, almost a museum piece. Not a scratch. Check it out. Even the plastic on the rear window is unblurred. Thirty-two thousand eight hundred four miles of purring, unrestored, numbers-matching history."

Hahva whistles.

"And it has three wipers," she says.

"You got it," I say. "Thirty-three and a third percent cleaner windows."

For a moment I feel sick. I feel wishful and ashamed, larcenous and haunted. A part of my father's history is sifting through me and it recognizes me as craven.

I have never even sat in this car.

"How Press and I coveted this thing," I say to Hahva, circling the E-Type. "Our father would never let us ride in it. Not even touch it. One night when my father was out of town Press stole the extra key and fired it up in the barn, but even he didn't have the guts to put it in gear. He just sat there for twenty minutes in the dark of the barn, revving the engine in neutral, me standing behind that beam, afraid to even sit in the passenger seat."

Six years after that I promised Karina Thiergartner that I would take her to the Totally Tiki prom in it but I couldn't even work up the courage to ask. I took her in my brother's heaving International Scout instead. It backfired in the lot and spat soot onto a girl's frock and angered her boyfriend, which is why my mouth is swollen so much that I look like Daffy Duck in the photos.

Hahva reaches out with a fingertip to touch the curve of the hood and I almost tell her to stop. But the car doesn't crumble. Sirens don't sound and flares don't ignite. It seems almost incredible that she grasps the handle and opens the door.

"Now's your big chance."

"For what?" I manage.

"Don't you want to get in?"

"I don't think we should," I say before I know it.

"Come on, chicken. We'll just sit."

"I don't know, Hahva."

"It smells so good in here."

"That's Connolly leather."

"Mmm."

Hahva puts one leg into the footwell. She is ginger, exploratory, as if testing the temperature of a hot tub. Then, in one easy movement, she is in the passenger seat. She looks at me with the surprise-surprise expression of a magician's lovely assistant who has just emerged inexplicably from a cloud of smoke.

"Jesus, Hahva."

She closes the door and then she is inside a sphere containing the legend of my father—his cocoon of pride and disdain and secrecy. It is that easy for her.

"Come on in." Her voice comes to me muffled through the canvas and glass: "Water's fine!" She leans across the gearshift and opens the driver's door to me.

The key to the E-Type burns inside my pocket.

I could fire it up if I had the guts. I could drive it right out of here.

"This is stupid," I say weakly. "I know what you're doing but it doesn't mean anything. I'm not being chicken. I just don't want to scratch the leather or anything."

Chicken noises—*baaawk baaawk baaawk baaaaaaaaawk!*—issue from the car.

"All right," I say. "Fine. If it will appease you. Christ."

All in one motion—the way amateur skydivers force themselves out of the airplane—I surge forward into the E-Type.

It takes me a second to orient. The seat is too far back; I cannot reach the pedals; because it is adjusted for a taller person I cannot see out the rearview mirror; the wheel is also too far away and I nearly hyperextend my elbows reaching for it. I try without success to ignore a shoes-too-big-to-fill impression.

"That wasn't so hard, was it?" Hahva says brightly, thinking she is helping. "Too bad we don't have the keys."

I want to be able to revile the E-Type. I want to be immune to it, to deny that it is a failure of my childhood hope, to forget that I ever wanted it for my own, that I ever secretly wished I could be a worthy recipient. The leather smells faintly of my father and the gearshift glints like poisonous candy and I concentrate so hard on making myself strong so that I will not want it, but I do. I do want it. I do I do I do.

The Terrapin 1.1

The Terrapin Bar is knuckley and fast. I had forgotten the feeling of walking into it, pushing through the door in Press's exhaust, seeing all the glass bottles like soldiers at attention, doubling in the mirror, saluting your return. Inch—a nickname describing the length of the fuse on his anger—is still behind the bar, unchanged by time. His face is as pink and bristled as a ham and his hands are as fast as a magician's serving up the damage. Shingled with street cruelty and grisly mortal know-how, he was born to preside over a register.

Press, dropheaded and low, lines through the bar to our old banquette in back. In our seats, in the weakling moldering light, my brother is more visible. His eyes are spoked in red but are more focused than they were this morning. He is still needley and straight even after years of saturation. The only part of him that is affected is his face. It used to be sharp and taut, his profile tomahawkish, but now it is sodden and emptied except for the beaky protuberance in the center of the wad of flesh. All these years his body has been loaded up with drink and sloth and greed and pornography—a vice frigate. How does it remain so lean? The genes of our ramrod father.

"Something to drink, little brother?" he says. "A brag?"

"A what?" Hahva says.

"A *brag*," Press repeats.

This is a syllable I have not heard in over a decade. I had almost forgotten it.

"I don't drink anymore, Press."

"What, you were serious about that? God, I thought that was a joke."

"No joke."

He looks at Hahva for verification.

"It's true," she says. "Hasn't had a drink since he was twenty-two."

I clench my stomach when she says this. Hahva doesn't know the truth about Jordana Mochnik and my night of drunken disgrace. She thinks I didn't finish my dissertation because of an ideological crisis. She doesn't know about Leon Flanders signing my discharge, disgust in his eyes. She thinks my professional neutering was a choice made in good faith with a clear conscience and not in a moment of drunken rage with emergency equipment.

"Really?" Press asks with a private unconvinced look for me.

"Really."

"That sounds very dreary. Have you found Jesus, too? Was he in the lingerie section, as I've always suspected?"

"Just get me get a soda, Press."

"And for you?"

"The same," Hahva says. Normally she would have a Seven & Seven, but she is demonstrating solidarity.

My brother contracts and submarines through the struggle of the bar. When he's gone Hahva emits an aspirated laugh.

"You know, I've been trying to get out of places like this for most of my life. But your brother—all that money and he chooses to come to a place like this. I don't get it."

"My father has money. That doesn't mean that Press does. Besides, we've had an arrangement with Inch since high school. My brother gets freebies in exchange for smuggling an occasional bottle of top-shelf from my dad's cabinet."

"That doesn't make any sense. Why doesn't he just drink your dad's stuff at home? It's already free."

I shrug: Isn't it obvious? "He needs to get out of that goddamn house."

All around us in the bar people are buckling just out of sight but when I turn to look they are somehow miraculously still in their seats, unfallen.

"You know," she says, "I've been trying to identify the smell of this place since we've come in. It's really quite remarkable."

"Yes. It seems a bit like fouled vacuum cleaner bags."

"And expired nonoxynol-9."

"Hot birdcage and Bakelite."

"Carpet glue."

"Combined with liquefied mushroom."

"And just a dash of mildewy drywall."

"And a *soupçon* of soiled urinal puck."

"Hey," she says, "what is with that 'popodopoulos' stuff?"

"Beats me," I say.

"And was that Worcestershire sauce he was drinking this morning? Blech. Why? Why, I ask you—why oh why—does anyone drink Worcestershire sauce?"

"It is a nostrum of long standing. If you see Press drinking Worcestershire sauce in the morning it indicates he's nursing a hangover."

"Nastiness."

"Come to think of it, if you see Press do pretty much anything in the morning it indicates he's nursing a hangover."

"Hard to believe he's your brother."

Father and Son

Behind Hahva, in the polluted corner, is a TV hanging from chains that is playing a commercial for diesel dualies or work-grade denimwear or deer-hunting weaponry or something. A rugged cowboy-hatted father is teaching his son important man-lessons like how to rope steers—and, offscreen, presumably how to handroll cigarettes on horseback and spit a good plug while squinting meaningfully at the blazing horizon—all set against a mournful harmonica. When the mustachioed father swats his son in chummy congratulation after a successful roping my heart quails.

Why didn't my father teach me how to rope cattle? Or how to fight? How to drive the E-Type? Anything? Despite all he's done I can't help wishing—I have wished my whole life—to be the recipient of his attention. Maybe it's juvenile, but I can't help thinking—bitterly, bitterly—that this is why Dex died: my father's supreme indifference to us.

He didn't care enough to keep an eye on Dex that night at the lake, and Dex died. And yet I long for him to teach me something. Even something stupid. Give me whittling, I'll take it. Give me papier-mâché doll-making, fine. I'm not proud, I'd even settle for learning how to affix a spare tire or analyze P/E ratios or make unravelable sailor knots. Anything, anything. Even how to tie a tie, for God's sake. Then I could attend cocktail parties and think to myself, Nice four-in-hand,

Jack. Just like your father's. Yep, you're a real chip off the old block. In this light I see you have his chin, too. Very handsome.

But then I confuse myself. Why do I want to be like him? Why do I want to learn from him? He keeps Pressman in indentured servitude in the basement. He broke my dream of being a concert pianist. He killed Dexter.

Why do I still want these things from him?

The Terrapin 1.2: Bzzzz Bzzzz

"So far the family Tennant is not exactly as I imagined," Hahva says.

"I don't know why you wouldn't believe me. I told you."

"You didn't, actually." When she gets nothing from this she says, "Why does everyone seem more concerned with tidy floors and drink glasses than they are with your father's life?"

I make a teetering scalelike gesture with my palms upturned.

Hahva looks for a moment like she is going to protest my evasiveness but then she simply stands up from the banquette and fights her way to the bathroom. Press burbles through the crowd, with drinks borne aloft like a handful of torches. They pass each other unacknowledged.

"Where's Florence Nightingale?"

"Cut it out, Press. What's the matter with you?"

"What do you think?"

"I don't know," I say tiredly. "That's why I'm asking."

Press makes a pinched gesture with thumb and forefinger and waves it in front of my face. "Bzzzz," he says. "Bzzzz bzzzz."

"You're on crack? That's the matter with you?"

"No, little brother, you are the matter. You think you can just fuck off for years and then come back here and start buzzing around like a fly on shit?"

"I have no idea what you're talking about. Is someone a piece of shit in this metaphor? Because it sounds to me like you're the piece of shit."

"I'm not the piece of shit. *Dad* is the piece of shit."

"You're going to have to explain better than that, I'm afraid."

"You know what I'm talking about. Dad's dying, Jacko. You heard Bess. He's fucked. And suddenly here you are, after all these years, buzzing around the crypt, looking to play make-up."

At this I almost laugh. "You have no idea why I'm here, Press. But I promise I have no interest in salvaging a relationship with Dad."

"But you are interested in the old man's money, aren't you? Hey. In a way I don't blame you. Parading your little woman around in front of him. Sound strategy. Do I need to make odds on how long it's going to take for her to start talking about children? Nothing like grandkiddies to mend fences and open wallets and whatnot, is there?"

"This is your theory? That is the stupidest thing I've ever heard."

"Then why are you here? And don't give me any shit about helping."

"You wouldn't understand."

"No? Maybe Flo can explain it."

"What does that mean?"

"Get real, Jack. First time she fucked you did she know who your daddy was?"

"I don't think I want to have this conversation."

"Look at yourself, Jacko. You're not exactly Casanova, are you? Prematurely balding, ridden with nervous tics, so awfully sober all the damn time, teaching at a third-rate institution in Boll Weevil, Georgia. And you're snacking on a fine Turkish delight like her?"

"She's not Turkish."

"Do the math, dumb-ass. Why do you think you're in bed with Miss Benetton Universe?" Press kicks back contemplatively in the banquette and suddenly I am the little brother again. I feel like I did in the old days when I was Press's acolyte. He would assume exactly this position and regard me critically, debating whether I was worthy of enlightenment. My eyes start pricking with tears and I wish for the thousandth time that I could respond with anger instead of fear. "Look at the facts. Hahva's a self-improver, right? She's a pipe cleaner so she works out—with impressive results, I might add—to build a new body. It's evident she wears knockoff shoes and imposter perfumes. And her accent. Her accent, Jacko. The diction is nearly perfect but I am still detecting something very *necky* about it, aren't I?" Press's mouth squints in thought. "What is it? Straight Georgia? Alabama? Miss-ah-sih-pah? That kind of accent doesn't just disappear by luck. How was it accomplished?"

"You don't know what you are saying, Press."

"She's trying to climb out of the gutter. And good for her. Why shouldn't she? But she's trying to climb out of the gutter on your family tree, Jacko. It would be advisable to bear that in mind."

"You're wrong."

"Maybe, maybe not. But my recommendation, my double-barrel formula for safety and happiness in this earthbound life, is a vasectomy and a six-pack. Cover your bases."

"Whatever."

"Oh, and you might want to also think about the various misfortunes that might befall you if you try anything cute vis-à-vis the inheritance," he says, filliping my skull and mussing what's left of my hair. "Just a friendly warning from your elder brother."

The Terrapin 1.3: Robbie Milesakakapediles

Honor requires that I essay a retort but before I can get anything out a woman extrudes from the carbon fouling of the bar. She is a teapotish bottle blonde with oriole streaks in a stonewashed miniskirt and five-and-dime Jody Watleys. Her mouth is a pink rubbery peel that moves more than necessary when she talks.

"Pressman Tennant," she says. "Have you been avoiding me?"

"Yes, I have," he says with an exhalation of fatigue. "I owe you money."

"You owe everybody money."

"Then perhaps I have been avoiding you for more sensible reasons."

"You should be nice to me, Pressman. I'm on a mission of mercy."

"You've taken a vow of silence?"

"I thought you'd like to know that Musser is here."

"Don't they have health codes in this joint?"

"He hasn't seen you yet, so you could still make a clean getaway."

"Fuck that fucking pole monkey. Sixty grand a year up and down a fucking telephone pole. He can just fuck right off." My brother prestidigitates a flask from somewhere on his person and upends it over his empty glass. Tawny liquid ignites the milky ice. "I don't owe him a fucking penny. That's some bullshit right there."

"Just because you were too drunk to remember nine grand doesn't mean it didn't happen. I was at that game, Press."

"I didn't lose that hand. I was drunk but not that drunk."

"It wasn't high/low, honey. It was just straight hold 'em. You would have been looking good if it were high/low, but if you're sitting there married to the felt with a six-of-diamonds high when Musser shows four cowboys, well, you do the math. And beat it out the back way, sugar."

"I'm staying right here."

"I wouldn't recommend it. He's all fired up tonight."

With her chin she indicates the corner. In the cone of grainy pewter light on the pool table I make out a nose-heavy, viper-headed guy leaning into someone, menacing him at beerpoint. Behind his back he cups a cue ball in his hand. The other guy is holding Musser off with his stick. I've seen this matchup before; it never goes well for the guy with the stick. Through the barroom static I can make out something that sounds like, "My bowtie would crush your ram!"

"Bowtie?" I say. "Ram? What the hell does that mean?"

The woman regards me for the first time. "Well, that means Chevrolet, silly. And Ram is Dodge. Where you from, doll, Mars?"

"This is my little brother, Jackson, *hight* Jack. Jack, Roberta Miles, goes by Robbie Milesakakapediles. Perhaps you've heard of her."

"Another Tennant? Goodness gracious."

"Bounty," my brother agrees.

A molten tongue issues from the pocket of her mouth and roils at me. "Well well well. You never told me you had a brother, Pressman."

"I wasn't sure I did. He's a big professor down south. Aren't you, Jacko?"

"Roberta," I say, changing the subject, "what do you do?"

"Robbie, please," she urges, sitting down next to me in the banquette. The batterish skin of her thigh rubs against mine.

"Um, that seat is taken."

"I'll just keep it warm, then." She gives me a humid, evaluative look. "No cigarette? No drink?"

"He respectfully declines," Press says.

"A Tennant who doesn't smoke and doesn't drink? Honest? You belong in the circus. Or maybe Guinness."

"Robbie's a journalist, Jack."

"Really? I wouldn't have figured."

"And what would you figure a girl like me would do?"

Rub cars dry in bikinied semipornographic postures at back-highway auto washaterias, I think. Volunteer as test subject for experimental cosmetic surgeries. Designated flopgirl for GLOW, the Gorgeous Ladies of Wrestling, perhaps with a stage name like Nicotine Nanette or the Push-Up Avenger.

"Um, entertainment lawyer?" I say. "Fashion designer?"

"Aren't you a darling? I just love you Tennant boys. But no. I write for the *Huntfield Gazette*."

"She has a column," Press says. " 'From the Horse's Mouth.' "

"I cover foxhunty goings-ons."

"Goings-*on*," Press says.

"No. I mean plural. More than one goings-ons."

"Right. Sorry."

I can't imagine why my brother would associate with a gossip columnist. It would split my mother's atoms if word of my father's condition were bruited around Huntfield, much less published in a sleazy gossip column.

"It's not Page Six but it's a paycheck." Then, at Press's ogling: "Hey, are you looking below the neckline, buster?"

Press's hands shoot skyward. "Hey! I was just exercising my constitutional right to look around and your tits got in my way!"

At which Robbie giggles, the pink peel splitting open.

"Can't be too much horsey news around this bar," I say, hoping this might dispel her.

"That's why I'm here."

"She has kind of a hate-hate relationship with her subjects," Press says.

"You can only spend so much time at the Bit & Bridle or the Jolly Porter or whatever before you want to shoot someone."

"Here's a question for you, Robbie," Press says. "Why do all the towns around here have names that sound like antidepressants? Linthicum, Timonium, Padonia. Why is that? It seems like an extraordinarily cruel paradox to me that a place that so conduces to depression should have names that evoke such medication. What do you make of that, Lois Lane?"

"Beats me. Why do these pricks feel the need to name their houses?"

"Yeah, like those assholes at Hunt Run Farms."

"Bugle Manor," I say, remembering.

"Nor'easter Estate," Press says. "Their kid scratched up my Scout."

"You hit him when he was skateboarding in the parking lot, sugar."

"The Grove."

"Sundance Acres."

"Brightwood Place."

"Foxhall Farms," Robbie says.

"No, no. The Laindons are all right," Press says. "You remember when we took Brody's Gator out for a joyride that night and ran it through the fence and into their pond? They winched us out of there and drained the engine. Never said a word to Brody or Dad."

"Oh yeah. Nice guys. Are they still around?"

"Dead," Robbie says. "Franklin Laindon got it with the boom coming about during a storm in the Virgins and Eunice followed six months later. Heartbreak. No. Wait. She was crushed by a chandelier at the Belvedere. One of the two."

"Damn. Those two were all right."

Raising my soda, I say, "To the memory of the beloved Laindons."

"Here here."

"So, Pressman," Robbie says after a respectful silence. "I hear the old man's under the weather."

"I thought you came to this bar to get away from foxhunting gossip."

"Inquiring minds, Pressman."

"Well, if you must know, he's had some stomach irregularity. Too much pheasant in his diet, no doubt."

"Mmm. Maybe I'll have to pump your brother for information."

"Take it easy with Jack, Robbie. He's spoken for."

"Boo hoo," she says with a viscid pout.

"Why don't you come over here, my pretty remorafish?"

As Robbie relocates to Press's side I suddenly realize that Hahva is standing by the banquette. It's unclear to how much she has been a witness.

"Oh," I say. "Hahva. Hi. This is Roberta—"

"Robbie, silly. I told you." An unprivate pink sliver of tongue rolls at me.

"Robbie," I say. "This is Hahva, my girlfriend." This I enunciate very clearly. "Robbie is—"

There is an ear-clearing moment of repressurization as the women regard each other. Now is the appropriate time for Robbie to make signals that indicate harmlessness and innocence. Now is the time for the deprecating shrug and comradely handshake. The oh-is-this-your-seat? But none of this is forthcoming and Press is predictably silent, basking in the glow of the uncomfortable ambiguity.

"A friend of the family," I finally say.

"We were just talking about Papa Tennant's illness," Robbie says as Hahva sits down. "How is he doing, Hahva?"

Before she can answer I say, "He just got back from checking out a steeplechaser in Lancaster today and we haven't seen much of him yet. He's recuperating. Mainly just sitting around today."

"That true, Hahva?"

"Sure," she says before I can tap her leg under the table. "He's sitting around."

This is not a lie, exactly, but it is probably the closest Hahva has ever come. I can hear her mother's prognostication: that Tennant boy will take you straight to hell in gasoline bloomers.

Something verbal transpires by the pool table—it sounds

like "Blood Man's coming!"—and Musser swings the cue ball in a wide accelerating arc that terminates at the guy's hairline. There is a clear ceramic sound of inelastic collision and then the guy slumps to the floor. Inch hurtles over the counter into a wild scrum of colors and teeth and hands and bottles.

"Battle stations, people!" Press declares.

"Whoops," Robbie says. "Time to go."

"Good idea," I say.

"Tallyho," cries Press, downing the last of his smuggled brag.

"You take me to the nicest places," Hahva says as we slip out.

Outside the parking lot is scored and blasted, knotted up in night. We bullfight through the full assembly of skirted lowriders and stenciled flatbeds to Press's Scout. A handlike leaf attaches to the delicate bones of Hahva's ankle and she gives me a look that I don't reciprocate: yes, Press is going to drive. His mouth is fimbriated in alcohol sap but he is steady, straight with his own gravity, as balanced as a throwing knife. A big block Firebird with glasspacks shrieks to life and holeshots on the scrubgrass and into the street. It has always been this way.

Pressman Montcalm Tennant, Uncharitably Considered

"He's lewd, crude, suggestive, disrespectful of his mother, his suffering father, his brother, his brother's girlfriend, I might add, and his own apparent girlfriend—"

"Sex vassal, more like," I amend, to which Hahva shudders in the sheets.

"He is an alcoholic, a bigot, a vulgarian, very possibly a level nine unhealthy individualist, or a self-destructive, with a rampant id and delusional self-contempt and serious displacement issues. Self-inhibiting, alienated despite elevated verbality and effusiveness, probably dangerous to himself or others. He's demonstrated amorality and a refusal to engage the reality of his father dying, which indicates some monster blockage and emotional paralysis. I suspect he feels acutely ashamed about what he perceives to be his failures, especially as he compares where he is in his life—the cellar, figuratively but also literally—to others at his age. Plus he's just mean and selfish and predatory and overall DSM-eligible and I don't like him at all, not one bit, and I cannot understand for the life of me why you let me get into a car driven by him tonight after all those drinks."

"He has nice hair, though," I say. "Right?"

Pressman Montcalm Tennant, Charitably Considered

What Hahva doesn't know is that although he is all of those things, Press is also my hero. He helped me survive in this house and was the only person who ever stood up for me. We were united in suffering, a nation of brothers, the two bragateers. He was the bounteous giver of support, moral and immoral. And he included me. Whereas my father wouldn't let me even touch the damn E-Type, Press would take me for rides on his Toaster Tank. Whereas my father wouldn't acknowledge or even speak to me, Press let me come down to the basement and sit on the Everlast—the only position of honor ever accorded me—and have a few brags with all his high school friends. Whereas my father refused even to teach me how to throw a jab, Press was my constant protector. Among other sticking-up-fors, he notably:

1. smote the hateful oriole

2. silenced my cachinnating critic at the Juilliard audition, and

3. the biggest of all: he put the kibosh on the routine, nearly daily beatings I got from Kasimir Kakmuzh and saved my beloved *White Pages*.

As I think about this, something uncomfortable pops inside me, as a bulb expiring, and I decide to tell Hahva about memory number three.

"Kasimir Kakmuzh was a guy who bullied me in middle school. He was on some kind of international exchange program for challenged kids or something. He looked like he was eighteen years old. I was twelve. And he had singled me out for abuse. All the time. He beat me with his hands, a bike chain, a Smurf umbrella, a pair of vise grips, a broken-off car antenna, you name it. He was savage. I was too embarrassed to tell anyone, though, and so it kept coming. One day Kasimir Kakmuzh—Kakmuzh: 'like a man' in Russian, if you can believe that—discovered one of my prized possessions. A copy of the *Bell Atlantic Greater Baltimore Metropolitan Area White Pages*—long story: don't ask—that I always carried around with me. He stole it from me, shredded it while I watched in front of a crowd of kids, including this girl Karina Thiergartner who I had this giant crush on."

"Why was the *White Pages* one of your prized possessions?"

"I never told anyone but word must have gotten back to Press because the next Monday the *White Pages* mysteriously reappeared in my backpack. A little torn up, it's true, but it was back. And that morning Kasimir Kakmuzh wasn't waiting for me at the bus stop. Or in the hallway. Or at my locker between classes. Or on the playground after school. In fact, after that he never looked at me again. He was still at the same school but it was as if he disappeared."

"Why did you love the *White Pages*?"

"No one could have made that kind of impression on anybody but Press. I know he came to my rescue again. He was always doing that. Through my whole life he has been the only person I could count on."

"Jack, will you please tell me what was the big deal with the *White Pages*?"

What I Could Tell Hahva 2: The *White Pages*

I am not ready to talk about this one yet.

For a while, and only as a kid, I wanted to be a writer. Pressman had a brand-new Commodore 64 on which my pianist fingers would pick out stories in bird-fast movements in the slurry nighttime darkness of the basement. The problem, I knew, even then, was that I couldn't write about the only subject I ever had: Dex. How do you conjure emptiness? How do you describe a void? How can you render a Lemon-shaped hole in the heart?

You can't. I couldn't. So I wrote about invented people. People that did not matter. People I could find by letting my fingers to do the walking.

In adulthood, as a grad student in New York, I understood that many writers had such talismans or employed similar superstitions of habit to aid their work. For inspiration Cervantes read the writing on pieces of trash he found blowing by in the street. Hemingway famously sharpened twenty pencils each morning. Dorothy West locked her door to write. It helps Joan Didion to sleep with her manuscript next to her at night. But for me the only thing that helped was the *White Pages*. Among those hundreds of thousands of names in the greater Baltimore area I found people who knew things other than unending loneliness. I found Benji Singaram, who sold everything he owned to start a used car lot but went bankrupt because he couldn't bear to part with any of them. I found Myrtle Groggins, truck stop psychic. I found the Petruzzi Potato Sack twins, carnival fugitives, who eked a living plying their skills on the street, one lunging step ahead of the vengeful ringmaster tracking them down.

I couldn't write about Dex, so I wrote about the owners of these names.

In the *White Pages* I found what so many other children found in regular storybooks: companionship. A reprieve from the void. Safety in numbers. Invisible friends. I felt, in reading the *White Pages* and typing out stories on my brother's Commodore 64, the same thing I felt while sleeping with the Everlast or watching reunions under the Arrivals/Departures sign at BWI or playing Diceman or hammering out Beethoven or talking with Leon Flanders or having a midnight brag with my brother in the basement: less alone in the world.

I treasured the *White Pages* in the manner of a pet or a stuffed animal. I kept it on me at all times. I humped it to school in my rucksack and wedged it under my mattress, next to the beloved flip-flop, at night. I tucked it covertly under my chair at restaurants and hugged it to myself as if it were a pillow while watching movies. Sometimes, when it just wasn't practical to have it on me, I would tear sheets out and stuff one page in each pocket.

I am armed, I said to myself, with names.

Imagine my horror when in grade six the bully Kasimir Kakmuzh discovered my love sealed meticulously away in a secret zippered bookbag pocket like a heart packed in ice, awaiting transplant, delectably vulnerable.

The Veto Power of the Ass President

I do my best to appease Hahva by complimenting her shoulders and convincing her to let me bite the knife-edges of her hands. Then I acknowledge how bravely she is keeping things clean. All her clothes are heaped in the closet out of sight and there are no sunflower seed shells/opened Lunchables containers/empty cans of Ensure littering the floor. Or shoved under the bed. Or hidden under the nightstand. Or stashed in a drawer.

This, I know, is a big deal for Hahva. She lacks even the most basic clean-up logic. When she was still a girl in Louisiana she took all her bedside items—clock, lamp, ballerina figurines, even certain jewelry—and glued them to the table because she got sick of moving them to dust. Another time she hit a cat with her car and tried for days to find the owner, keeping the carcass overnight in my grill so neighborhood scavengers wouldn't get at it. ("What do you mean that's crazy?" she said, outraged. "Dead meat is *supposed* to go in the grill, jackass.")

Bob and weave: the biting and blandishment strategy works and Hahva doesn't take me to task for not talking about the *White Pages*.

We start getting ready for bed. As I push the two single beds together for the night I watch Hahva undress. She conscientiously throws her clothes in the back of the closet. Down to her mismatching underwear, Hahva strides back and forth between bedroom and bathroom, her long legs opening and closing like scissors, filling the room with the heated promise of sex.

"Lincoln's winking at me again," I say.

"Cheeky presidential bastard," she says, twisting to show me the imprint on her ass and moving almost within range. "Can you tell what he's thinking?"

"I can't quite make out his expression. Please take a step closer that I might discern."

Five years ago, when Hahva was still in school working on her MSW, she burned Abraham Lincoln into her ass by mistake. She drove this '76 Buick Skylark that had vinyl upholstery covered pointlessly—perilously—in brown metal buckles. The Skylark didn't have any air-conditioning and in the summer the vinyl got scorching. The placement of the metal buckles made it virtually impossible to sit safely but Hahva devised a system of contortion by which she could sit on the scorching seat without touching any buckles. The necessary position required that she cock her left knee to her chest and rest her foot on the vent, as if she were preparing to kick the dashboard through the windshield and into the atmosphere. She refined this stance to the point of reflex and could drive nearly unimpaired.

But she didn't count on stray coinage. Coming back from Tybee Beach one day when the Skylark had been cooking unshaded on the asphalt for hours she sat down in her traditional buckle-free spot directly on top of a penny burning with the total nuclear heat it had absorbed over eight hours in the summertime Georgia sun. Abraham Lincoln has been there ever since, presiding over her ass. His profile is branded clearly into her right gluteus, alert and knowing but also interested and maybe more than just presidentially involved. Is he ogling the other cheek or does he just want to make sure peace reigns across the fruited plains? It's hard to tell.

When she walks the bunching of her muscle can make it look like Lincoln is winking at you.

Sometimes during sex, if I have a vantage point, this unnerves me somewhat. I feel like either 1) I can't live up to certain expectations or 2) I don't have the necessary moral fortitude to engage in carnal acts in front of—let's be honest: directly in the stern bearded face of—the sixteenth President of the United States. This is the supreme veto power of the Ass President and once or twice, here or there—three, four times, tops— this has been my downfall.

Tonight, alas, all systems are not go, but it is not because of the veto power of the Ass President. Tonight it has another, more dire source. I feel a pelvic shyness for the same reason the sofa never saw any action during high school: the supreme anaphrodisiac power of this house. Even as an adolescent, when my libido should have been ravening on such modest fare as *National Geographic* and black-and-white Maidenform ads in *The Baltimore Sun*, I was so vanquished by this house that simply to work up the courage to take matters into hand I would have to retreat to the woods and kneel with a flashlight clenched between my teeth and commit impassioned acts of frottage upon a section of a graphic relief map that contained the Ural Mountains. (I did this not only because the friction of that particular range was immensely pleasurable but because when Kasimir Kakmuzh brutalized me I could masturbate on the Urals and think to myself, "You may have beaten me today, Russian thug, but I will never be inferior to you, for I have fucked the mountains of your homeland!")

But now I resolve to make a stand. Things are different now, right? I am not the same person. I am not the little brother. I am not the apprentice clown. I don't brag anymore. I am independent; I have successfully defected from this house, returning only by choice. In a few years I could probably even pronounce the name Dexter without weeping if I really wanted to.

But when Hahva eases into the blue sheets next to me and I detect the familiar odor of her skin—seaweed and earth—which under normal conditions pricks certain nerve clusters in my brain and makes me superdynamated with lust, it seems to have no effect.

It's quiet . . . *too* quiet.

"Is it Lincoln?" Hahva asks at last.

"I think it must just be fatigue," I say, wondering how this lie will hold up in the future when I have no excuse for fatigue. "Think the chopper has bought the farm for tonight."

Scoreboard

House: 2
Me: 0

Excerpt from the Lexicon of Pressman Tennant: Pregret

Unable to sleep, I start to toe-first it downstairs for a glass of water but am tripped up. On the steps Press has left a note taped to an empty tumbler next to a bottle of Lagavulin. The scalpel-cut handwriting reads:

> PREGRET: a punitive feeling of regret that is experienced before one commits an act that would normally produce regret. A common feature of the recidivist and the coward. Although powerful, pregret is a redundant and irrelevant emotion. For example: if one is already experiencing reproachful and anguished feelings of pregret about the prospect of drinking again, should one not at least be allowed the pleasure of the act?

The tumbler is smoky Murano glass and heavy, the darling of gravity. In a lunar spotlight, clutched in my hand, it looks martial, as if awaiting engagement. It is waiting to be filled the way a gun waits to be loaded.

That's Why You Came, Right?

It isn't easy, but I force myself downstairs and return the scotch unopened to the cabinet. Then, in the kitchen, filling a new glass with water at the sink, I see that a light is on in the erstwhile billiards room. It is Bess, sitting next to my father on his small cot, filling a hypodermic needle with Dewar's.

"I know what you're thinking," she says to me. "Bess was here. Right?"

And sure enough, the billiards room has been transformed to Bess's specifications. All the baronial appointments—the antique Brunswick full-size, the vintage Balabushkas I was never allowed to touch, the period ivory balls, the Eames chairs—have been replaced by curious therapeutic items that look at once deadly and toylike. There is a battalion of scented lotions, swabs, a pincushion hosting a single pin, some prehensile rubber apparatus, inflatable balls of various sizes, a walkie-talkie with a red light glowing perched above the cot, multicolored sponges, a bucket, a coffee-sized canister of something called Thick-It, a logspill of straws, a minifridge, a bungee cord, an electric device that looks like a princess phone, and lots of medications in orange cylinders. Where a picture of my father and Barry Goldwater clasping hands used to hang is now a hand-drawn sign that says CAN'T IS A FOUR-LETTER WORD. Where the cases of Lagavulin 16 and crystal tumblers used to be stacked is now a portable stereo and, hilariously, CDs that my father would execrate, among which I see *The Great Muppet Caper Soundtrack* and *John Denver's Greatest Hits*. Facing my father's small cot is a TV that is playing a never-ending game of slow-motion Pong, the glowing white ball bouncing hypnotically back and forth on the screen.

"I know it looks crazy," she says about the scotch, "and you probably shouldn't say anything to the others about it, but your father has had DTs since he bled out. You can't tell because there's no visible shaking, but he feels like he's shaking, and the sweats and fever are bad. This is the most humane way. He'll be off it soon," she says cheerfully. "Won't you, Gil?"

Bess injects the contents of the needle into my father's IV and then swabs his mouth with a Dewar's-soaked sponge. "Might as well give him a taste, right? Pleasures are few and far between these days. Right, Gil?"

My father's eyelid closes with rapture while the scotch spreads through his palate. I do not tell Bess that my dad takes his drink at precisely six o'clock to the militarily precise minute every single day, and that if he is even a few heartbeats over six p.m. he becomes enraged. I also decline to tell her that he never drinks the blends, that she should really be doing that with an Islay, maybe the Lagavulin or some Laphroaig, even. Anything but Dewar's.

"Right," I say. "Good thinking."

"I see you and your father have something in common."

"We do?"

"Insomnia. He's had it ever since he stroked. Did he have it before?"

"Beats me."

"You mind if I say something?"

"Go ahead."

Bess leads me out of the room and closes the door so my father can't hear.

"I noticed you really didn't look at your father this afternoon."

"Yeah, well," I say.

"Look. I've only known your dad for a week. I have no idea what kind of father he is. But I can tell you that he is a fantastic patient. He's trying as hard as he can."

"That's good."

"I hope you'll pardon the candor here, but don't snow me, Jack."

"Sorry," I say sheepishly.

After a long moment she says, "Want to know how most locked-in patients die? Lack of attention."

"What does that mean?"

"The feelings of abandonment, of isolation, are so powerful that the body shuts down. It's like he is living in a deep hole and can't get out without your help. If you leave him down in it, he'll die."

"Mm-hm."

"It sounds strange but if your father is going to have any chance at surviving, let alone improving, you are going to have to literally love him back to health."

"You seem like a real nice lady. But there are a lot of things you don't know."

"I know he needs you. He told me."

"That must have been a neat trick."

"He also asked me to make sure that you came up to see him."

"You mean my mother asked me to come up."

"No," she says, holding up a Ouija board. "He asked me."

"He communicated from beyond the coma?" I can't resist making some spooky noises as I wriggle my fingers to indicate the presence of the supernatural.

"This is how you talk to your father, Jack. You point to all the letters on this board and he blinks when he wants you to stop."

"And he what? Blinked to you that he wanted me to come up?" An unfortunate *I Dream of Jeannie* image comes to me.

"Exactly."

"I hope you won't be offended if I tell you right now that this whole thing sounds pretty fantastic."

She shrugs. "I'm through with him for tonight. Just go in and sit with him for a while, O.K.? He's still feverish and it takes forever for him to get to sleep. He can't adjust himself, obviously, and if he happens to be in an uncomfortable position there's nothing he can do about it. I do my best, but I don't always get it right. So. Just go see him. Do what you can to make him comfortable."

"I don't know."

"You're here, aren't you? Might as well reach out. That's why you came, right?"

In the Hole Together

How he has changed. The dry paper-cut slit above my father's chin is now a flaccid oily fishmouth tinseled with sebum and spit. The skin of his face is putty-wet, purple, a flayed plum. His once shovel-hard forehead is now oysterish and veiny. And his ray-gun stare is gone. A puddled, mossy void has replaced it. He is there but only marginally—mechanically. He is alive, at best, in the way that analog clocks are alive.

Everyone else is asleep and here I am with my windup father. He looks at me. I look at him. And I realize something: my father is no longer the master of silence in this house; he is its victim. He is hurtling now toward the Big Silence, the Unbreakable Silence, the Eternity Mute, while I can sit here as long as I want. I can speak or not. I can deal out the wordlessness. He can't leave the room. He can't ignore me. He can't refute, refuse, dismiss, disdain, or deny.

If I were to say, "It's your fault about Dex," he couldn't vise down on my finger.

All he can do now is listen.

Clutching my father, all that dead weight, by the lapels of his nightshirt I pull him up against the wall so that I can look at him squarely. The blanket has fallen off him; he is not wearing any bottoms. His penis is curled like an obese seahorse and is resined in the sweat of alcohol withdrawal. There is a tube sprouting from the glans leading to a plastic bag still hidden in the covers. It is a mortifying moment. I feel it in my gut—a vacuum feeling—and at my temples. I cover him up again—clumsily, hastily, with as much embarrassment as the discovery itself—during which his eye looks modestly away from me. It occurs to me that he is trying to spare me the discomfort, but it doesn't help.

I still can't get rid of the scraped-out feeling in my soul.

Then I do something I don't understand. In the deep armistitial quiet of the room, the house, the night, while outside the pastures roll in blue silence, I sit down next to my father on his cot. I unbutton the neck of his nightshirt. I reach out with my hand, through the flannel material, and touch his chest. I can feel his heart beating. It is the first time I ever have. It has an irresistible rhythm and meter. For a long time I listen to it, feeling its incomprehensible message pulsing in my hand. The skin is warm and malleable. It seems expectant and ready, like new clay waiting to be kneaded into life.

Then I take his hand in mine and put it on the crown of my head. Even lifeless his thick fighter's hand feels inescapable and immensely heavy.

An unknown quantity of time passes.

My father's eye makes quick birdlike saccades up and down.

The white ball on the TV screen pings and pongs.

Outside the Invincibles are folding.

I don't dare say it, but I am thinking: *Killer.*

Something shameful and bitterly chemical roils in my stomach and I have to sprint into the bathroom, where I vomit riotously into the toilet. I sit there, momentarily frozen. Then there is a violent superatmospheric rush in my ears as I realize that everyone—Press, Hahva, Bess—is wrong. I am not here for the inheritance. I didn't agree to come here because of the do-gooder influence of Hahva Finn, trisyllable of hope. And I certainly didn't come home to help take care of my father.

I have come home to punish my father.

Part Two

What I Do Remember: The Origin of Brag

The day of the funeral it was raining but not overcast. It seemed to me, at five years old, that it was some kind of sign that it was all a terrible mistake. God had screwed it up—Dex wasn't supposed to be dead; it was a terrible mix-up, a clerical error in my big brother's disfavor—but it was too late now. Death was untakebackable. The only thing he could do was send me a God-note. "Dear Jackson, Please accept this freakish, cloudless, blue-sky rain as an admission of the wrongness of the events of last week and my regret about your future grief and all the failures that will accrue from your heartbreak . . ."

Inside the funeral home the air was complicated and heavy. It smelled processed, thick with medicinal perfumes, but also rubberized. The rain, the sadness, the congestion of human body heat, the strange fumes—it all smelled like wet balloons. But what I was feeling was failure: I hadn't been there. Press hadn't been there. Dad, whose job it was to be there, hadn't been there. Mom had been at the store; only she had dispensation from guilt. But the rest of us had failed Dex, and here we were.

I wanted to tell him that I was sorry.

I know there must have been noises in the viewing room—it was chock-full of adults I had never seen before, and whom I resented for pretending a claim to Dex—but I didn't hear anything. People shifted on their feet, drank from plastic cups, munched dip-crested carrots, and muttered small reassurances to each other without producing any sound. To me it was like viewing a silent movie.

There was a makeshift line for Dex's sled-sized coffin; Press and I teetered forward until it was our turn. It happened very suddenly. We looked up and there was no one left between us and Dex. Some voices behind us asked where our parents were; didn't they want to walk up with us? I felt some hands on my shoulders and utterances of safeguarding. Strange adults were afraid for us viewing Dex. So was I. But Press wasn't. Nine-year-old Press turned around, not letting go of my hand, and scolded the crowd. "We don't need our parents," he said. "We can do it by ourselves."

Ten empty feet stood between me and Dex. I felt a little dizzy. I was ashamed, too. I didn't want to be there. Press squeezed my hand, trying to reassure me, but every shuffle-step forward I took felt more and more dreadful. I was approaching something I'd never be able to come back from. The steps I was taking were final steps. I took a timid left, a shaky right, walking the plank.

I didn't take the last step. I stopped short. Press tried to pull me forward but I wriggled out of his grasp. My hand, still hot and swelling from being gripped so hard, retreated into my jacket and found the single orange flip-flop occupying the secret pocket. With my thumb and forefinger I worried the orange nubbed surface, imagining that I could discern the difference between my sweat and the residual sweat that Dex had left there. It felt like a communion.

It was the closest I came to Dex that day.

But Press dared proximity. As he tiptoed toward the box, his heels rose up from the shag carpet worn thin from the heartbroken leanings of an unimaginable number of the bereft and grieving. His head bent low, then lower, then lower still, until he was a shocking, jeweler's distance from what I knew was our brother's face. He froze there for a long time. His legs were shaking from the effort of staying elevated so long and I could see the tension in his back.

Out the window above him I saw two birds, orioles, jagged streaks of greasy black and beacon orange, tittering on a telephone wire. It seemed obscene to me that these birds were enjoying themselves, flapping and twitching and buddy-buddy, in plain view of my brother's casket. Suddenly I hated them—I had to put the hatred somewhere, and I wasn't brave enough yet to put it on my father—and I wanted to make them pay.

I sprinted outside, grabbed the nearest rock, and tore around the back of the building, hurling the rock at them as hard as I could. But I was so young, and not especially athletic, and even adrenalized by rage and grief I couldn't get the necessary elevation. My rock limped upward in a sagging arc before peaking at about ten feet and then breaking into a dejected free fall back toward earth. My tearful missiling didn't produce even a single ruffled feather. The birds just cocked their heads improbably sideways and regarded me with unreadable olive-black eyes, staring me down. I clutched another rock and hurled that, too, achieving no better results. Up, pause for a second, sink back down. Up, freeze momentarily, plink harmlessly on the asphalt. Up, stall, fail. I kept trying, but it was useless.

Then a rock sizzled over my head, on a tight thread straight toward the power line, and—*foom!*—one oriole exploded into a black and orange cloud. The other one beat it, fast.

Press patted me on the shoulder. I got it for you, he seemed to be saying. I understand. I'm with you.

The rain had made his blazer shiny and his hair hang in yarny streamers in his eyes. I noticed he had a leather-bound flask in his hand, the same flask I had seen my father drink from while hiding behind a plastic ficus in the viewing room. With one hand Press tilted the flask at me—cheers—then put it to his lips and drank. The first drink of his life.

For a long moment his cheeks puffed and froze; then he spat out a copper liquid violently onto the ground at my feet. He tried again. This time he didn't hold it in his mouth. He swallowed it right down, hacking out a gustatory, appreciative cough. The action seemed nearly incomprehensible—thrilling and illicit and miraculous. I was too young to understand precisely what liquor was, but I knew something momentous was happening. Press was changing. Not into an adult, but into something not kidlike anymore, either. Something more advanced. And stronger.

Press took another swig and his eyes filled with tears. He made a discreet animal noise in his throat.

"Does it hurt you?" I asked him.

"Nothing hurts me," he bragged, and took another drink.

The Big Question

The question I was thinking that day as I stood watching Pressman drink for the first time is the same question that has tormented me for the past twenty-seven years: was it an accident, or did Dex do it on purpose?

Rematch

The next day, before we are to convene with Bess to get a lesson in administering therapy, my brother and I have a rematch. Quizzical birds, demented with their constant astonishment at the world around them, regard us from the fence as we descend to the countersunk croquet pitch, clutching our mallets like bildersticks. When we approach too close, when our hate static becomes too powerful, they explode into cacophonous flight and watch, circling us from above. The horses, too, make truffling noises of anxiety and retreat to the far side of the paddock. The only one who doesn't seem to perceive it is Hahva, who is pushing our father around the grounds in his wheelchair. At the fence to the near paddock she bends down the stalk of an Invincible, giving him a noseful.

The sight of her kindness with my father—and her fingertip and nosepoint communion with Invincibles—makes uneasiness shoot through me. It seems all wrong. It seems like a betrayal.

"Well, let the games begin," Press announces.

He is already liquored up, hale and windblown and buzzing in the canting morning sunlight on the croquet pitch. As we play Press displays with admirable aplomb his rapier-ease with the mallet, swinging it in graceful pendulum movements between his legs—textbook—while I insist on maintaining my cramped golf-putter style.

"Good shot, little brother. Nearly hit the wicket."

"Keep talking," is my riposte.

Press finishes the course first and becomes "poison." For three turns I dodge him between wickets and try to shake him with long defensive shots, but he hunts me down inexorably. His ball collides—*click!*—with mine and I, poisoned, am vanquished. I hadn't even made it to the back half of the course.

This is a familiar scenario.

Press and I apprehend the sputtering tuba note of a beater diesel wheeling around Manor Road. When it rattles into view, even from this distance, we can see the viper-headed features of Musser, who is leaning out of the rusted cab, brandishing a bottle overhead. His arm axes down and there is only a slight delay before the sound of glass shattering on our mailbox reaches us.

"Stellar," says Press. "Take a guess who gets to clean that up." Something in my brother's expression deforms. The tight lineaments of his victory are reduced to a sag of defeat. There is a deadness and sudden animal desperation in his eyes; he looks like one of Gorky's broken laborers. "I've already been up this morning fucking aerating the lawn." I know what this means, and despite myself I sympathize with it: to aerate the lawn you don specialized shoes with metal spikes and walk over every inch of turf, creating oxygen holes for the grass. It doesn't even do anything. My mother just insists.

My brother commences a plaintive catalogue of his manual subservitude. He keeps the interior of the house up to exacting Mom-specification, doing all the sanitizing and vacuuming and Windexing and polishing and lint picking and laundering and folding. He does exterior work on the house involving gutters and paint and wall mending. He feeds, bathes, grooms, monitors the horses. He mucks the stalls. He does it all. It's not backbreaking work, he concedes, but it makes him feel like he's twelve years old. It's degrading. If one of Mom's bags of nontoxic volcanic granules becomes saturated and needs replacing, he gets hell. If an errant hair is left in the sink in his own damn bathroom, it is evidenced in front of his fucking nose, he says, accompanied by an insulting question. "Do you know what this is?" she might say. "Haven't I told you to clean after yourself?"

And if it's not rectified, he says, the liquor cabinet gets locked up.

"It's like I'm their fucking wump or something," he says.

Wump: this is a Turnbull Academy term. I had forgotten it. White Underpaid Maintenance Person. My brother laughed at them back then. He's not laughing now.

"That clusterfuck Musser gets sixty grand a year up and down a goddamn telephone pole. He didn't get that job because he's a supergenius either. He got it because his father—a forklift operator at Southern States—put a word in with BG&E. A forklift operator! But he helped out his kid, didn't he? Dad has connections with everybody on earth and he won't even give me a loan to start a business. Or, God forbid, pay off certain pressing personal debts. It's not like I wouldn't pay it back."

Press spits askance.

"Fucking pole monkey."

"You want to start a business?"

"Yeah," he says. "No. Yes and no. I don't know. I just don't want to keep on living like a jerk. It's too fucking much. I can't live like this. I don't even know how I got here." For the first time since I've been back my brother isn't emanating hatred for me. He seems almost conspiratorial—brotherly.

I almost ask it. I almost say, "I don't know how you got here either. You had made it out. Why did you ever come back from California?"

"Want to hear something uncharacteristic?" he says. "Of the old man, I mean? There is no will. Which means one of two things. He either never envisioned dying and therefore disregarded the subject of last will and testament, or two, the jury's out on what to give to whom. Who knows, maybe he wants to get a closer look at progeny number two before he doles anything out."

"I already told you. I'm not interested in the inheritance."

"You know what really burns me up about it? Bess. You know how much this therapy is costing? Fifty grand a month for the private treatment and various therapeutic devices. That is over sixteen hundred dollars he is costing us—you and me— each day he keeps on breathing in that lump of a body of his."

"You are begrudging our father lifesaving treatment?"

"Lifesaving," he snorts. "Yeah, it would be just like that virile fuck to hold on for years, wouldn't it? He's going to pauperize us if he keeps on with that therapy."

"I guess you're screwed, then."

"Not necessarily."

Press's eyes acquire a piratical gleam of relish.

"Although it is entirely possible that he might survive for years, it is also quite possible that an accident of some sort might befall him shortly. If he were to perish sooner rather than later, well—imagine what we could do with an extra sixteen hundred dollars a day. To say nothing of the whole megabucks schmeer."

"What are you saying? You want to kill our father?"

"Kill is such an unseemly word, and it's not apt. He's already dead, Jack."

"You're kidding."

"Am I? He's eating up our inheritance, Jack. Yours and mine. For what? So he can twitch a pinky? So he can swallow his own applesauce? It's not like he has anything to look forward to. He won't be wiping his own asshole in this lifetime, will he? We're not stealing any life, Jackson, we're just . . . upping the schedule."

"You're fucking crazy."

"I'm not talking shotguns or anything. Nothing hideous. I'm saying, hypothetically now, what if one of us messes up with his therapy? It's complicated business and a strong wind could kill him right now. We're not qualified therapists, are we? All those pills and their exact dosages. It's a lot to remember. Who knows how much is too much? We were never good at math in the first place, and we're not registered nurses, after all."

"This is sick."

"Think of the money, Jack. He never did any goddamn thing for us. Did he talk to you about women? Help you apply for jobs? Did he ever let you even take a ride in his fucking E-Type? Did Mr. Heavyweight Prizefighter ever show you how to throw a jab?"

"No," I say, fingering the key in my pocket.

"No. And there are certain other failures we could mention, aren't there? Didn't he rob us of something else? Do you think—"

I can't stand to hear the name spoken out loud. I stop him before he can say it. It is probably the first time I've raised my voice to my brother in my life. I certainly have never had the guts to tell him to shut up. But he does. He waits a respectful duration—honoring the dead, maybe—before renewing his pitch.

"He wasn't a father to us, Jack. And now, after all these years, what can he do for us? A father should do something for his only sons, shouldn't he?"

"So you're saying that at last, the one thing he can do for us is to—"

"Die. Yes. And we can take his money—our money, Jack—and put it toward our lives. I could get out of that fucking basement at last. Start some legit business. I wouldn't have to clean a vent with an extractor brush ever again, or take any more humiliating orders from Mom. And you, Jack. You could start a new life, too. With all that money you could go back to grad school, finish your degree somewhere. Redeem yourself. Put all that Leon Flanders shit behind you."

I can't remember how much I have told Press about my disgrace. I know I've drunk-dialed him a few times since that day with Leon and the Disciplinary Committee, but surely I didn't tell him everything.

"Nothing happened with Jordana Mochnik," I insist.

"Hey. Who's judging? Who cares if you did or you didn't? Either way, there's no reason to suffer for the rest of your life over that one misunderstanding, is there? I've suffered enough. Haven't you?"

"I don't want anything that Dad's money can buy me."

"Oh no? Well, what about her?" Press says, indicating Hahva. She is standing amid the bee-flux of the garden, soaking up the ravishment of the sulky flowers and the aerated lawn. "Don't you want to give her a chance at something? She's had it hard just about long enough, too, hasn't she? Are you too pristine to accept your rightful inheritance to give the woman you love a chance at a good life? I'm not talking a new car, Jack. I'm talking a whole new life. Freedom. Is that beneath you?"

Outsized, thuggish ants—ants raised on rich Maryland fare, who have breathed unprocessed Huntfield air—scrimmage over my tattered sneaker in a kaleidoscope of rage and business. We eat our own, they say to me. The weak, the sick, the old. It is an evolutionary imperative. It's a mistake to attach morality to it. The next generation must thrive.

Against my will I start fondling the idea. Press's words, luxuriant and hot, osmose despite my efforts; they acquire a stark reasonableness. They become sensible, streamlined, euclidean.

I consider what kind of ring I could get for Hahva with my share. How it would be for Hahva to feel X-less for the rest of her life. McGurk wouldn't have to sell my car for me. I wouldn't have to live in a nail-filled apartment with no insulation. The words of colleagues and the Philosoraptor couldn't hurt me. The censure of Leon Flanders wouldn't hurt as badly. I could get a badass Elizabeth Taylor brilliant-cut diamond in a tasteful claw setting with mongo baguettes up and down, incredible scintillation, and retina-frying light return geometry.

Oh yeah. I can imagine that.

I scrape my tongue painfully against my chipped tooth to maintain clarity, thinking: Henry James Pye, Robert Southey, William Wordsworth, Alfred, Lord Tennyson, Robert Bridges. It takes a moment to stabilize, and when I do I start laughing. I can't stop. I laugh and laugh and laugh. The mallet drops from my hands and I have to brace myself, hands on my knees. Press is walking around me, circling in easy lynxlike movements.

"God," I say, recovering. "You had me going there for a second. I thought you were serious. I really thought you were serious."

Press smiles too, but it only lasts for a moment. Then he shrugs, and the fishhook under his nose uncreases into nothing.

"Aren't I?" he says.

McGurk Calls

"How's it going at Thornfield, Professor?"

"Don't call me that."

"Right. Sorry. How's it going at Thornfield, Adjunct?"

"Fine. Got any good news?"

"Kelly Blue Book suggests that rusted-out '87 Dodge Omnis whose driver's windows are held up by wedged-in chopsticks rarely fraternize with good news."

"What if they have an aftermarket erosion sunroof and the optional Tilt-a-Whirl power-unassist steering?"

"Does nothing to further the cause, I'm afraid."

"So nothing?"

"Nope. No soap. Well, no definitive soap. I had one guy come look at it last Thursday. Said it had the appearance of the carcass of a Micronesian turtle he'd seen on TV, only rusty. Georgians aren't accustomed to rust."

"It's still got New York tags. That can't help."

"Ah, entropy."

"Well, shit."

"Should I keep the ad in the paper going?"

"Yeah. I'll send you a check. And can you park it with the For Sale sign in the window at the Waffle House by the Salvation Army on the weekend?"

"Easier requested than done."

"What do you mean?"

"It expresses a certain reluctance at ignition."

"Five seconds on, five seconds off. It should start in about a minute."

"I'll try again."

"And if you can, try to warm it up before the buyers get there so they don't see it struggling to start."

"Done."

"Thanks, McGurk. You're saving my ass."

"What's left of it. Even in the quiet summertime department hallways there are breezes of Jack-related scandal ruffling certain collars."

"Fuck. How bad?"

"Not good."

"Graphic?"

"Not a blow-by-blow, pardon the pun, but the essentials are there. Inappropriate contact with a student."

"Fuck. Is the nature of the contact they suggest lubricious?"

"Is it lubricious? He asks is it *lubricious*? Do you know who we are dealing with?"

"Shit. How specific has it gotten?"

"I haven't heard the syllables 'Jordana Mochnik' yet, if that's any indication."

"Thank God for that."

"Probably it's just as well you're up north this summer. Maybe by the time you get back they will have found a new target."

"Hey. I haven't heard anything about renewal of classes for the fall. Shouldn't they start sending out contracts soon?"

"Maybe. I'm not sure."

"Really? You're not sure? Have you received yours?"

There is a pause on the line. I know that right now McGurk is sheepishly staring at his shoes and folding up his lumberjack frame. He feels bad for me and doesn't want to admit that he has classes lined up. But why shouldn't he get his classes? He did not "knowingly and willingly abuse the power of his office to vitiate a student." Nor did he receive "immediate expulsion with censure."

"It's O.K., big mick. You deserve those classes. Besides, my papers are probably stuck in the mail getting forwarded to Maryland."

"No doubt. I'm sure that's where they are," he says, a little too brightly.

"Right," I confirm.

"Hey. Um. You sure you want to go forward with selling the Omni? I mean, it shouldn't happen—it won't, I'm sure it won't happen—but if September rolls around and you don't have any classes and you've sold your car for Hahva's ring, that is going to represent a certain financial hardship, won't it?"

"I've got it covered."

"So keep selling?"

"Keep selling."

"Roger."

"And drop the price another hundred bucks."

"Again?"

"If we don't I'll never be able to do my madcap dance while claiming that my prices are insane."

"You got it."

"Thanks."

"And hey, Jack. Take it easy up there. I don't like the idea of you spending so much time in that house. I want you back here in one piece and without jodhpurs."

"Don't worry. I'll be back soon and I'll be the same old me."

"I'd like to believe that."

Therapy

Even in broad daylight the room is steeped in my father. It is implacable and unknowable, spit-shined and ready. We are still only its guests. We nevertheless constellate bravely around my father but Bess is the only one close to him, cotside. The rest of us are flung out along the ambit of the room, still playing our parts.

Mother: the exquisite, she is impeccable, coded, unreadable.

Press: straight-backed and ever-ready, sipping a fuming brag and cola that isn't fooling anyone.

Hahva: eyes dilating with guileless care, hands clasped in Victorian empathy.

Me: looking silently on, planning escape routes, quizzing self avidly. Alabama: Yellowhammer. Alaska: Willow Ptarmigan. Arizona: Cactus Wren.

Bess: self-possessed as a yogi, tranquil and evenhanded, explaining to us how we are all expected to help.

Sometimes, she starts, it is possible to slow or reverse paralysis simply by movement. So every three hours we are to massage his limbs and fingers with scented lotion. She picks up his arm and bends it repeatedly at the elbow joint, making salute gestures ("Aye aye, cap'n!" she says affectionately). Then she kneads his hands with patchouli-scented lotion that causes my mother to sniff delicately.

She shows us how to use Thick-It powder to turn tap water into a glue-smelling sludge that is easy to swallow. She inflates the physioball and we clumsily drape our father over it and rock him back and forth like a baby. On his face we use the electrostimulation machine to improve musculation and prevent sag. Bess demonstrates on me, applying a cold greenish gel to my cheek and firing it up, making my fillings vibrate painfully and my eyeball stretch like a bowstring. We are instructed how to affix and clean a tube attached to my father's side that is filled with a turbid whitish liquid. The Play Machine feature on the televised Pong game is explained. The Ouija board is demonstrated; she runs her finger over the letters and every time he blinks she stops, until he has spelled out a word that she records on the cotside legal pad. Bess stands back and regards the pad.

"I must have spelled this wrong," she says. "Islay?"

"It's pronounced *eye*-la," I correct. "It refers to a region of Scotland that produces the best single malts. Lagavulin, for example."

"Yummers," Press agrees, smacking his lips.

Then Bess takes out a small inflatable beach ball with a picture of Jesus on it and starts throwing it at my father, who sits there blinking every time it bounces off his head or ricochets off his shoulder or dribbles out of his hands unmolested.

"He's not much for catch, is he?" Press says.

"Not yet," Bess says.

"Isn't that, um, rather humiliating?" my mother says.

"Sure is. It's excruciating. Especially for a big colonel like Gil. Isn't it, Gilly?" she says sweetly, batting him in the nose with the ball. "Can't you play catch with Jesus? Jesus wants to play catch with you. Why won't you play, Gil?"

"This is undignified," my mother says.

"Exactly," Bess says. "It makes him highly motivated to catch it. How much do you think he wants not to get clocked by Jesus?

I want Gil to play catch with Jesus three times a day for twenty minutes at a time. Oh. And, Adair, you have a lovely home but we need to brighten the place up. Music and TV. Maybe some art. Nostalgia. You know. Memory plays a big part in recovery. For example," she says to my mother, "what was your song?"

"Our what?" she asks, uncomprehending.

"You know, a romantic song that you two shared."

"Sometimes we listened to oldies."

"I mean a special song. Something from your past. Something you shared together."

My mother says nothing.

"Like, what did you play at your wedding?"

"Pachelbel, I suppose."

"And what did you dance to? You know, your song?"

"Dance?" my mother repeats, as if it were the most irrelevant thing she had ever heard.

"Well, how about some photos then? We could put them around the desk, here."

Bess receives blank stares. There are no photos.

I know what Press is thinking: for this we are paying $1,600 a day.

"Well, good thing I brought Ducky, then."

From her bag Bess produces a miniature rubber ducky and laces my father's fingers around it. Using her own hand over my father's she squeezes, making a shrill quacking noise.

"Ducky speaks! After twenty minutes with Jesus I want you to spend twenty minutes with Ducky. I want Gil eventually to be able to make Ducky speak on his own, but in the meantime you can help. That's three times a day, twenty minutes of Ducky time."

Bess releases her grip and encourages my father to squeeze on his own. His right index finger twitches to the tune of half a centimeter, causing Ducky to tilt almost imperceptibly and inducing in Bess perfervid celebration.

"You gave Ducky the business, didn't you, Gil? You keep going and one day he'll be quacking for his life!"

My father's eye flickers wildly and an unheralded tear rolls down his face.

Bess wipes it away with a towelette and says, "Don't worry about that. With locked-in syndrome emotions are very near the surface. He'll cry if the phone rings. He'll crack up if your shoe is unlaced. Just the way it goes with LIS.

"Now for the tough stuff. Breathing. The ultimate goal of reestablishing full pulmonary autonomy is to achieve the phonatory breath but right now we're just working for comfort. When Gil was checked into the emergency room he was already losing control over his breath. Remember that, Adair?"

"The nurse asked me if he always snored that loud."

"But he wasn't snoring, was he?"

My mother examines the chitin of her bevel-perfect French manicure. "No," she says.

"He was struggling for breath," Bess says, apparently to me. "By the end of the night the struggle was so bad that his body was lifting off the table. Only his shoulders and feet were touching. Finally they put him on a respirator not because he would die but because his body was exhausted. That was the last time Gil enjoyed any significant autonomous movement. That's what we're going to try to get back. Starting here. First thing we do is prime him with frozen glycerin swabs for deep pharyngeal neuromuscular stimulation."

"You gag him?" Press says.

"You gag him. Show him you mean it." From the minifridge Bess extracts what looks like an elongated Q-tip and inserts it deep into my father's throat, forcing a rale of phlegm to erupt. "He's already warmed up this morning but normally you will need to do two to three hundred reps of this before starting work on the phonatory breath. Which goes like this."

Bess attains a deep kung fu stance before my father's body, hands to his chest.

"Breathing is trickier than you think. The inhalation is easy. Automatic. It's the exhalation that's tough. Letting it out. We can help him by pressing on the thorax on the exhale like this. You have to get close to him. Listen to the breathing, get his rhythm." Bess puts her cheek against my father's bare chest, which is already chain-mailed in spit, closes her eyes, assimilating something, and then pushes forcefully. "And *ooomph*. Wait. *Ooomph*. Like that. On a rhythm. It's a lot like dancing."

Distaste is stenciled on my mother's face. There are telltale corners of linen kerchiefs protruding from her sleeve and I understand her dilemma. To clean her husband's spittle will so enfilth the linens that perhaps it's better to leave his chin unwiped. It's mainly a question of frequency, she's thinking. If he is going to drool constantly, then she can get away with tidying up at long intervals—what good will it do to dirty a kerchief when ten seconds later another will need to be sacrificed? But if the current mess represents only an irregular frothing, then she might very well clean him without any gloves. She does the mess math in her head, astutely observing the rate of spit discharge, then covertly tucks the kerchiefs back into her sleeves. She will wait. Moments later Bess, perhaps intuiting that no one is going to provide the assist, wipes the sputum with a cloth that is always perched parrotlike on her shoulder.

"Who wants to try?" Bess cleanses her face of my father's

saliva and rubs dry one lens of her enormous Swifty Lazars. No one volunteers. "Jack, step right up."

What choice do I have? I step right up and Bess directs me through the process. I put my hands on the incalescent spit-slicked rubber of my father's chest and lean in, per Bess's insistence, ear first. His ghoulish mouth is sealed up with white gluten and his breath is weak and distant. It sounds as if it has another source besides my father, as if it is coming from beneath the bed or from hidden speakers in the corners. Shallow waves of soupy breath descend upon my face.

I push.

"Good timing, Jack. You've got his rhythm. Now, Gil already has good respiration. So let's take a shot at achieving the phonatory breath. By pressing on the thorax this way you increase the amplitude of phonatory movement to the point of sound production."

"Speech?" Hahva asks.

"Not yet. But close. Watch. Jack, would you please? And Pressman, would you like to assist?" Bess instructs Press and inserts him into her place. In position, with my brother looming over me, I see through the fog of my father's breath that he has the same fleshy semidetached earlobes that I have. They look just like mine, like undersized lima beans. I have never noticed this before about my father.

I wonder if Dex had them, too.

Again I push on the exhalation. As I do this Press plugs his nose and a guttural, walrusy noise erupts violently from my father. "Bravo!" Bess says. "That is a very favorable factor! Excellent work, boys. You're bringing your father back around. You should be proud."

Press gives me a private poisonous look and retreats to his

position by the wet bar. I know what he is thinking: if we are expending energy on speech therapy, survival and even improvement may be assumed.

"This therapy seems sort of dicey to me," Press says. "Isn't there a risk of choking?"

"Yes, there is. You have to be very careful when gagging and when plugging the nose. Sometimes if Gil is unresponsive you might go beyond the limits of therapy and . . . well, the best rule of thumb is to be persistent but not too persistent. If he does not gag for you or produce the phonatory breath, then back off and let him recover his normal breathing pattern before starting again."

"I see."

Press's face hardens with cruelty and cunning, and again I know what he is thinking.

Dex as Therapist?

If he were here now, being conscripted to care for our father—to help save the man who did not save him—what he would do?

Anything?

Should I?

The Barbasol Incident 1.2

Over coffee the next day, while Hahva is still upstairs, my mother explains my selection. She has an appointment with a wheelchair specialist in Sparks; Hahva isn't family and it wouldn't do to have her touch my father; Bess is a physical and occupational therapist, not a barber; and earlier this morning Press reported feeling "*merde*-y."

There is no escape. I am to shave my father.

When my mother leaves for Sparks I am again alone with my father. It makes me feel puny and malleable and I have to sit still, looking out the window, until it passes. The Invincibles, I see, are already exploded, and despite myself I have a twitch of pride. They are no feckless hothouse droopers. They are robust and full of themselves, ready for the elements, full of push and thorn. Their faces are turned toward my father and me, into the sunlight, as if issuing a dare. They make me nervous, staring like that, and I fit the handle of the razor into the chip in my tooth for relief but it does not fit.

"All right," I say to him at last. "I guess you're going under the knife."

Approaching my father it occurs to me that there may have been another, more private reason my mother declined this job: he is covered in an entire night's worth of uncleanliness. Either she didn't even wipe his chin this morning or he is producing fluid at an alarming rate.

As I scrub him with a hot towel I get a complicated feeling. I feel brazen and elect, priestly and wishful. Touching his face, I apply the shaving cream and I can't help remembering how he looked that day at Annapolis, putting his hands on the Barbasol-covered cadets, talking to them, teaching them, straightening out their jabs, teaching them how to bird-wing their shoulders around their jaws, showing them what they needed to know to avoid being hurt.

Llullaillaco, I think, Guallatiri, Láascar, Cotopaxi, El Misti . . .

It takes me a few minutes to fight myself calm, but I do. I keep my hands steady and work in smooth, regular movements. I pull the razor from his ear down his venous cheek, terminating at his jawline. My father uses an old Solingen straight razor that he sharpens regularly, so the blade is fine and it goes quick. I have to touch his nose to get his upper lip and nothing alarming happens. Despite the unnerving appearance of the long blade I am relaxed. I am even relaxed enough to laugh momentarily out loud when I consider giving him a soul patch or a goatee.

The whole thing goes so smoothly that when I get to his neck I am startled when my first stroke cuts him. A red efflorescence the bold color of an Invincible spreads out in the white cream as I realize my father must shave his neck up. Most men do this, I know, but I have always shaved my neck down, and I just assumed that my father would, too. But when I try a stroke going up I realize that he doesn't. He is an up-shaver, all right. When I understand this it seems grotesque that I wouldn't shave up on my neck also. Wouldn't I be an up-shaver too if my father had shown me how to shave? Why didn't he want to show me how to shave like him? Isn't that something a father should do?

It's ridiculous, but this makes fissures of pain open up inside my heart.

I am entranced in this for a while before I realize that something is wrong with my father. His eye is tracking around the room and his body is hot, dappled in sweat. His mouth is cracked and it occurs to me that he may be dehydrated.

"Are you thirsty?" I ask him.

The eye clenches shut.

"I guess that's a yes."

I finish his neck harmlessly, going up, then clean the cut and wipe the blood off my hands. At the former bar, while the Pong machine plays itself silently, I fill a glass with water and mix in some Thick-It, and then, as with a baby's bottle, I test the solution. It is puddinglike, per Bess's instruction, and it tastes, as she said it would, remarkably like wallpaper glue.

I have spooned the entire glass of Thick-It into my father's mouth when I realize that he is unappeased. His eye is still agitated and sweat is still bursting through his pores.

"Do you want another glass?" I ask. His eye flicks open and closed. No. Then, remembering what Bess said about how his body temperature can swing wildly, I say, "Are you hot? Do you want me to take the blankets off?" But the eye flicks again. Coughing delicately, I say, "Do you require the bathroom?" Again I receive a flick in the negative.

Then I get an idea. "Want to try to say it?"

He does. I slide a pillow behind his back to take the pressure off his spine, retard my breathing to match his, put my hands on his chest in a resuscitant position, just like Bess taught me, wait with the patience of a surfer for the right wave, and then push hard. We attain a phonatory breath but it doesn't amount to much.

He produces an urgent apneic eruption that sounds precisely, mortifyingly, like the noises Dex made when he went under the water.

"That was a bad fucking idea," I say, mostly to myself. Then I see, at the end of the bar where the tumblers used to be, the Ouija board peeping out from a hedge of multicolored sponges and scented lotions.

"Can you spell it?" I say.

The eye clenches affirmatively.

Propping it on my father's lap, I put a finger on the A at the top corner, then retract it. "You blink and I stop on that letter, right?" The eye confirms this. "All right. I'll go slow."

It only takes a few tries for me to record what he wants. My ruined finger, spoiler of Liszt and Beethoven, spells it out.

L-A-G-A-V-U-L-I-N.

His tortoisean eye fills with water and stares at me, wet and beseeching, and I realize I am in an unprecedented situation. My father wants something of me. He has an absolute need that only I can grant. Against my will a lifetime of memory floods over me. Why didn't you teach me to shave? Why didn't you trust me with the E-Type? Where were you when I was getting beaten by Kasimir Kakmuzh?

Where were you when Dex needed you? You were drinking, weren't you?

Why should I give you a drink now?

If I have really come back to punish my father, I think, this is it. My big chance.

I want to say the word: *Killer*.

But it's no good. Although my heart swarms with vengeance I find myself unstoppering the Lagavulin, pouring some into a plastic cup, drawing a small shot into a syringe, and slowly injecting it into my father's IV. A few moments later, when his condition does not improve, I administer another dose. Then another. Ten minutes later when I wipe the sweat off his skin it does not reappear so quickly, but his eye is not pacified. He still blinks with importunate fervor and I understand his anguish.

I pour a finger of Lagavulin into the cup and soak one of the small sponges in it. Then I unhinge his cowcatcher jaw and swab his tongue and the vault of his mouth with the scotch. I keep spreading the liquor onto his taste buds until his finger twitches with ecstasy and his eye quits flickering, stabilizes, then finally closes and he falls asleep, princely and innocent.

I wish I were braver.

The Jester Tove in His Prime

That night Hahva and I make a startling discovery.

So far during our stay I have treaded through this house with the care of a sci-fi character who adventures into the past on a chronotour and is minded repeatedly not to step off the prescribed path lest it ruin the history of just about everything. Like a good protagonist I have stayed far away from any unsanctioned territory, but tonight Hahva complains of leaving her book in Georgia, so we venture into the study to look for some reading material.

And boy do we find it.

Next to a copy of Jacques Gautier D'Agoty's harrowing anatomical prints, Hahva finds a leather-bound notebook whose spine reads *The Tremain School*. Of course that's the one she picks up, not the nearly priceless, totally unfoxed eighteenth-century folio full of magnificent, entirely unvarnished four-color plates bound in spectacular red half morocco over glazed green boards.

Naturally.

"Oh my God," she says after a breathless perusal. "Jack, you won't believe this."

Outside the window gypsy moths pull up and down in the night air. When they hit the glass, dust clouds explode from them like powder from a gunshot.

"You've got to see this," she says. "Really."

Hahva leans in close to me with the book, pulling me into her intimacy sphere. The glossy black-and-white pages whir by under her fingers, fanning to me the mildewy scent of illicit history. She stops on a page devoted to recording the hijinks of the Slithy Toves: a Jester Society.

"Yeah," I say. "Fantastic. Can we go back to bed now?"

"You're not looking close enough. Do you see who the Jester Tove is?"

Upon closer examination I perceive the features underneath a tufted harlequin cap: plow-throated neck, air-cleaving nose, cowcatcher jaw. What at first confounded identification, I see now, is the expression. Assuming various contortions of mirth and mischief—peering out from between a hedge of skirted legs under a tablecloth; looking up from all fours on the turf of the football field while the pelican mascot of the Bancroft-Ash School sprawls, just-tripped, behind him; measuring out a thick pour of liquid from a jeroboam into a punch bowl while a beehived schoolmarm closes in, hands outstretched as if about to tag him—is the mouth of my father, smiling. In some of the shots the smile cracks so wide across his face that his eyes are reduced to slits. When this happens his cheeks attain a hilarious chipmunky puffiness, giving him, incredibly, an air of unpremeditated jollity.

My father, cracker of jokes.

My father, troublemaking agent of fun and deviltry.

"This is ridiculous," I say.

"Keep going."

Captions made inscrutable by private humor describe my father's Slithy Tove achievements. *Most Likely to Defenestrate. Rector of the New Church of Sturm und Drang. Lemon Meringue Found to Promote Hair Growth, Shine.* Under a picture of a sprawling ibex mascot one reads *Tennant Scores Only Sack in 102nd Annual Tremain/Turnbull Spoon Title Game.* In a tandem shot, in front of a scoreboard reading TREMAIN: 6, VISITOR: 31, there is the frozen image of my father streaking behind a withered school official wearing Turnbull colors, and snatching from his upraised hand an enormous silver spoon. *Jester Tove Tennant Brings Spoon Home After 34-Year Absence,* it says.

"And look at this one," she says. "He's musical."

The next one is a collage that features my father at an upright in what appears to be a church, playing, or pantomiming, in various postures of freestyling abandon—feet on the keys, backwards, underleg, behind the back, using the knuckles instead of the fingertips.

"So he's posing for the camera," I say, feeling a hot wave of nausea come over me. "That doesn't mean he plays."

"Flip to the next page."

The next page celebrates, in scattered photos, the performances of the Tremain Orchestra, in which my father, in a rigid posture that adumbrates the military bearing he would perfect in later years, mans a concert grand piano. It cannot be a Slithy ruse. Even if they had found a way to splice my father into one of the shots they could not have given his body the authority it has at the bench. The stance is austere but natural: the elbows are at textbook elevation but the shoulders are unbunched, the hands arched and spread with Liszt-like dominance.

My palate floods with sickening water. Can it be true? Can my father be a pianist too?

"Can you believe it?" Hahva says.

Why didn't he ever tell me he was a pianist?

"It's crazy, right?"

Maybe he was waiting until I got good enough.

"Look how young he looks."

And I never got there.

"He looks like so much fun, doesn't he?"

He never considered me ready to be told.

"And look. You two have the same jaw!"

Because of my ruined finger.

"What a super find!" she exclaims. "Who knew you had musical genes?"

I reel with possibility: if this can be true, what could my father have written to me in those thirteen letters?

I Receive the Assist

Sitting at the Bösendorfer in the darkness of an unfamiliar concert hall I pound out *Pathétique* Sonata's first movement in *allegro*. At first I am fluid and easy, possessed of the same mindless authority that I used to have with the bottle. Every atom in my fingers is finely attuned to the savagery and tenderness that Beethoven meant for the piece: a love song, with battery. The audience, I see, is filled with rows of identical luminous figures with severe mouths and attitudes of imperviousness—my mother, hundreds of her, arms crossed, chins upturned, waiting for me to commit the same error I always do.

Dex is nowhere to be seen.

I can feel the moment rushing toward me and my body becomes clenched. Then, as Hahva conducts me to the crossover and the old dread starts to mount I suddenly realize there is another body at the bench with me, its arm extended in mime-like waxy flexibility above the keys. I apprehend all this too quickly to process usefully; in the zeptosecond of the crossover my partner's pointer finger hammers down on the key, providing the assist. My hand smoothes over his and plays seamlessly until the crossover reappears, when once again the pointer finger hammers down on the same key I can never reach.

My partner commits the only action of which he is capable, covering for me the only action of which I am incapable, and we play the sonata to perfection this way, my gargoylean father and I.

Pop Quiz

Q: If this is such a sweet dream, why do I wake up from it in tears?

A:

The Bösendorfer Speaks

Two days later we run out of pretexts for being out of the house at night and end up gathered together in the living room. Press lolls in the corner. Hahva struggles to maintain the distance I've requested in deference to my mother's idea of proxemics. My mother stands with soldierly rectitude below her own portrait, an image of her own pitiless perfection. My father's chair has been retired and stored in the basement—at a dignified distance from Press's gutter-picked furnishings and protected from their emanations by a heavy linen drape—and into that old space by the fireplace Bess wheels my father in his new electric chair. (According to Press, bitterly: $28,500 as equipped with power tilt, articulating casters, and a Qtronix joystick controller for the day when he regains enough motor control to direct it.) My father produces his own physics; the light of the room eddies around his motionless feet as his eye punches holes in the air.

We all concentrate on ignoring the dioramic falseness of the room.

"I have an idea," Press says. "How about some music? A sonic treat for our weary auditory canals, which have, it is clear, been awfully good all year long."

"Oh no," I say under my breath.

"I think that's a great idea," Hahva says.

"Yes, fabulous," Bess seconds.

"I'll pick something out," Hahva volunteers. "Where is the stereo?"

"*Mais non.* We can do better than that. We are in the presence of musical genius tonight. A fleet-fingered Bobby Fischer of the ivories, with the passion of three Picassos and the speed of a mongoose smoking coolies."

"You play the piano?" Hahva asks Press.

"Not I, alas."

Hahva looks curiously at my mother, who remains imperforate.

"Warmer," my brother urges, and then, when her eyes, incredulous, turn to me, "Hot! White hot! Burning up like a paper cup!"

"Jack?" she asks, aspirated with disbelief. "You are a piano Bobby Fischer?"

I know what she is doing right now. She is thinking back to the faculty parties where it was inquired of the guests if anyone could play something on the piano and no offers were made. She is remembering the many times Rodney begged someone to play James Brown on the Ark's donated upright. She is recalling her shock when, after I took her to the symphony in Atlanta—a two-hour round trip in the quivering Omni—I described Daniel Barenboim's performance as "flabby and rote" while she marveled at it breathlessly with the rest of the Woodruff Center lobby crowd idiotically gushing about his celebrity.

> (Fatuous Symphonygoer One: We are so honored by his presence tonight. It was so . . . such a . . . bravado performance. So passionate. A tour de force.
> Fatuous Symphonygoer Two: Yes. He elevated the music to the ethereal.

Hahva, overhearing: Oh yes! I agree. It was so moving!
  Don't you think so, Jack?
Me: Yes, it was quite good for a one-handed tone-deaf
  robot with Parkinson's.)

"Jack plays the piano?" Hahva finally verbalizes.

"Play isn't the word," Press says. "He inhabits the piano. He embodies the notes. He *is* the music."

"Hardly," I say.

Hahva appeals to the room for support. My mother looks on, uncracked and revealing nothing. Press grins. My father's eye flashes up and down, indicating anything. Bess is no doubt considering what proverb applies to this baffling situation.

"You really play?"

"Show her, little brother. We should all like to hear something."

"Oh yes," says Bess, putting her hands together in a prayerful semaphore of do-gooder enthusiasm. "Please do."

"No," I say. "I don't feel up to it."

I am assailed by a chorus of pleas. Everyone wants to hear a song. Oh come on, Jack. Be a sport, Jack. But I will not be a sport.

"Sorry," I say. "I can't really play. It's been too long."

My father's eye starts blinking and Bess leans in to him with the Ouija board, drawing her finger across the letters, deciphering. Then she holds up her scratch pad, on which is written in Bess's curlicue-ridden script: PLA PLS. It is the only time I can think of that my father has asked for anything. It occurs to me that Bess might very well be lying, that he might have really blinked LAGVLN PLS. But Bess seems as incapable of lying as my father is of asking. Which improbability is afoot here?

"All right," I say.

I get up and Hahva peels away from me to let the stranger next to her pass unhindered. When I step into the shadow of the Bösendorfer it pierces my heart like a knife. I don't want to do this. Music is the purest form of memory. Your muscles remember the movements required to strike the correct keys. Your mind remembers the progression of notes and chords and keys. And your heart processes it all. This is what people are referring to when they speak of the heartbreaking tenacity of old songs. When the sound enters your ear you literally vibrate with memory. You assimilate it bodily.

"I'll take any requests."

Hahva wants to quiz me. She asks for Billy Joel, the Beatles, Johnny Mercer. She wants Cole Porter, Scott Joplin, "Jesu, Joy of Man's Desiring," some execrable Hans Zimmery garbage that I make up on the spot. Kid stuff. Then, perhaps suspecting some kind of trained-monkey ruse, she orders a Magnetic Fields song that we both heard for the first time last month, which I reproduce easily and without error. This, after all, is my talent. On this song I let myself have some fun, involving the nine extra keys. It is totally capricious and extraneous but what the heck. The Magnetic Fields are one of the few bands that might have a use for these lowballs anyway. The notes are so low that you can hear the individual ticking of each string.

Let them eat cake, I think. Ha.

With every song Hahva's eyes grow wider with disbelief. From the bench—once again my seat of power: the Bösendorfer is giving it up; she is in my thrall—I cannot tell if Hahva's pupils are dilating with delight and wonder or with the shock of betrayal: yet something else about me she did not know. Another classified item to which she was denied clearance.

A knife-edge of one hand enters her mouth.

For a while I notebind the room. My brother sinks lower into the cushions. Bess's eyes behind her Swifty Lazars glaze with pleasure. Even my mother is affected. Her snaptight backbone flexes bowlike; her shoulders relax. She attains a posture almost fallible. My father's eyelid closes. Hahva bites her other hand for balance. And then I go for too much. I start playing *appassionato* and the memory of the audition comes to me. "Permission to start again?" The sound of shucking corn floods my ears and I miss a crossover, an easy one, a baby step.

A bright ribbon of hatred flashes before me.

"Whoopsie daisy," Press says. "An unseemly error."

One is talc. Two, gypsum. Three, calcite. Four, fluorite. Five, apatite.

"Are we to believe that this concludes tonight's performance?"

Earth is 980 cm/s^2. Mars is 371. Jupiter, 2,312.

"Well. Our Jack is a silent genius. Bravo," Press says, clapping. Bess does not perceive the irony and joins in the applause.

"I've never heard anything like it," she says. "My heart lifts up to the Lord."

"Hallelujah holy ghost and Virgin Mary praise God amen," Press says.

"Well done, Jackson," my mother intones from her position.

My father's eye blinks at me and a gurgling, drowning noise escapes his throat.

Hahva is conspicuously silent, a sign, I would like to hope, merely of her pleasure.

"Aren't you proud of your man?" Press asks her. "I hope so."

Hahva says nothing but chevrons of clenched muscle appear at her shoulders and the saddlesoap burnish of her skin goes nuclear and mottled in a way that assures me I can abandon all hope.

* * *

"Didn't you care for the performance?" Press asks when everyone else goes upstairs.

"How did you learn to play like that?" Hahva says, a question that is really an accusation.

I shrug and dig a fingernail into my scalp. Guru Nanek Dev, I think, Guru Angad Dev, Guru Amar Das, Guru Hargobind.

"He learned to play like that by dedicating his young life to music. Didn't you, Jacko? When normal kids were out playing with other kids or bonding with siblings Jack was at the old piano bench."

"What is he talking about, Jack?"

"Nothing."

Guru Har Rai, Guru Harkrishan, Guru Gobind Singh . . .

"Nothing? Nothing? That should be your fucking personal anthem. 'Nothing,' by Jack Tennant. Lyrics: none. Just an instrumental, only without any instruments."

"You can't have an instrumental without any instruments, Hahva."

"Are you being a jackass to me right now? God, Jack. I leave Georgia, come all this way. To be with you. In this . . . fortress of solitude . . ."

"It was your idea to come, remember. You asked for it."

"I didn't ask for you to totally abandon me once we got here. I didn't ask for you to turn into some monster of silence. I didn't ask to be dropped amid all these . . ."

"Assholes?" Press provides.

"And then to be . . ."

"Abandoned?" he contributes.

"After which you continue to treat me like some kind of . . ."

"Stranger?" my brother finishes.

Press, chock-full of caligulan pleasure at his own strife production, drains what's left of his brag and shakes the empty bottle as if divining something. He stares into it as if into a crystal ball—bragomancy—and, with his arm kerning over Hahva's shoulder on the sofa, says to her, "Jacko has many secrets, does he not? Perhaps I can be of assistance in revealing some. How about this one. You know the way regular people maintain hope chests? In which they keep precious items they want to include in their happy future lives? Stuff for their weddings, their families, beloved heirlooms and whatnot? Well, Jacko keeps a Pain Box. What stories it contains! What story would you like to hear from the Pain Box?" He's building, his speech becoming faster and more urgent, *stringendo*. He's really enjoying this. "The relationship of the *Greater Baltimore Metropolitan Area White Pages* to love? The story of the nine-millimeter pacifier? The real reason Jack never got his PhD?"

"That's enough, Press."

"The *White Pages* again?" she says, nearly outraged. "What is with the *White Pages*? What's a nine-millimeter pacifier? What does that even mean? And what are you talking about, the real reason Jack never got his PhD?" Hahva presses. "He didn't like New York."

"Shut up, Press," I say.

Press stands up, the voltage in his eyes crackling. My brain sends signals indicating I should step down but I ignore them and move my body toward him. A hard insect hatred riles in my stomach.

I try to stare my brother down but his eyes are full of reflex and dare. He is all cockstrong readiness. His body is rapidly calculating all the configurations of leverage and thrust it could produce if called upon. It knows the eventualities already. No doubt his body regards this as an exquisite delicacy: the rare opportunity to thrash the little brother, in front of the girl-friend, no less. It has been waiting for this for fifteen years. Ever since I escaped from Maryland.

Neutered by capitulation, I step aside.

Maybe it's the seigneurial chinner he's flashing at me. Maybe it's the accumulation of a lifetime of humiliation and vic-timhood. Whatever the reason, I snap. It happens fast. Without preamble of thought, I take a wild swing at my brother.

My instant target is his cowcatcher jaw and the smile at-tached to it, but Press feels it coming and slips the punch. My fist skids off the dome of his skull, a stone skipping across wa-ter. He does not even reel. Then, in violation of everything I've always heard my father preach, I do not follow up the punch. No combination is forthcoming. No jabwork. No cheap shots. No spray-fire of crosses or hooks or uppercuts. We just stare at each other. My body heaves with exertion and anxiety but Press, even though his face is alive with electricity, remains loose and unclenched. I've seen him in these moments before. My brother's violence is callikinetic, mesmerizing as a snake charmer. His grin splits into a wide smile that adumbrates the worst.

I feel my eyes close, bracing. For a long time nothing hap-pens. When I finally open my eyes again I see my brother throw back his head and let out a wild vandal laugh.

"Now that, little brother," he says, "*that* was assertive."

Scoreboard

House: 3
Me: 0

Reservation for One at the Everlast

"You've hurt yourself, Jackadopupidopoulos," my brother says to me downstairs in the basement. "I've got something for that."

From his minifridge he extracts a flexible plastic pack glowing with swimming-pool blue gel and applies it to the knuckles on my ring and little finger. His hand touches my hand. "Don't you know you can't hit with those two knuckles?"

"I know," I say sheepishly. "Guess I forgot."

"Bad memory?" Press says.

"Always."

"I heard that," he says. Something sympathetic now passes between us on a subaudible fraternal frequency. "That was a good hack you took up there. If you hadn't telegraphed by cocking back so far it would have done some real damage. I doff my hat."

"Thanks."

"Hey," he says, nodding to the ice pack, which I have removed momentarily. "You need to keep that on there for twenty minutes. We can't have you with asymmetrical knuckles. Mom will freak."

"All right," I say, uncertain of the care he is suddenly taking.

From the window comes a moist percolatory cooing sound.

"This a boys-only club or can anyone join?" a voice says. Even from this distance, in the weak light, with only her head protruding through the window, I can see the clotted arachnid bristle of Robbie's mascara-encrusted eyelashes; even in the heavy brag fog of the basement I can feel her heated pleather presence.

"Sure, come on down. We're recuperating."

"From what?"

"Just some sport. Have you come by for refreshment?"

Robbie makes her sectional passage through the sliver of window—head, thorax, buttocks, and legs—and materializes in a venomous lump on the concrete. Now I can see her fully. Her slap is applied with Nutcrackerish flair: saucerish ketchupy daubs on the cheeks, relish-green circles around her eyes, fancy mustard hair. She closes in.

"Unless you Tennant boys have something else to offer."

"So that's one for you. And for you, little brother? A peg of brag?"

"No thanks."

"But it's magically delicious."

"Thanks but no."

"Oh come now. I know what you're going through. You don't get any extra-credit points for denying yourself. Don't be a sucker for pregret."

"Nothing for me, thanks," I manage to say when Press passes the opened bottle under my nose. Despite myself, I breathe deeply from it. I should be repulsed by this odor—I have spent nearly two decades disciplining myself against it—but I am not repulsed. The sensation is glorious. Particles of liquor enter my nostrils and scorch delicate hairs. My nose twitches, my body twitches. I want a brag. I want to sit down on my Everlast with my brother, my wretched brother, and have a few.

"Don't give in to pregret. Live a little."

"I'm not resisting anything. I'm just indifferent."

"Suit yourself," he says, taking the bottle away.

Press pours the drinks—ginger ale for me, flat and iceless—and I shuffle around the basement, trying to blow the smell out of my nose. Then, with my back turned and thinking, 1936: Paul Muni, 1937: Spencer Tracy, 1938: Robert Donat, I hear Robbie emit a squeal of terror. When I turn around my brother is ecstatic with fury, looming over Robbie on the Everlast.

With murderous precision Press says, "What. Have. I. Told. You. About. That?"

"About what? About what?" Robbie pleads.

"About sitting on that punching bag?"

"Oh God," she says, leaping to her feet. "I'm sorry. I can't remember a thing like that. It's just a stupid punching bag. O.K. already. Jesus."

When Press recovers and tries to smooth out his feathers he cannot hide his embarrassment. He tries to avoid looking at me but cannot. He shrugs.

"No one can sit on the Everlast?" I say, my heart filling with love.

He shrugs again.

"I should have known," Robbie says. "He's a fucking lunatic over that thing. 'Fifteen years and no one's touched that bag.' Like he should get some fucking medal for letting shit lie around." When Press says nothing to this she scoffs. "This one day last year I happen to be overnighting and, just to be nice— as a favor—I start to tidy up down here. You know, sweeping up the broken glass and mouse shit, throwing away the take-out boxes. And this bag that has been sitting here on the floor for fucking ever, making a home for spiders and vermin, I swear to God, this fucking punching bag I start rolling so I can sweep under it and I almost get decked. Hate to say this to you, kid, but your brother's a freak show." Robbie's fear has been replaced with resentment. "Will you threaten to hit me if I move that nail gun, asshole?"

Press still cannot look at me.

"No one's sat on the Everlast all this time?" I say. "Since I sat on it?"

After a long moment he says, "It's been reserved."

I walk to my brother. He looks suddenly small and beaten, his shoulders collapsed. His body is shaking minutely with something that seems to be fear. Perhaps it's suffering. Maybe it's memory.

This is a movement I have never seen him make. When I was twelve he laid down his Toaster Tank on Jarrettsville Pike going forty. He was wearing only cutoffs and an old pair of Stan Smiths. No helmet, no jacket, no shirt, no gloves, no long pants. He laid down the old boxer on a patch of sand—its Metzlers were already scalped, front and back—and then skid-ded thirty-five feet, bare-skinned, on the asphalt. His body stopped at the intersection by Coen's Handi-Mart and Coen told me, four months later, that Press peeled himself off the road, seeped inside the double doors, and said aloud to a crowd of astonished onlookers, "Hey, you guys carry Band-Aids? I think I'm going to need the big ones, though. That and a six of Mickey's Big Mouths, please."

Over that summer he grew a thick, fuming scabjacket all over his torso but never emitted a syllable of complaint, never made one gesture of pain.

And now my impervious brother—my oriole-killing, Russian-smiting, Toaster-wrecking, brag-taking brother—is quivering with tenderness and sorrow over my Everlast.

My Everlast! Mine!

The Everlast, it occurs to me, is to my brother what the orange flip-flops are to me: an inviolate talisman of love. I cannot believe it. He has been guarding it for me all this time.

I want to hug him. But I do something better.

"Hey," I say. "What does a guy have to do for a brag around here?"

"What?" he says, looking up.

"You heard me," I say, thrusting a tumbler at him. "Load it."

Nothing Hurts Me

It is just like the old days: sitting around the basement, accelerating. I am on my Everlast, Press is on the edge of the bed, and Robbie sags on a cylinder of rolled-up carpet. Press drinks with great formality. When Robbie receives the bottle she throws it back and her condiment-colored makeup flashes stroboscopically in the weak light. On my turn I hold the bottle under my nose, assimilating the preview. Then I bring the glass lip to my own and give the bottle a deep, sucking soul kiss. At first I resist it. It burns and my swallow is awkward. I gag and cough discreetly as the nerves in my throat and stomach ignite at the passage of liquor. After a few drinks, however, my amateurism disappears and I become fluid and full of grace. My body remembers this in the way that it remembered the Bösendorfer. I hold the bottle easily between two splayed fingers and I accomplish my motions with an efficient, practiced legerity.

I am attuned, mindful and mindless at the same time, all reflex—a bottlesharp.

Then my brother initiates a very old ritual.

"Does it hurt you?" he asks as I swallow.

"Nothing hurts me," I brag, and take another drink.

The True Story of Jordana Mochnik, Spurned Student

Something else I had forgotten about brag: the feeling of infinite possibility. Tonight I might very well go to the Terrapin. Or play some Diceman. I won't worry about the spillage of the Bösendorfer beans and Hahva's anger. Hell, I might even spill some additional beans. Why not? I want to demonstrate solidarity with my brother.

"I can't remember how much I ever told you about Jordana Mochnik," I say.

"Not much. Just that the affair is the reason you got the boot from your program."

"Juicy!" Robbie exclaims, delighted. "A Tennant in disgrace! Who knew?"

"That's not quite true, Press. She is the reason I got the boot, but there was no affair. Listen to this. You're going to like it."

I can't help feeling a painful twitch in my heart when I think about the scandal. Leon never believed my claims of innocence. Six years I was friends with him. Six years. The only reason I attended that program was because I knew Leon was there. For years I had read his work on the short story writers of the Russian Revolution and I felt in him, long before we ever met, the same sympathy to human weakness and travail that I had myself. He knew darkness. He knew failure. He knew the wild hunger for escape. We had the greatest relationship. I covered his classes when he was on vacation. We played poker with faculty and select grad students Tuesday nights. He would drop by my office hours and ask me what I thought about this or that Babel piece. I helped his wife make bundt cakes for faculty parties. I babysat for his children.

Once I nearly told him about Dexter. I came so close.

It was winter. The heat pipe in my East Village apartment was busted and I was spending a lot of my nights at the Korean laundromat, keeping warm. Leon walked by on his way back from introducing someone or other at KGB and saw me huddled up next to a dryer, reading Gogol in the unflinching fluorescent lights. Like something out of Dickens, he swooped in, pried me out of my seat, and took me to an enervated, sawdust-littered ye-olde-style saloon a few blocks away. He fed me, but all they had to drink was beer. They were nearly fascist about it.

You had about four seconds to say "Bitter" or "Lager," or else the efficient, harried, nearly wordless sexagenarian server would scurry away in disgust. If you managed either word before the deadline, and he approved of you, he would bring you whatever number of beers he intuited you would need. They had liquor, no soda, no juice. I didn't dare ask for water. What I got was bitter.

Leon put a few quick pints away in a gesture of game camaraderie—"*Na zearovie!*" he cried every time—while I covertly poured my drinks down the urinal during trips to the bathroom. But I couldn't sustain the ruse. Leon was enjoying my company. He was talkative. Sooner or later he would notice. So I started sipping on a pint of turbid bitter and almost immediately became pricked with semidrunkenness. I couldn't help it: I started thinking about Dex. I wanted to say something. I wanted him to know. But I couldn't figure out how to start.

Leon was talking shop—I still remember: it was something about modern war-writing's debt to *Red Cavalry* and the conflation of the profane and the sublime in battleground imagery—when he sensed that something was wrong.

"Hey," he said. "You know what, though? Sometimes the critical enterprise is just so . . . academic. You know? Sometimes I get so sick of it. What do you want with you on your deathbed, anyway? Your Robbe-Grillet? Or the woman you love? Am I right? Fuck Manthia Diawara, I say. Screw Judith Butler. Forget all that Post-Althusserian rabble. Sometimes if you've got something hard in your heart you just need to talk it. You just need to say it. Sometimes that act, just getting it out, helps. Don't you think?"

It was an invitation. He wasn't prying, but he knew I wanted to say something. And I did.

I wanted to say: my brother is dead.

That's it. Simple and true. Contained in that confession—unalloyed, unmitigated by critjargon, plain as the blade of a knife—would be the whole encyclopedia of my heartache. That's all it would take. "I had a brother," I could say. "He's dead now."

Leon would understand it. Maybe then it would make some kind of sense to me.

Instead I said, "Totally," and had another drink of bitter.

God, how I loved Leon for that. He was always there for you. He always helped you. He would never abandon you. If he had told you he would watch you, he would be there watching you. And not drinking.

I think I wanted him to be my father. It seemed like he sort of felt that way, too.

But I was wrong.

Leon's testimony during my Disciplinary Committee hearing was, "It is my belief that Jackson Tennant did knowingly and willingly abuse the power of his office to vitiate Jordana Mochnik. I regretfully must therefore recommend to this committee immediate expulsion with censure." During my hearing there was no evidence of any involvement with Jordana Mochnik except her elaborate architecture of lies; it was Leon's testimony alone that sealed my fate. Why didn't he believe me? I'll never know. I don't care about Jordana herself—it is simply her nature to lie. I do not blame her.

But Leon: why? Why wouldn't you believe me?

"So I had this student. Jordana Mochnik. She developed this thing for me. Don't ask me why." I wait here for my brother to say something—was she on drugs? did she need glasses?—but nothing is forthcoming. He listens in attentive, respectful silence. "She began stalking me, basically. My office hours, the apartment, the coffee shop. She'd just show up.

She was always asking these salacious questions in class. She licked lollipops suggestively. It was preposterous, a Lolita caricature. I tried to disregard her but it was impossible. She showed up once at a faculty party—Leon Flanders was there, I am pained to say—and made all these gestures of ownership: putting her hands on me in front of others, drinking from my glass when I put it down. I wasn't even attracted to her. I mean, I wanted to be, in theory. She was beautiful and nineteen years old and I was lonely as hell. It was flattering. But we had nothing in common. And she wasn't the brightest. In one of her stories she spelled 'hard-on' without the hyphen. Hardon. One word. Like it's an atomic component. Proton, neutron, electron, hardon."

"Brainiac," says Press.

"The more I refused her the more extreme her efforts became. I should have gone to the department about it but I didn't want to do anything official. Even if I was cleared of wrongdoing—and I couldn't be sure I would; Jordana Mochnik was so pretty and so young and I was, well, me—there would still be a formal record of the suspicion. I didn't want to engage in all that. I just wanted it to go away. I thought I could reason with her."

"But you were wrong," Robbie provides.

"She finally became vindictive. Back then I had this Vespa. One night she sneaks over to my apartment and sabotages it—she Armor-Alled the seat."

At this Press bursts into a gust of appreciative laughter.

"Resourceful girl," he says when he recovers.

"What?" Robbie asks. "What does that mean? Armor-Alled the seat?"

"She sprayed Armor All on the leather seat. Armor All is a protectant for plastics and rubber. You spray it on tires and the dashboard and so on. It guards against ultraviolet damage. Keeps things shiny, basically."

"But it is also prodigiously slippery," Press says.

"Exactly. So the next day I fire it up and run it to class. I'm late so I'm speeding. Everything seems normal until I try to come to a stop. I was taking the FDR and when I pulled off the exit and started braking hard I slid off the seat, racking myself on the fork and spinning into a wreck. It was quite a digger. I jackknifed over the handlebars and the scooter tumbled over and over until it smashed into a guardrail.

"It was too much for me. I didn't go to school. I went straight to Mars and started drinking. It didn't take much. I stayed there all afternoon. Late in the evening Jordana Mochnik arrives. She starts applying herself to me. I was grieving. I was drunk. I was vulnerable. What can I say? I succumbed. She pulled me behind the amplifiers and we started kissing." I remember this moment with a complicated pleasure. She was fleshy and malleable and the force of her carnal willingness, her hungry submission, was almost irresistible. Almost.

"Then I had some kind of flash of clarity and I pulled away. I told her that I was sorry, that we couldn't do this. I wiped her lipstick from my mouth on the edge of my sleeve. I remember how she looked at that gesture with such horror, such contempt. She reached into her purse and extracted a bottle of Armor All, sprayed it on the seat of my pants, and said, 'Rest in peace, Vespa.'

"It took me a moment to realize what she meant. I hadn't suspected her. I had plenty of enemies in the department and in my neighborhood there were any number of idiots who would delight in random sabotage. But then I understood. I exploded. I mean, I detonated. I grabbed for the nearest object. I wanted to hit her so bad. That was my impulse. I can't deny it. I wanted to hit her repeatedly with something hard. What was within range, what I grabbed, was a fire extinguisher. I remember shaking. I remember cocking my arm back, pulling it high above my head—"

"You need to stop telegraphing," Press says. "You'll never connect like that."

"I had it way back, ready to bring it down, to smite her with the fire extinguisher. I remember how plush her self-satisfaction was. She was radiant with smugness; her face was pillowed with it. God did I want to hit that face. But I didn't. I resisted. Instead I leveled the business end of the extinguisher at the opening of her sweater and fired it off."

"Ha!" goes Press. "Bombs away! I love it!"

"I didn't exactly stop, either. I proceeded to jet her with it mercilessly until I emptied the canister. And it was not the travel-sized shorty. It was a fat, full-sized scuba tank canister that produced surprising velocity. I mean, it had recoil. While I was spraying her no one noticed. We were safely hidden by the amplifiers and the surf sound of the extinguisher covered her yelling. After I sprayed out the whole tank, though, plenty of people heard her scream. I was discovered by a dozen witnesses standing over her 'in a posture of menace' with the fire extinguisher in my hands. Apparently I was still squeezing the trigger even though nothing was coming out.

"When I came out of the daze of fury, as I stood there over Jordana, who was wild-eyed and frosted like a Christmas ornament, I said to the witnesses crowding around, 'This is a *non*smoking area. Anyone else want to light up?' None of them thought it was funny. Neither did the Disciplinary Committee."

"I do, though," Press says. "I congratulate your sense of levity in the face of disaster."

"Thank you."

"So giving Jordana Mochnik a money shot from an extinguisher got you expelled?"

"No. Hosing her down didn't get me expelled. It was a lapse in judgment, I'll give you that. A bad decision, clearly. Spraying her down would have gotten a strong reprimand, no question. But the DC gave me the boot because Jordana used that incident to fabricate a story of our 'affair.'"

"Uh-oh."

"Right. She described the extinguisher incident as an act of lovelorn retribution. She claimed that I had manipulated her into a sexual relationship, that I had been preying on her for months, extracting 'favors,' threatening to fail her unless she performed carnal services."

"Va-va-va voom," Robbie says, oiling closer to Press.

"She said that night at Mars she was breaking up with me and that in a jealous rage I attacked her with the fire extinguisher. You know what else? She tried to describe the accident on the Vespa as caused by grief. When I told the DC that she had Armor-Alled my seat she made these big innocent What Is He Talking About, Your Honor? eyes and Leon completely bought it, which made me crazy. I might have exploded a bit at that point, which did nothing but further validate her version of things."

"But it was basically just her word against yours?" Press says.

I nod.

"But this Leon Flanders guy, your pal. He knew you well, right?"

"I thought he was my best friend," I say. "At the time."

"Why didn't he stick up for you? Surely he could have testified about your character."

"That right there is the heartbreaker. I don't know. I suspect I'll never know."

Even now, thinking about Leon Flanders hurts me. He *believed* that I had extorted sex from Jordana Mochnik, that I actually coerced her, that she was an innocent. I can't help thinking what I overheard the Philosoraptor say in the lounge that day: Tennant couldn't get hired as an assistant prof at East Wyoming State Technical Community Vocational Junior College. He couldn't get a job teaching pigs to shit.

"I called Leon a few times afterwards, when I had moved to Georgia, but he gave me the polite brush-off. He was my advisor and I needed a letter from him for the job at Georgia but he wouldn't write one. I hadn't worked closely with anyone else; I had no one else to ask for a letter. Imagine how awkward it was for me to apply for a job with no recommendations and DC proceedings on my transcript."

"What can you do about it now?" Robbie says.

"Now?" I say, putting down another fizzing mouthful of brag. "Nothing. I'm pretty much finished. I think I might already be fired."

"They might not know the real story, but we do," Press says, raising his brag. "A toast to my brother, firefighting man of action."

"Fuck Leon Flanders," Robbie agrees. "Fuck Jordana Mochnik."

When we drink the toast together I feel the saline sting of tears forming in my eyes. I leverage the bottle over my mouth and feel the molten liquid enter me. My Everlast, my brag, my brother.

This is the way I deserve to be loved.

Scoreboard

House: 3
Me: 1

Jackapopudopoulos Goes 'Night 'Night

Upstairs in our room I am astonished to find the beds pushed together.

"What was that?" I hear Hahva say as I start unlacing my boots.

"What what?"

"You were singing something."

"No I wasn't."

"I heard it."

"Not from me, you didn't, sister."

"You were singing," she reaffirms. " 'Nobody knows' something something something."

Dimly it registers that I was singing a spiritual. I repeat the words, basso profundo, in my mind.

Nobody knows the brain cellicide I've seen. Nobody knows but Seagram's.

"I don't sing. I don't dance. And I don't do windows."

"Jack," Hahva says, incredulous. "Are you drunk?"

"I am not drunk. I am a teapot, short and stout. Would you like to see my handle?"

"Jack . . ."

"Or perhaps my spout. It has an interesting feature."

"Jack, did Press make you drink something?"

"That's Jackapopudopoulos to you," I say grandly.

"Oh my God. You *are* drunk!"

"Oh dear. Besmirched by unseemly allegations. Please not to bruit."

"Let me smell your breath."

"I must respectfully decline."

"Come over here already."

Still sporting one boot, I limp to the bed.

"Why didn't you tell me about playing the piano, Jack? Did you think I would be mad that you play the piano? What was it, Jack? Why does everything have to be such a secret?"

Covertly extracting the orange flip-flop from under the mattress, and clutching it protectively to my chest, I think: if I told you about the piano, that would lead you to the broken finger, which would lead you to confrontation with my father, which would lead you to Dex.

"Hip bone's connected to the—*bah-bah*—leg bone!"

"What?"

"Hunh?"

"What did you say?"

"Eh?"

"Jack. Why didn't you tell me about the piano?"

"I forgot?"

Still fully clothed, with one boot on, I pull myself under the covers and roll away from Hahva, my back to her.

"And now you're trying to hide that you're drunk?"

" 'Night 'night," I say sweetly.

As I feign sleep Hahva keeps trying. She asks some questions. She makes further allegations. Recriminations about my silences. Criticisms about my sudden burst of semiviolence against my brother. Assertions that she's been abandoned. And she tries to wake me, but she is so destabilized by my drunkenness that she only taps my shoulder with a timorous prodding gesture. Finally she gives up and rolls away, giving me her back.

For the first time in two years we go to sleep this way—silent, unhappy, addorsed.

The Effects of Brag 1.1: Solidarity

The next morning I wake up with my mouth full of mothpowder and poison. The terrain around me is familiar but has a vortographic confusion, so I give my visual cortex a grace period before moving. Once I am upright, my brain nougat starts dieseling and I decide, after a couple of shaky moments, to take this in baby steps. I need to reassert my grasp on the physical world one element at a time. I grasp the mattress elastic. Elastic still snappy. I turn on the light. Electricity check. I overturn a glass next to the bed and it spills Worcestershire sauce on the marquetry. Gravity O.K. This is progress. America was built on progress.

As the room materializes around me I have the clarity to see that there is a moment in which it would be possible to backtrack. Hahva arises from bed, turned away from me, and stretches with her hands over her head, her back fretting with muscle. She is, consciously or subconsciously, displaying her shoulders to me, affording me the opportunity to say something like, "I'm sorry about last night. I didn't mean to dump ugliness on you, but I figured that if there is anyone on earth with shoulders strong enough to take it, it must be you." But I do not say this. The shoulders receive no comment; Hahva receives no apology.

Instead I stagger in a broken clockwork out of the room and descend downstairs to the kitchen, attired in only my dirty T-shirt and boxers. Press is already hunched over the sink, drinking from a mug. When Press hears my footwork—I take pride in my noisy gait; no longer for me the impotent, sock-padded tiptoe around the house—he hands me wordlessly, and without looking up, my own mug of Worcestershire sauce. When I take it from him I see that we have the same knuckle-knobbed hands with the same widdershins whorl of hair on the back. I upend the mug over my mouth and instantly I feel revitalized, fulgurated into existence.

"I can say this now," Press says after a while. "Welcome home, Lieutenant Boscovich."

The Effects of Brag 1.2: Hate Math

Midnight, out in the garden, with a spade and a boxful of blue urinal cakes procured from Coen's, I stare down the Invincibles. They live up to their name, I am thinking. They are a

Floribunda but their petals do not burn in the sun. They have strong graft and union. Practically immune to mildew, black spot, balling, rust, thrips, and aphids. Good cutter, good repeater. Plenty hardy enough for Maryland winters. And their blooms, although dense and rich, are nearly perfectly symmetrical; they look like the explosion of a red bomb on time-stop film. When Karina Thiergartner saw them she put her face deep into a blossom and stayed there for a long time.

"You did this?" she said, incredulous.

Yes, I did that. And now I am doing this. In my delirium the hate math makes perfect sense.

LIVING ROSES = IMPOTENCE + SUFFERING × HATRED (FAILURE)

whereas

DEAD ROSES = RELEASE + ASSERTION × PEACE (TRIUMPH)

The horses sense it and back away to the far side of the pasture. My knees damp from the dew in the grass, I dig shallow holes and bury a blue puck under each Invincible. If they kill the roses too quickly my mother will recognize the signs of recent digging, so I wrap each flaky puck in a bonnet of thick paper towels—like Hahva's sandwiches, I can't help thinking—and earth over them carefully. Once, when I have to snap a thick shoot that is in the way, I have a surging idea that I am killing my own children and I almost retch into my own hole.

Waterloo, I think, fighting down my gorge, Blackfriars, Millenium, Southwark.

When I am done I go down to the barn to return the spade. Under the cover are the sumptuous lines of the E-Type.

Why hadn't this occurred to me?

Feeling malevolent and sure, I remove the cover. It is elasticized around the corners and pops off like a bedsheet. Intimate. Underneath is the pearly Cornish Grey paint and thrilling chrome. I circle it a few times, rubbing my bent finger down its skin while the key inside my pocket burns against my thigh in outrage.

Silently I unscrew the gas cap and insert a spadeful of fertilizer into the opening. Then I get in the E-Type, put the top down, grip the steering wheel as hard as I can, and discharge hot tears into the dry fibers of the carpet, the rich gutters of the leather.

"Killer," I say out loud for the first time in my life.

The Effects of Brag 1.3: Renunciation

While sober at the house I continue to feel desperate and submerged—sand-trapped. I am sad and guilty about Hahva. I think I am doing wrong. But when I drink I feel exultant, a geyser of possibility, airborne. Everything seems right.

Nothing hurts me.

How did I get along without this feeling for all these years?

Something else remarkable happens. After a few days of bragwork I stop quizzing myself. I could care less about reciting pi into triple digits. Fuck Tony Award winners, I think. Fuck cicero and agate conversion. Fuck alphabetical organization of capitals, both foreign and domestic. Fuck the periodic table of elements, also-ran Derby horses, phobias all the way from aardvarks to zephyrs, all the patron saints and their dumb-ass causes—"Excuse me, Saint Venerius, but you can go fuck your lighthouse keepers, O.K.?" and "Saint Benedict, sorry to bother you, but you and your speleologists can blow me now." And fuck, last but certainly not least, all those smug dumb fuckers on the jacket of *Sgt. Pepper*. That's right. You heard me, Tyrone Power. Fuck you. Fuck you, Aleister Crowley and Aldous Huxley and T. E. Lawrence, you shirt-rending, camel-humping fuck. Mae West, fuck you and your smart-ass mouth. William Burroughs, I'll have a hangover of sorrow tomorrow, but you, sir, may go forth and fuck the hole you made in your own wife's head. Poe, Wilde, Marx, Dylan—both you Dylans—go fuck each other from hell to breakfast. Tony Curtis, I loved you in *Sweet Smell of Success*, but guess what? You may go fuck Burt Lancaster; he must feel left out. Linder, Bell, Dors, Handley, all you other fucks I've never heard of, fuck off for never having been heard of. To those of you I can't remember: you know what you can do, too.

I'll never utter you again. You have all been bragged into oblivion. Good luck on the other side.

And that's not all. I still avoid walking in the shadow of the Bösendorfer but I am less victimized by my extracranial brevity. One day I wake up with my hair in a beluga-headed Angro and do not care. After showers I eschew all blow-drying and setting rituals. When I don my shirt I do not painstakingly pull out the neck into a wide hoop; I recklessly yank it on right over my head, manfully raking my scalp.

The Invincibles are absorbing poison hourly. The E-Type is out of commission. I have renounced my desperate rosarial system of quizzing. I am lionlike, almost as strong as Press.

Anything could happen.

Scoreboard

House: 3
Me: 4

Accusations of Trevority

From my hiding place on the stairs, staring between the scalloped balusters, I spy a disconcerting scene of intimacy between Hahva and Bess. At the table, under the chandelier, with her Swifties on the surface between them, Bess cleans gleaming ultrasound conductor fluid from Hahva's hands. She would be pleased to know how biblical this looks.

Bess asks about her childhood and Hahva spills it. She tells her about her life in New Orleans, her family's generations of military service—and how that produced her Celtic and Sicilian and Israeli bloodlines—and she even tells Bess about her shot at being a ballerina. Hahva gives Bess the whole scoop: the fellowship, the cruelty of the other, wealthy dancers, even the way the teacher put a chalk X on her leotard whenever Hahva spoke. I bristle at this jealously; Hahva only recently told me about this. Why should Bess have this level clearance already?

Then, with a gastric bubble of distress, I realize that Hahva has embarked on a new subject—me vs. the ex—and I have to fortify with some extra braggadocio.

"I was seeing this other guy at the time," Hahva is saying. "Trevor. He had a lot going for him, and I thought at the time that it was love. We'd been together two years, through most of my MSW. I liked his family. He was an engineer but he worked in alternative energies. Photowhatever cells for cars, water cooling for houses instead of conventional A/C. That sort of thing. It seemed noble. Is noble, I guess. I thought it signified a kind of emotional generosity; it just seemed to follow that he would be nice to me."

"But he wasn't?"

"I felt like an accessory a lot. I wasn't personally a cause of any happiness. I was an interchangeable agent of it. I was Girl X. But Girl Y could have just as easily made him feel like that. Am I explaining this right? I think he got pleasure from the display of kindness to me. He was much nicer to me at parties than he was in private, I think because it enhanced his image in a way. It flattered his public sense of self. It had a value as a spectacle but not as an act itself. At parties he would just chat away. He would involve me in the conversation. He'd tell stories that included me, that celebrated me for something or teased me in a gentle, flirtatious way. All night long he'd go like this—icebreaker, cheerleader, confidant, reaching out to touch my arm. 'Isn't that how it happened, Hahva?' he'd say, putting his hand on my back. 'Wasn't it fabulous?' he'd go, kissing me on the neck. It was great.

"And then we'd leave the party and he wouldn't hold my hand on the sidewalk. In the car there wouldn't be any more stories. He wouldn't ask me my opinion about anything. He wouldn't even look at me. If I said something he'd get real serious about the traffic. 'I'm driving!' he'd say. 'I'm trying to look at the road, Hahva. I'd like to get us home alive. Is that all right with you?' "

"That doesn't sound very nice."

"There were other things. During Trivial Pursuit he couldn't stand to wait one second while I considered where to move. 'Orange or green, Hahva, orange or green! Wild card or science and nature! Wild card or science and nature! Wild card, science and nature already! It's not that tough!' "

"Yikes."

"Really. And all the time, after sex, regardless of whether I had mine, he would roll off and lean back with his hands behind his head like he was the CEO of the bed or something, and then he'd go . . . Oh, wait. This is too much. I shouldn't say this."

"It's O.K.," Bess assures her. "Who am I going to tell?"

"Well," Hahva says, giddy with the pleasure of the illicit, "after sex, he'd lie back and say—" and she whispers something to Bess that induces her features to flex in an attitude of dawning hilarity and the Styrofoam squeak of her voice to give way to a balloon-screech peal of laughter. Yes sir, she is really enjoying this.

"Oh my Lord," she says when she recomposes. "What does that mean?"

"Beats me."

"So when you met Jack you realized you didn't love Trevor after all?"

"Not exactly. Not at first. I was still trying with Trevor. It seemed like I was supposed to. I was a social worker, he was so socially conscious. He was a cyclist and had these long muscles."

"Nothing wrong with muscles."

"He was tall and had this beard and this long hair. Jack said he had a 'foppish neogranola Robin Hood pseudohipster look.' After we broke up, Trevor would sometimes drunk-dial me and when Jack saw the number on my cell he would make this bow-and-arrow gesture. *Ffffffffttt*, he'd go, making shooting-arrow noises at me." Hahva whistles. "Boy did he ever hate Trevor."

This makes me regret my eavesdropping. I'm not sure I want to hear anything about Hahva's sex life with another man, even in dispraise, and I certainly don't want to hear about his hair.

I send Hahva a telepathic signal: can we just leave the hair out of it, please?

"When I met Jack I thought, well, here's someone different. The first thing that made me notice him was how he was with the residents at the shelter. He was so gentle. He wanted to know their stories. Gail, Fern, Miss D. I overheard one of the night staffers ask him why he was working there in the first place and he said the strangest thing.

"He said, 'I am working here because the Ark is headquarters for everyone who never got loved the way they deserved.'"

"That *is* a funny thing to say. Funny, but sweet."

"He was always saying things like that."

"Don't take this the wrong way, Hahva, but that doesn't seem like the Jack I've met."

"I know! He's been so secretive. Why are men like this? They all like to think they are spies. They have these secrets they must keep from you. What do they think will happen if they tell you? Let the air out of their tires? What is it? What are the stratagems they are hoarding? If Trevor took the trash out without me knowing he thought he had scored some fantastic victory. One time I came home and had an entire phone conversation with my mother, some of which included Trevor, I might add, and then forty-five minutes later I find him in the bathroom. He hadn't wanted to let me know he was home and so he just stayed in there the whole time, sitting on the edge of the tub, listening to my conversation with my mom. About him! Eerie, right?"

"Eerie, really. Creepy."

"That's why I've been so frustrated with Jack. I thought that by coming here it might change something. That it would present Jack with some kind of change. I thought any change would be good. Like what you were saying about Gil— neuroplasticity. But I was wrong. He didn't become more open. He became even more closed off. I don't think we've slept in separate beds twice during the entire two years we've dated, and now, for the past three nights in a row, even though we sleep in the same room, we have slept in different beds. We hardly see each other during the day. We don't talk. He spends all night in the basement with his brother. For the last three days we have only really communicated by notes.

"I rented this movie tonight." Through the railing I see Hahva wave a plastic case that is pigmented suspiciously like a love story—all peach tones and bronze. "I thought that if we did it like this, that if we could spend some time together when we didn't have to talk . . . but I don't know. It's probably a dumb idea. He's been so different since he's been here.

"It's like," she says, pausing to chew on the knife-edge of her hand, "it's like he's becoming more and more Trevor-like by the second up here."

Effects of Brag 2: X Marks the Spot

At first it is not disastrous. At first I try to put all references to that foppish neogranola Robin Hood pseudohipster—including but not limited to charming sex-noises and unflattering comparisons with his secretivenessness, his long muscles, and his curly locks—out of my mind. It works, sort of. Hahva and I proceed with cautious détente, some of which is aided by geometry: the TV is virtually unviewable from either bed while disunited; if we are to watch the movie we need to push the beds togetherish. Which we do. The beds are within three feet of each other. Close enough to evoke a thrilling sensation of semitogetherness and possibility—her body, even in the batting flicker of light from the TV, looks like a muscled glyph of hope—but far enough away that she cannot, I am nearly positive, detect the odor of brag on my breath.

The movie is a bad choice. Not a bad movie—quite moving, actually, subtle and urgent and unmaudlin, a story of a young love cut short by easily identifiable evil; no troublesome ambiguities here—but given my state of mind, a very poor choice. Toward the end, when you can see it coming, The End, when the girl starts succumbing to the sickness eating invisibly away at her insides, Hahva and I start expressing divergent responses. Which is to say she starts getting tender while I, in my separate but proximate bed, go ramrod with disgust. After the girl expires with her husband clinging to her in the tiny hospital bed, the movie commences a soft-dissolve to his lovelorn memories of their incredible time together. As the scenes shift from flirtatious first encounter to dating banter to full-thrust romance and marriage to dire career strife surmounted together to tragic diagnosis and speedy deterioration, Hahva starts making rapid-fire anapestic sniffles.

But I become rigid—I mean, my body goes vacuum-packed—with repulsion.

As Hahva makes a move to peel back the sheets—she may be coming my way, I process too late—it comes out. I can't help it.

"This is ridiculous. They want me to be sorry for him? Why should I be sorry for him? That permed dye-job fuckwad. That ungrateful follicle fuck. That—"

"Jack?" Hahva says, stopping midpeel, one leg out of the sheets, one still inside, like a track star frozen over a hurdle.

I gesticulate at the screen emphatically. I have never reacted this violently before, but then again I have never sad-movied while drunk before, either.

"Look at all he has! He had *years* with her. They met in undergrad. Dated all through college. Got married. Went through law school. Then they move to New York City—*New York City, for fuck's sake!*—and have years there. Think what he has to remember her by!"

"But she's gone," Hahva says, looking at me as if I'd just crushed to death a spectacular butterfly because I couldn't be bothered to step over it. "It's so sad. He's lost her."

"Lost? Who cares? Everyone dies. Big deal," I say. "And sad? I don't feel sorry for him, that greedy fuck. Think of all the memories he has. The pretty snowball fight on the quad. Seeing her cheer for him in the stands at the hockey game. Finding her on the doorstep late at night after that fight. The rides in the car, the studying on the sofa together, the meeting of the parents, both good and bad. I bet he knows all sorts of things about her. What books she likes. If her eyes were brown. How long her fingers were. If she likes herpetology."

"Herpetology?"

"If she smiles extra big for photos. If she knows everything there is to know about baseball. If she has strong feelings about uncapped toothpaste or zippers or *Mutual of Omaha's Wild Kingdom*."

"Toothpaste?" Hahva says. *"Mutual of Omaha's Wild Kingdom?"*

"And I bet he knows if she loves oranges!" I say savagely. "Then every time he eats one he can think of her, can't he?"

Before I know what's happening I've fastballed something at the TV screen, now filled with the image of the bereft staring wistfully out over Central Park, and I'm muttering out loud in garbled anger code. Hahva tips forward over the edge of her sarcophogine single, surveys the floor, tilts back, regards me quizzically.

"What was that?"

"Eh?"

"What did you just throw at the TV?"

"What do you mean?" I try to replicate her investigatory movement but I must have had more brag than I thought and I tumble forward blindly into the sheets. When I disentangle myself I see that Hahva is holding before my face a single orange, child-sized flip-flop.

"Hey. Where did you get this?" she says, turning it over in the bluing light of the TV. "And why does it say 'Dexter' on the heel?"

My organism revolts. I haven't heard the yoking of those two syllables—Dex, ter—in what seems like decades. And no other human being has ever laid eyes on the flip-flop since that night in August nearly three decades ago.

Its magic is its secret: I go a little berserk.

I issue some sort of threat, then importunity. I act outraged. I pretend I was just kidding; I have never seen it before, how odd ha ha ha. Hahva won't give it back; she wants to know what the hell is going on with me. Instead of explaining I make a mad swing for it but end up on the floor. After grappling with the air for a few seconds, getting straight with gravity, I lurch at her bed. We wrestle. The animosity of the past few days—the drinking, the notes, how Trevor-like I've allegedly become—make her dig in. Hahva is stronger than I am and refuses to let go. I hear words, pronounced in what seems to be my own voice, of fourth-grade peeve.

"Give it! Give it!" I hear coming from the general direction of my mouth.

We tug-of-war. Even as I yank away at it, I know in some submerged, higher-functioning part of my brain that it is going to end in tears, that physics will not look kindly upon the violent stretching of a thirty-year-old piece of kid-worn, mattress-flattened, tear-softened foam rubber.

It doesn't. My beloved flip-flop emits a puffy, aerated noise of surrender and separates into two jagged pieces, wishing-bone style. We regard each other in astonishment momentarily, then, like a locker room scene, check each other out comparatively. How big is yours? No, how big is *yours*? It takes a second for me to comprehend what has happened exactly. When it does, it hurts.

My stomach clenches as if in preparation for a blow.

I am drunker than I thought.

"Just fucking give it to me, Hahva," I eventually say. Stunned, she does.

"Jack, will you ever tell me what is going on with you?"

"Will you ever quit your fucking snooping?"

"I didn't snoop anything! You threw it at the TV, idiot!"

This is true but it does not pacify me. It makes me madder. I try to pull back but I can't. I am too hurt, and I have too much brag momentum.

I exhale deeply and feel searing thrusters of brag in my throat.

"You know what I feel like sometimes? I feel that your ballet teacher was right. Hell, maybe I should put an X on you myself. Maybe a big black one, in permanent ink, right there, over your big mouth. A big fat-lined Sharpie right on the kisser. X marks the spot. Maybe that would shut you up for a while. Yep. X you right up good and proper, Hahvakakapediles." When I say this last part I pinch the skin around her shoulders as if wielding a body-fat caliper.

Then, incredibly, I hear myself say, "I think maybe you'd better go home."

The meanness spreads between us like a toxic spill. No one says anything else.

Another Note

In the morning Hahva's bed is made and there is an informative note on the pillow. It is admirable for its brevity, its unembellished straight-to-the-pointness. My students, I can't help thinking, could learn a lot from the rapidity with which the thesis is asserted—and from the flawlessness of the dialectic.

Your father isn't the one who is sick, it avers. You are the one who is DSM-eligible.

It also posits: You have tried so hard your whole life to be the opposite of your father. The Great Plan. And now you are just like him: silent, drunk, and cruel.

Don't call me, it postscripts. I'm unable to talk, as my mouth has been X-ed.

Asshole, it additionally appends.

Lemons

What I want more than anything right now is a mandarin. I don't even need the weirdos. Just give me a good, old-fashioned orange, I think. I'll do anything for it. I need to stabilize. I need an orange to hold on to.

But I have to make do with some blushing oblong rindy thing with prickles. Cutting it open, I look intensely into the constellation of seeds, its starry universe full of rich ovarian promise. Then something in my chest ruptures like an ice floe: the bottom of the bowl is lined with lemons. I start crying. I can't stop. I sob and sob and sob. Tears fall in curtains onto the lemons below. I pick one up and examine its slicked yellow surface. It looks cratered and remote—lunar—but also germinal, as if it were a new lemon planet forming new life. I press the wet, cool rind to my face and feel its will to give.

Through the window I can see that the first of the Invincibles are dying. Vaguely I wonder if the E-Type's engine has disintegrated yet. My mother enters the room and says that she is sorry Hahva got called back to work so suddenly.

"Me too," I manage, turning my back to my mother while my eyes keep pumping the lemons full of water.

Baaawk Baaawk Baaawk Baaaaaaaaawk!

Hahva is as good as her word. She refuses to pick up her phone. I call all that day and all that night to no avail. I want to leave a message. The object is to apologize, maybe even explain, possibly tell a microscopic truth about Dex, but for some reason I am too chicken. Her outgoing voice message intimidates me. Her voice sounds terse and businesslike.

It sounds like the voice of someone else.

It makes me too scared—for reasons I don't understand—to say anything.

Bad Idea

This is a bad idea—it can only hurt me—but when you have a dead brother, you can't help thinking, What If?

Bitterly, I imagine how different everything would be right now. Not just for me, but for Press too. Think of it: no funeral, no pilfered hip flask, no precocious bragging, no adolescent bragging, no twentysomething and thirtysome-thing bragging, no dropping out of college, no ignominious return home from California, no series of lost loser jobs, no basement tenancy. Maybe no soul-disposaling lifelong brag abuse problem at all.

And me? With no safetying to grad school there would be no Jordana Mochnik. No smashed beloved Vespa. No debilitating career besmirchment. No humiliations galore like selling dog food door-to-door and delivering phone books to make ends meet, no Philosoraptor mockery in the hallway.

I never would have met, and lost, Leon Flanders.

Because he never went under the water at Lake George that night, there would be no Lemon-shaped hole, no billiards room outburst, no ruined finger, no "inappropriate compensatory action," no agonizing "Permission to start again?" I would have aced the audition. I would have got the scholarship. I would have escaped the house and moved to New York City. I would have made it as a pianist. Right now I could be performing in metropolitan symphony halls and contributing to movie soundtracks with Sir Elton and shooting cell phone commercials with Yo-Yo Ma. I would have health insurance, an apartment without exposed tetanic nails aimed at your skull, a normally functioning car. I could even buy a real engagement ring and retain the normally functioning car.

I wouldn't have met Hahva as a ruined academic with a terminal degree in a dead-end adjunct job at a third-rate institution in Boll Weevil, Georgia. I would have met her in the Woodruff Center lobby one night after a thrilling performance as understudy for an infirm Daniel Barenboim. She would have admired my powerful performance of Liszt, courtesy of ten fully functioning digits, and she would have found my head, shaved with a bare-knuckled Mr. Cleanian aplomb, erotically appealing. (And she would have been impressed by my manly invulnerability to the fearsome veto power of the Ass President, too, I might add.)

Our first kiss wouldn't have been under the sputtering canary light of a streetlamp in the parking lot of a cinder-block homeless shelter; it would have been somewhere slick, somewhere glamorous, somewhere with a lot of glass and polished leather and silent-flushing toilets. Somewhere that indicated a future of hope and bounty. Somewhere that suggested we would be somebodies.

But most important of all: I wouldn't have been drunk last night. I wouldn't have said the awful things I said. And no matter how successful a pianist, how virile, or how rich—no matter how I acquired the ring; no matter what quality ring I acquired—she would be able to entertain my proposal.

Hahva would still be here.

McGurk Calls Again

"Jack," McGurk says again. "You still there?"

"Yeah," I say.

"For the third time, do you want me to drop the price again or what?"

Hahva's note is in my shirt pocket. I clutch at it through the cotton.

"Hey. Come back, Jack. You're needed for some dialogue. I'm on daytime minutes here."

"Sorry. What was the question?"

"Jesus. Do you want me to keep trying with the Omni, or

what? Because unless someone bites pretty soon the profit from the sale will barely exceed the cost of advertising."

"What? Seriously?"

"No, not seriously. That was a joke, Jack. But just barely. Has something happened to you up there? Rarefied air causing an oxygen shortage? Sustain a head wound falling off a steeplechaser? Because your brain has an unusually mushlike aspect right now."

"Just kind of . . . hungover." My hangover, in fact, is a girandole of cerebrovascular agony. Spectacularly complicated pyrotechnics of pain flash before my eyes and penetrate the coils of my brain. I feel gristled, worked over, a part of the street, a worthy associate of my brother. But it's good. The pain makes me feel less lonely.

McGurk whistles. "You? Fucking hell. You inhale too close to your brother?"

"Something like that."

"Well, I don't want to sound like your grandmother or anything but take care of yourself."

"I am."

I can picture McGurk right now: hunching over, making himself as small and sympathetic as he can, even over the phone. He is my friend. He only wants what is best for me.

"So you want me to keep it up with the Omni?" he says finally.

What happens if I sell my car but have no Hahva to give a ring to?

"Jack!"

"Sorry," I say. "Sure, keep trying with the Omni."

"You don't sound so sure."

"No. I'm sure. I want you to sell the Omni."

"O.K. then. You're the boss."

"Thanks, big mick."

There ensues a pause in which, I know, McGurk is considering how probing he should be. "Hey, did you ever get those
contracts in the mail? Are you set for teaching next term?"

"Yes," I lie.

One Is Forward

"You're stoned," Press says. "Six is forward."

"One is forward, idiot. Six is back."

"No, six is forward." Press pinches thumb and forefinger
together and makes a smoking gesture.

"One is," I maintain.

This is the only thing that makes me feel less miserable:
my brother, a bottle, and Diceman.

"Who has the better memory?" I say.

"I do."

"You have no memory. At best you have a creeping suspicion about the past. I, on the other hand, forget fucking
nothing."

"Except for how often you are just plain old fucking wrong."

Press and I are wandering through the brittle Huntfield
night, casting our die while the stars overhead make prophe-
cies we are not meant to understand. We are also having trouble remembering the rules. One is forward, I propose. Two
left, three right, four drink, five drink, six back. Press is not
convinced, but it does not matter. The rules are flexible. We
know we are rolling to the Terrapin and will contrive any ex-

ceptions to get there eventually. But I am convinced I am right and I am not going to knuckle under.

"It's six, my man."

"*Au contraire, mon frère.* One is forward. Six is totally counterintuitive. Why would the last number indicate forward movement?"

"Because one is drink."

"Christ."

"What?"

"Every fucking number is drink to you," I say. "One is drink to you. Two is drink. Three, four, five, six is drink to you. Googolplex is drink to you. It's a fucking miracle we've moved ten feet."

"I have a very eloquent and ineluctable rebuttal to that."

"Ineluctable? I'd like to hear that. Go on. Hit me. Ineluctate."

"Hit you?"

"Hit away."

"All right," he says, raising his hands back-fisted, a fey mockery of John L. Sullivan–like old-timers. He shadowboxes me with each syllable he utters. "Because one through six means drink for you too, you fucking alcoholic motherfucker."

I reel histrionically. "Ouch. You got me. Truth hurts. But you know what? Waste not, want not," I say, leveraging the bottle over my mouth.

"I never understood that. If I were to waste a drink—"

"Major hypothetical here."

"—If I were to waste a drink I'd still want one. Wouldn't you?"

"Absolutely. You know what else I never understood? Why you can't have your cake and eat it too. I mean, you have your cake; it's eaten. Good for you. You eat it; it's also eaten. What's the diff?"

"I concur," Press says. "Baffling."

"Life is full of confusion."

"Like lunch today."

"I assume you refer to the pickled beets?"

"The pickled beets," Press affirms. "I am not so sure about the pickled beets. Why did they bleed all over the place?"

"Unseemly," I agree. "And they looked so angry."

"They have been subject to vile treatment."

"Softened against their will."

"Undermined."

"Made to leak."

"There are grudges being held."

"Confusion reigns."

"You have to be willing to make allowances under such circumstances."

"And remember their architecture? How they were stacked?"

"Gehry-like."

"Not their best selves."

"Very uncomfortable, I'd imagine."

"And unapproachable. I can't help feeling that a salad should be in service to the diner, not the other way around."

"You were daunted?"

"It was unclear whether they were meant for consumption or demolition."

"I would have gotten the personal pizza, myself," Press says. "Eliminate the element of chance."

"Well, now I know," I say. "Bell Biv DeVoe."

Press shifts nervously on his feet. He looks like a kid about to commence on a book report in front of the class.

"Little brother," he says. "It's been tough being here alone all this time. I might have missed you a little bit while you were gone, Boscovich."

"I might have missed you some, too," I say.

Now we are awkward. Press looks into the ramified branches of the trees; I look up at the stars blurring through tears. Then I work up the guts to spit out a question I have wanted to ask him for nearly fifteen years.

"Hey," I say. "Can I ask you a question?"

"As long as it doesn't involve binomials, trinomials, any kind of nomials."

"Why did you really leave California to come back here?"

"What?" he says, really concentrating on those branches.

"You came back from college. You had made it out. You were free. You had a scholarship and everything. You never had to set foot in this state again. The whole world was out there for you. You could have done anything. But you just came back home and never said why. I never understood it. I still don't understand."

Press squints at the treeline. He takes a swig. I see the muscles at the joint of his jaw contract.

"Where else can I get free brag?" he says suddenly, and swats me on the shoulder.

I Am the Blood Man

The Terrapin is a Mardi Gras of Day-Glo and nylon cappery. A brave sampling of protoerotic teenies and dirty dozens of Robbie's cognates profuse through the cultures of men at the pool table, the TV, the smoking corners, the keno machines.

A glozing of hackmen and gassers, spring-loaded and slumping with vice, defend their positions from the stools. Young and old, aspirants and lifers, they are all heartbroken puppets, splintered and worn and eroded in ways they don't understand.

Who will notice me? they want to know. Why aren't I chosen? Who will love me? When will it end?

I knife through the crowd, my jaw cleaving the air, the molecules sliding right off me while Press follows behind. Now drunk with my brother, in our bar, my sadness is dissipating and is being replaced with bragvision. I have full bottle clarity. All is known to me. The movements of the patrons are revealed to me in advance, their breaths measured before they're made. Amplitude, frequency, valence, there is nothing I do not anticipate.

When the cetacean form of Robbie heaves to our banquette I acknowledge her with an air of inevitability. I know where she has been. She is laminated in neon and the peaty, horse-hot exhalations of other men. Grinning pinkly, she bestows an adhesive kiss on my brother's cheek—making an invisible palimpsest of the kisses of how many other men?—and says, "You two started without me. Boo."

"Can I make up for it with the traditional fare?" Press says.

"Sloppy joes?"

"It is meet."

Press stands and fishtails through the crowd to Inch at the bar.

"You wouldn't know it by looking but that man orders a mean sloppy joe," Robbie says, looking about her with owlish alertness. Her chaotic hair moves in time-delay; her earrings make wind chime noises. Then I see why: in the corner, watching with luscious prurient interest someone else playing the $trip Poker video game, is the guy who was thrashed by the pool table. He has a face like a flatfish and his mouth is now crenellated with ruined, shattered teeth. When the guy at the machine rotates on his stool, savoring the removal of a portion of merry widow, the viper-headed features are clear.

Musser.

"They're here," she says.

"I see that. Why didn't you tell Press?"

"Would it make any difference? He's so stubborn. He's convinced he didn't lose that money. And I can't make Musser lay off anymore. I think it's best just to say nothing and hope Musser doesn't notice."

"You were making him lay off? How?"

"How do you think, silly?" she says, puckering demonstratively and revealing the nicotine-colored papillae and the squalid viscosities of her mouth.

"But no longer?"

She shrugs. "Men have short attention spans."

"But you've been consorting, at least, with Press for over a year?"

"That's not attraction. That's just laziness, honey. Press doesn't like leaving the basement too often."

"Well," I say, "it is very homey."

"Sloppy joes and spirits all around," Press exclaims when he sits down, passing around our plates and glasses. "Don't say I never buy you anything nice."

"You seem in awfully good spirits tonight," Robbie says.

"Diceman is very invigorating. Good for the liver. Or is it the kidneys? Who can keep them straight?"

"Someone who drinks like you should know," Robbie says.

"Pshaw," I say.

"Well, maybe it's the soul, then," he says, winking at me.

"You are in a weird mood tonight," Robbie says. "I've never seen you like this. You're almost . . ."

"Ineluctable?"

"Childlike. It's very eerie. What could be the cause?"

As he starts formulating a sentence—he is looking at me; presumably I am going to be accredited the source of my brother's improvement—a pool cue cuts laterally across my line of vision, fat end first, stopping, briefly, at the point where Press's jaw meets his ear, before it fractures in a cloud of splinters and skitters under the table. I blink. When I look next I see my brother on the floor, blood trickling out of his ear, his mouth opening and closing in the manner of a baby signaling hunger. Musser stands above him with the tapered end of the pool cue in his hand, waving it like a baton, leering with his friends. Our die has been knocked out of my brother's pocket and has tumbled to the floor: one.

"Blood Man's here!" Musser exclaims happily. He pulls back a boot and kicks my brother in the ribs. "Consider this your first overdue notice. And here is your service charge," he says, and kicks my brother again. This time there is a crunching sound inside my brother's shirt and his leg twitches like a dying insect. "And your late fee." My brother has rolled into a fetal position, clutching his face, leaving his back exposed. Musser kicks him in the spine.

The guy with the teeth points at me, laughing. "Hey. Check it out. What's the fat little fuck doing with his hand?"

It appears I am chewing on the knife-edge of my hand. Munch munch, I go. In mortal dread, in neutering fear. Nibble nibble. Snack snack.

They both look at me and laugh. It is the vibration of pure failure and grief. It is the sonic expression of the playground I am hearing, of the locker room, of Kasimir Kakmuzh shredding my *White Pages*, of Jordana Mochnik gloating as I limped out of the DC hearing in disgrace, of the Philosoraptor—"Tennant couldn't get a job teaching pigs to shit"—of my colleagues whispering in the hallway and lounge and back rooms at faculty parties.

Of Leon Flanders, beloved traitorous idol.

Of two flip-flops nudging the pilings of the dock, waiting for me to rescue them.

Of my father, smelling of scotch, dripping lake water from his empty hands.

This obscene filament of memory burns in me and my cells go dense and nuclear with hatred.

"He looks pretty pissed, Musser," says Teeth.

"What you going to do?" Again Musser laughs moistly, his keeled throat throbbing as he guttles his beer. "You going to gnaw us to death? You going to—"

Then it happens. My jaw mousetraps shut. My body curls into a tight italic of rage. Midsentence my clenched fist sickles through the air and connects solidly with the pointed tip of Musser's jaw. It is my father's uppercut—faster than thought, no excessive motion. I do not cock it unnecessarily. I do not shovel. I do not telegraph. It is efficient, geometrically perfect, a heatseeker. It has a clean powerline from the deep magnetic core of the earth through my pelvis and straight up to the polestar. Musser's head bobbles on his neck; then he slumps to the floor, bloody and volant, his eyes knocking around his skull. Teeth retreats a half step, his arms raised in a cross over his face—protective, submissive, fearful—as I step forward.

Then there is a chaotic venturi crush of bodies at the door—Inch is coming—but I make no move to exit. When Inch appears in front of me he skids to a stop, his face a latticework of throb and astonishment. "Jack?" he says, frozen in a postoperative confusion, piecing the image together: Pressman Tennant, fetal; Musser, floored; the weakling Tennant standing above him, a boot bearing down on his neck.

"Jack," he says. "Is that you?"

I turn on Inch, feeling at once my brother's icy jitter immunity and also an exultant murderous rage. All the grief of my life—the demonology of all my memories—is now contained in my fists and I am going to put them into Musser and Teeth. And Inch if he tries to stop me.

As I close on Inch, his eyes widening, I hear the words come out of my mouth in spit and venom: "I'm not Jack. I am the Blood Man!"

Afterglow

Robbie unplugs a segmented cigarette from the corner of her mouth and exhales a cloud of dirty cotton. "Never seen anything like it," she says. My brother is finally asleep on his bed, with the same ice pack that he pressed to my knuckle now applied to the joint below his ear. "Double time. Musser and his asshole friend."

"That was the first fight I've ever won."

"Wouldn't know it by looking, Blood Man. Didn't do that bad by Inch, either. That was the first indication I've ever seen that he bleeds."

"Yeah, well, now we know that I do, too."

"You don't look so bad, considering. A swelling around the jaw."

"And creaking in the ribs."

"Just like your brother."

"Yeah?" I say. "Same places?"

"Almost identical," she affirms, pointing to the damage around my brother's mandible, then touching mine.

"Hey. Ouch."

"See?"

"See what?"

"You and your brother," she says. "You match."

Wings open and close inside my chest when she says this.

"Oh."

Robbie passes me the smeared cigarette but I wave it away. "I don't smoke."

"What better time to start?" she says. "When you're trying so much that's new?"

Robbie shrugs invitationally and offers the cigarette, which I take and inexpertly smoke.

"That was good," she purrs. "Real good. Have you considered any other new experiences?"

Robbie undulates closer to me. In the shark-gray light of the basement I allow myself to soak up the odor flurry of Robbie's sex push. She is inordinate, her features sagging under the painterly application of makeup, her skin overflowing in a rubbery top with straps of incomprehensible engineering.

I don't understand what I'm feeling.

"What are you looking at, Jack?"

"I'm just exercising my constitutional right to look around," I say drunkenly, "and your tits got in my way."

"You want another drink?"

My brother is turtling on his back, passed out cold.

"See?" she says, swelling up to me. "He's out. We can do anything we like."

Robbie hands me the bottle and I drain as much as I can.

"Wow," Robbie says. "You're so *firsty*." As she says this she leans into me—scent of movie butter and Barbicide—and starts kneading my penis through my pants.

"Why isn't your father hunting anymore?" There is a leathery slapping sound as my belt unbuckles.

I say something.

"How does that happen?" I hear the slow metallic creak of zipper teeth disjoining.

I say something else.

"And that is happening at home? How is everyone coping?" I feel a gelid frisson as cold fingertips rub against my skin.

"Robbie," I say. But this is as far as I get. Robbie closes her eyes, opens her lips to me, chin upturned, and extends her pointed tongue sharply into the air, offering a gory baby-bird kiss. I enter the soupy cess of her mouth, fizzing with bacteria, while my hands unfasten straps. Through the cumulonimbus of brag in my head—and as Robbie pulls my pants down around my ankles—something jackknifes painfully in my stomach.

What am I doing?

I Sturm and Drang against her but even the slightest movement produces inclement waves of vertigo and nausea. I close my eyes against it all and when I open them again I have been demoted to horizontality on the floor with Robbie hanging in the air above me. With my hands I desiderate that she cease and desist all genitalian interference, but it does no good. She is stronger than I am. When I try to syllablize a more formal protest she plugs my mouth with the mouth of the bottle. I am aware of liquid conduiting so rapidly from bottle to belly that gushing streamers of scotch lave what I still dimly perceive as my face and torso.

From her knees, sitting between my legs and my pants-bound ankles, the pink rubbery peel splits open and smiles. I see that her tongue is cleft like, and as red as, an engorged strawberry.

Later, through the distortion of haze and bragtime, I understand what has transpired. With a bowelly rupture of fear and disgust, and with elbows bent in capitulation on the concrete, I see the undressed form of Robbie on the floor next to me. She is blissed and glazen-eyed, not with pleasure but with victory. She has won something.

Reveille

In the morning, as the room assembles kaleidoscopically around me, I apprehend the grisly details. There is a dried confetti of predigested matter scattered around my head in a crownlike pattern. I am nakedish—shirted, but with my pants on the floor next to me, legs bent in genuflection. My boxers are nested like a wadded fig leaf over the delicates. And my hands are swollen and brown with the blood of other people.

There is no trace of Robbie. Pressman is still asleep, frozen in the same position, one hand above his head, preserved midgesture like a Pompeiian corpse.

No one knows about this but me.

I try to will myself to stop thinking about it but I can't. My brain spews with memory. I feel myself knot, condense, turn into something tiny and hot, then into nothing at all.

Straight from the Horse's Mouth to You

The next day an item runs in the *Huntfield Gazette*'s "From the Horse's Mouth" column.

COLONEL TENNANT AWOL?

If the first field has looked a little thin lately it is because of the prolonged and mysterious absence of one of the Huntfield Hunt Club's eldest and most venerable members, Guilford Tennant. Mum has been the word over the last month but recently an FTHM spy has informed us that the Colonel has been AWOL due to a stroke. Those close to the family tell us that Tennant has been released from John Hopkin's and is convalescing at home on his farm under the care of a full-time therapist and his family, including his second son, Jackson, an English professor from Georgia. Asked how everyone is coping, Jackson says, "Distillers all over Scotland are holding their breath." We hope that's what professorial types call irony.

You heard it here first, straight From the Horse's Mouth to you.

—*Roberta Miles*

"You see this thing?" Press says, waving the story at me. His face is changing colors from the beating, draining beetroot and blue. It is changing shape, too. Today it is fallen and peaked and pocketed—a doomed soufflé.

He tries to engage me in the conversation but all I can think about is Hahva.

"Yep," he charges on. "Guess who read it?"

I remember standing with Hahva under a cone of sputtering canary light from the streetlamp.

"No guesses?" Press says. "Not very sportsmanlike. Very well, I shall tell you. Mom read it."

We were listening to the rataplan of the rain coming down on the hot asphalt.

"Yep, one of her Hunt Club friendies called up asking about it."

The burned-cabbage smell of the chicken plant was vivid and heavy, awash in my nose.

"Mom of course thought you gave the quote. But you know what I did? Nope. Not that. No, nothing with the rubber chicken. Wrong again. It had nothing to do with echolocation. Bzzzz. Not even close. Stop already, you're killing me. What I did was—ta *da*—I told her that it was I, Pressman Montcalm Tennant, who gave Robbie the info. I figured you'd already had a hard enough time, what with Hahva and everything."

Some kids rattled past, drinking from paper bags while pushing each other in a grocery cart.

"No, no, stop it with the gratitude, already. Jeez. You're embarrassing me."

When they wrecked in the gutter the liquor they spewed out of their mouths looked like a spray of diamonds.

"But you know the crazy thing?" Press's features acquire an expression of confounded wonder, as if he were about to try to convince someone of the authenticity of a poltergeist manifestation. "She didn't seem to care about the article." He pauses here to see if he can get a reaction. His eyes goggle when he sequels, "Yep, she just laughed and said, and I quote, 'The poor dear left off the S in Johns Hopkins.' Then I said, 'But she made up for it with a bonus apostrophe,' and she laughed a second time. And then I said, 'Guess the S is for stupid,' and she laughed thrice."

When I kissed Hahva at that moment I felt hundreds of windows fly open inside my heart.

"She should have gone starkers at the bruiting of the news, but she just laughed a little and that was that. Hard to believe this is the same woman who would look at you as if you were a toilet ring if you made a single allusion to any Tennant family business in front of others." He gives me a chummy, nail-driving slap on my shoulder. "I'm with you, little brother. Curiouser and curiouser."

It made me wish that I had never kissed anyone else.

Caveat Imbibor

Apparently I have bendered myself downstairs. I find myself amid the gubernatorial furnishings of my father's converted bedroom, trying unsuccessfully to assist the weak force nudging my brain stem. The reason I am here is encoded somewhere inconvenient to retrieval; a cursory run over the nodes of memory hierarchy—brag, dress, brag, billiards room, brag—comes up short. Instead I try hard to focus on my father. He is propped up in his archvillainous chair, chin oiled in spittle, making chocking noises as he sleeps.

Now I remember. I came here just to look at him. In my father's face I look for clues to Dexter's features, but none of it—

his cowcatcher jaw, his corded neck, his eroded taurine health—makes any sense. I cannot imagine it. It is impossible to envision how Dex could have looked like him. He would, I fantasize, look more like me: of obscure provenance. Maybe he would have the same follicle fear. Maybe he would be unskilled at sport. Maybe he would have the same wimpiness and social anxiety and self-doubt.

With a powerful backwash of sadness I realize something else: it's possible Dex would have had some of my flaws, but he would never have said what I said to Hahva. He would never have done what I did with Robbie.

Now, looking at my sleeping father, I feel my error on me. It makes me feel thick and clotted, gluey with wrong decisions. I take another drink to try to macerate the feeling but it doesn't work. It's bonding to me. Dimly I wonder if Press's vulturous interest in our father's money makes him feel this way, too, and if it will ever stop. When will it become too late for us?

Is it already too late?

Suddenly I have to put my self-loathing on hold; there is incoming. As I duck behind the bar the door creaks open and Bess leads Pressman to the chair I just vacated. They sit. From my spylike prone position, ten feet away, I can detect the full pious thrust of Bess's heated, antiseptic presence. She is blinking at my brother through her Swifties. Her hair is mussed in a way that conjures an unfortunate Mouseketeer image, a fantasy seconded by her bantam ranking in weight class and her alert and hopeful expression. Sitting, she clasps her hands together prayerfully on her knees and gives off the impression—perhaps it's the brag talking—that she could be folded up and stored in an overhead compartment. It doesn't help that as she whispers to Press now, careful not to wake my snoring father,

her voice is rendered nearly incomprehensible by the Styro-foam squeak.

Bess's features assume the pursed attitude that presages do-gooder commentary.

"Pressman, there is something I ought to tell you about your father's stroke."

"What's that?" he says, his voice turbid with alcohol.

"I've already told your father this, but I think it's probably for the best if you don't repeat this to your mother. I think it would only cause her undue grief. Can I count on you to do that for me?"

At this I must suppress a snicker; most likely Press will not even remember this conversation tomorrow morning.

"Secret's safe with me," he says, obviously pleased to be holding up his end of the conversation with such syllabic aplomb.

"O.K.," Bess says. "You shouldn't drink, Pressman."

"Roger," he says. "Aye, aye."

"What I mean is that drinking caused your father to stroke out in the first place. It was alcohol that precipitated the stroke."

Press looks dubious.

"He drank his way into a coma?"

"In a manner of speaking."

"Well," he says, making a pledge-of-allegiance salute, "I hereby solemnly swear not to drink to that excess."

"I don't think you're getting me. Gil didn't stroke because of bad luck, or because of just one drink too many. He has a blood condition that made him susceptible. He has unusually thick blood. His hemoglobin is way too high. On the night of the stroke it was off the chart."

Press has a bottle stuck in his belt like Billy the Kid's six-shooter. While Bess regards our father momentarily he unholsters it and throws back a quickie.

"So what does drinking have to do with that?" he says, wiping the corner of his mouth.

"The alcohol dehydrated Gil. And his blood was already so thick that, on top of the drinks he had that night, he didn't have a chance. His blood basically just . . . sludged."

"In his brain."

"Correct."

"His blood sludged in his brain," Press repeats rhythmically, almost in a tune.

Bess adjusts her Swifties. "And the tragedy is that it was totally preventable. If he had been taking care of himself, if he had been going for checkups with his GP, this would have shown up in routine testing. He could have been put on a donation schedule or been given a regimen of thinners or just . . ."

"Not drink?" Press says.

"Or not drink," she affirms.

"But you can't know how much the alcohol could really have contributed, can you? I mean, maybe it wasn't a big part," Press says, seemingly, momentarily—and miraculously—sobered.

Bess attains an expression of impenetrable certainty. "His blood-alcohol was point one nine. It's not a coincidence."

"Point one nine isn't that drunk."

"It was more than enough to precipitate the stroke."

"So you're saying the drink caused my father to be locked in?"

Bess nods.

"And you think I am at the same risk? To become locked in?"

Bess nods again.

"I see. And we're sure this is hereditary?"

"Positive."

"I don't believe it. Drinking gives you headaches, not strokes."

"Maybe you won't get it today. Maybe not this year. Maybe not this decade. But you can never tell. Maybe one day you have one beer too many and you start feeling sort of dizzy, tingly in the fingertips, the tongue might get numb, and next thing you know you wake up three months later in a hospital, unable to move a muscle."

"It can't happen like that. I'm still young."

Bess regards him with a pitying look. It is as if she is witnessing a hilarious spectacle of childish futility—someone trying to attain orbit by running down a steep grade while flapping their arms.

"Your father has it. You probably have it. And Jack will have it. You're all at the same risk for—" And here she spreads her hands demonstrably before my sleeping father.

"Jack too?" Press says sharply. "But he's not at all like Dad."

What Bess says next makes me feel dizzy, pinpricked, nearly sleepy. My double helix doubles over. Do I hear this right?

"Of course he is," she says. "He's the same flesh. He has literally the same blood. The same genes. The same congenital risk. Jack is also your father's son."

Your father's son, echoes the hole.

Good News from Georgia

The next day my cell phone emits a polyhymnal jingle: unknown ID. Press answers it for me.

"Jack Tennant's wire," he says into the receiver.

He shakes his head to me: not Hahva.

"Yes. No. His brother. Hi there, Mr. McGurk. Very well,
thank you. Yourself? He's not available at the moment. Indis-
posed. Suffering from the ague. Sure. Shoot. O.K. Right. That
sounds very dreary. Aha. Greased lightning, ha ha ha. Sorry.
I'm with you. The hill. Who knew? Sucker every minute, I suppose. What's 'it' mean?" When he says this he perks with interest. "Private, huh? Nothing will induce you to speak? Fine
then. O.K. Yeah, I'll ask him. Yeah, I'll tell him." Press pauses
and gives me an evaluative look. "Yeah, he's great. I mean, under the weather at the moment, but yep, he's his old self, that's
for sure. All right, Mysterioso. Thanks again."

Press hangs up. "Good news. Your car's been sold. Your
friend said he went to the 'place,' as you instructed, and bought
'the one under your name' and is going to ship 'it' to you here
because he thought your need for it might be 'imminent.' I am
putting those words in quotes because your friend seems very
intent on maintaining some kind of confidentiality. An intran-
sigent fellow. Seems very pleased with himself, too. Said he
parked the Omni on a hill so he could pop-start it before the
customer looked at it. Crafty friend. I salute him." Press drinks

again from the mug. "Oh. And he said something about not seeing your online 'module' for course offerings this fall, that it's already past the deadline, and that if you haven't done it already you'd better send in your contracts or else. He sounded very businesslike about that.

"So what's the big 'it,' Jack? You getting rid of the car for another Vespa? A Toaster Tank? Is this cause for celebration?"

Pressman Montcalm Tennant, Peptalker 1.1

On my eighth broken window Press entreats me again to come out.

"It's like disco fever in here," he says, indicating the glass rubble. "Which is frightful. Disco is so out. And I'd appreciate it if you'd change into something other than my sheet. Don't you think you could sleep upstairs sometime?"

"I can't go back up there. I can't go back into that bed."

"Speech!"

"Don't be a dick, Press."

"Why can't you go back up there?"

Press is losing patience with me. Since that night with Robbie I have spent every day in the stygian basement, staring at the charcoal of the ceiling, the chalk of the walls. Press has made his brag runs upstairs for me and I strive to drink until the walls empurple and collapse around me. Then I curl up with the Everlast until I fall asleep.

"Hey," Press says. "Really. Lower lifeboats, Jack. You got to get your ass out of here. You're turning into, well, you're turning into me. And it just won't do. Certain trademark regulations obtain."

"Why don't you do something useful?"

He shrugs. "Drank them dry, you fucking sponge. All out. You're going to have to venture to the Terrapin with me if you're thirsty." When he receives nothing he says, "How about some Diceman? I'll get some provisions at Coen's and then we can take your hermit ass around breaking windows in public places. What do you say? Lots of windows out there in the free world and they ain't breaking themselves. Come on. Bestir yourself. What do you say? Look. I rolled a one. You're right. One is forward. Let's go forward.

"Through with breaking, huh? All right. How about we hit the city. Go get some Gunning's. They claim to have the best crab cakes in Baltimore, you know. Normally I like to try to stay out of the best-crab-cakes-in-town fracas, but maybe disputation is just what we need right now. I'll treat. What do you say?"

Press picks his way, heronlike, through the rubble. Then, using a shred of carpet to sweep up some of the shards around his bed, he sits down on his denuded mattress. His features flex *grave* and *aigu* with concern.

"Jack. I know why you're feeling so shitty."

I think: you have no idea why I'm feeling so shitty. You have no idea what happened with Robbie, what memories I must live with now.

"Why don't you just call her, already?"

Pop Quiz

Q: Given that *a*) if I do not talk to Hahva I can never be re-united with her, but that *b*) I cannot speak to her without confessing what happened with Robbie because of, at minimum, *bb*) the risk of STDs, to say nothing of my own *bbb*) punitive conscience that makes it *c*) impossible to live with myself unless I obliterate my memories with brag, then *d*) how can I call her on the phone, let alone *e*) ever get her back?

A:

Pressman Montcalm Tennant, Peptalker 1.2

"Bet I know what will help make things better. The inheritance, Jack. Sixteen hundred dollars a day. Plus a nearly unimaginable lump sum! Think of it. You could fly Hahva first class to Italy for a weekend in Venice. Propose to her kneeling in a gondola. Let her dunk you if she's still mad. Tell her you've bought her some fucking country estate outside Savannah and have founded a brand-new shelter for homeless Jerry's Kids or something. Then send an Imperial-class Cloudsplitter to pick her up.

"Think that wouldn't work as an apology? Think about yourself, Jack. Think about it. Just ask yourself what is fair. Has he ever done anything good for us? No. But he can do something good now."

"Die?"

"Die is right. And provide for the two children he has so far ignored. Hell, it would probably be a mercy. Probably would be the only thing his soul has got going for it."

Press doesn't say it, but I know what he is thinking: Dad killed Dex. He doesn't deserve to live.

I let the brute sadness hit me full force. Already I am drunk enough to glide around the room barefoot on thermals of my own production. I hear my brother say, "Ouch! Watch it, that's broken glass," but it does not seem to mean anything. Out one of the shattered windows my vision is full of horses and megaflora.

Vengefulness gnaws at me.

"That money should be ours," Press says. "Think about it."

Clarity

The next day a package arrives from McGurk. He has overnighted it, his note says, because he knows how close I am to bending knees. Inside the packaging is a burgundy velvet box that says in fancy gold script LUX, BOND & GREEN. I open it and in the undead fluorescent light of the basement I see for the first time what the ring really is: a cheap-quality stone of speck-like carat and quaglike clarity, weakly reflecting a few jaundiced beamlets of dirty light.

What did I expect from the income of a dead-end job in Boll Weevil, Georgia, and the sale of a decrepit Omni?

I throw the fuzzy box into the trash, teeter onto the Everlast and pass out, wake up two hours later, shamble back into the kitchen and extract the box, now slick with the bilious effusions of decomposing fruit, open it, and commit the ring to my pocket, where it cohabits with the key to the E-Type.

Perfect.

Jack and the Pain Box

That night the sadness is so dense it feels like a new element. No longer do I breathe oxygen; I breathe pure sadness. The food I consume, the waste I excrete: sadness. The basement is a cell of sadness. My eyes and ears are clogged with sadness. I am dressed in sadness, sleep in sadness, consume and am consumed by sadness, move through space in an invisible electron shroud of sadness, trailing sadness contrails.

There is no way I can keep this ring—gimcrack instantiation of my failure, agonizing reminder of Hahva's absence—with me. I need to put it where it belongs.

"Hey," I hear my brother say, "that's an injudicious amount of brag for someone so young. Maybe you should let me have that." Then he gets awkward, solicitous, his voice dipping into the lower register with concern. "Hey Jack, you know what? Maybe you shouldn't drink quite so much."

He is trying to warn me. He wants to tell me about Dad

and how we share the same genes and the same thick blood—
the same risk. But he's slow, and I don't let him get it out.

I push past my brother and pull myself hand-over-hand up
the banister. In the darkness I rattle out into the woods, beyond
the horse trails, to the dilapidated kiln where I buried the Pain
Box. I remove the flowers from the shovel and dig, scintillant
particles of window glass falling from my hair, until I hit something hard. I unearth the flameproof safe, slash my tongue
over the chip in my tooth, savoring the hot, penny-tasting
blood in my mouth, and open it. Everything is still there.

—container, minoxidil

—page 1066 from *Greater Baltimore Metropolitan Area
White Pages*

—label from one canvas Everlast ninety-pound punching bag

—document on yellow legal paper with addendums and
emendations in two sets of handwriting, labeled "DICEMAN:
Rules and Etiquette"

—rubber bite plane

—letter on Juilliard letterhead, blotted

—bottle of Lagavulin 16, opened but unsampled

—fragment of graphic relief map, Ural Mountains

—extra set of keys, 1969 Jaguar E-Type

—blue and white propeller emblem from 1972 BMW
Toaster Tank motorcycle

—bottle, Simple Green, empty

—passage from Saul Bellow's *Henderson the Rain King*,
Penguin Classics

—container of Barbasol shave cream, travel-sized

—section of preserved lemon rind, embottled

—one child-sized flip-flop, orange

—9mm Colt 1911 beavertail and case of hollowpoint bullets

There is no night static out in the woods. The stars pulse overhead and wings open and close in the trees and a fox, trippant and alert, looks on from a stump, but otherwise it's just me and the Pain Box. Before I commit the ring I can't help taking the items out of the safe and inspecting them. It's been so long but they have not lost their power. The Everlast label is still starchy from tears. The altitude of the Ural Mountains has been reduced several thousand feet by friction and sweat. The flip-flop is markedly less worn than the one I keep under my mattress, but it still has a muddy patina of freshwater and dirt on it, as if freshly plucked from Lake George. The print on page 1066 of the *White Pages* is smudgy and illegible but the bluing on the barrel of the beavertail, although scored with teethmarks, is still bright. I turn the gun over in my hands. Even loaded with only one hollowpoint it is much heavier than I remember.

Gravity pulls more powerfully on the gun than on other objects. The earth wants the gun very badly, I think. It wants you, too.

Briefly I wonder if this is how Dex felt about the water he swallowed.

I barely know what I am doing, but I do it anyway.

With sacramental care I fit the barrel into my mouth—the scratches still match up with the chip in my dentition—and then, kneeling in grass jeweled with numinous dew and with wild voluptuous tears bursting from my sockets, I squeeze the trigger.

In my skull there is the thunderclap vociferation of death. It all flashes by me: Kasimir Kakmuzh tearing the *White Pages* from my hands, Pressman winking at me when I take my first shot of brag at eleven, the sickening thrust of shame when I wipe the Barbasol off my face, my father's powerful fist wrapped around my finger, the judges at Juilliard shaking their heads, the many faces and many limbs and many joys of countless couples embracing under the Arrivals/Departures sign at the airport, Karina Thiergartner's face nuzzling the red bloom of an Invincible, Leon Flanders walking away from me in the hallway, disgust in his eyes.

Two orange flip-flops coming back to me on the waves at Lake George.

And Hahva, too, kissing me next to her car in the Georgia heat of the parking lot at night, her body jigsawing with mine under the starwork of nails in my abject apartment, giving Rodney the James Brown treatment at the Ark, babbling at me not to look in her backseat while I drive her home from the Manhattan, standing in front of bright blooming camellias in her wedding gown at the botanical gardens, playing in the surf at Tybee.

My bride. Why couldn't I have this?

There is a hot liquid in my mouth, leaking down my throat. It is not blood. It is not coming from a hole in my head; it is seeping in from outside my mouth—tears. I open my eyes and drink them in. They taste like ether, limestone, and solvent. Around me the night is unchanged. The silence is unbroken; no birds have burst from the trees; the fox looks on unworried from his stump. Opening the chamber I see the hollowpoint is still engaged, unfired.

Failure by a Marine sidearm? My father will be so ashamed.

Marveling, I point the barrel of the gun toward the earth and again pull the trigger. This time there is a heaven-splitting crack and a scattershot of dirt and twigs flies back into my face.

Report Card

"Where did you go last night?" Press asks me the next morning in the basement.

"Hunting rabbits."

"Big game."

"Sharp pointy teeth."

"Thick pelt."

"Tough to penetrate."

"Get any shots off?"

"One," I say. "Missed."

Press tsk-tsks. "Oh well. A for effort, I suppose."

Ducky Speaks

Later that day, already zombied in the basement:

"The hell is that?"

"Liszt, unless I'm mistaken," Press says.

"They have a stereo in the living room now?"

"That's Olivia Hofstadter."

"Never heard of her. She does an interesting Liszt. What label is she on?"

"Label?"

"She must be a European. Think I would have heard of her if she were an American."

"I doubt you've heard of her. And I'm pretty sure she's American."

"It's weird. So much pathos but a little amateurish in the execution department. She's not a sloppy player, really, just . . . undisciplined. But damn. So visceral."

"Like you?"

"Ha. Yeah. I guess."

"Yeah. That's what Christof said."

"Christof? He's still around?"

"You could say that."

"Cut the mysterioso shit."

"He's upstairs, Jack."

"Come on."

"What you are hearing are the weekly musical praxeological stylings of his star pupil. The maybe-genius—his second maybe-genius, I should say—Olivia Hofstadter, age twelve."

"Bullshit."

"See for yourself."

Upstairs I see he is telling the truth. The pouchy, elongated form of Christof is hunched over the piano, a little more pouchy and a little less elongated than fifteen years ago, but still rapt with attention for his pupil, his hand, as always, touching the bent side rim of the piano as if searching for a pulse. At the bench, in profile to me, in green corduroys worn white at the knees and a train of frayed threads at the heels—such attire! my mother must be thinking—is a dark-headed girl with improbably lanceolate, octave-spanning fingers. Five foot three but with fingers so long they look like an alien's, as if she has an extra phalanx or two in there.

Those fingers: no wonder she can play Liszt like that.

My mother sits elegantly cross-legged, observing. My father is next to her in his space-age wheelchair, Ducky enlaced in his motionless fingers.

"What the hell is this?"

"Hi, Jack," Christof says. "It's good to see you."

"Jackson," my mother intones. "What happened to your face? And your hands?"

"Who the hell are you?" I say to the girl.

The girl looks mortified. Her mouth, full of dull metal and agape, doesn't move to speak.

"Her name is Olivia," Christof says.

"Play that again," I tell her.

She closes her mouth and turns away from me. Her fingers spring to life. Christof puts his hand back on the bent side rim and closes his eyes, soaking it in.

"All right. Stop. Stop stop stop," I say. "It's remarkable. Granted. A little indulgent technically but also exquisitely . . ."

"Expressive?" Christof offers.

"Yes," I say reluctantly. "Expressive. It's like she's . . ."

"She's what?"

I breathe deeply. There's nothing to do but admit it.

"Like she's telling you a secret about yourself you've wanted to know your whole life."

"Remind you of anyone?" Christof says.

"But what the hell are you doing here?"

"She gets a lesson every week, Jack."

"But why here? Don't you have your own home?" I demand.

"She doesn't have a piano."

"She should get one. You can't go around mooching other people's Bösendorfers every damn week."

Christof clears his throat delicately. "Pianos are expensive, Jack."

"Bullshit. If she can afford you, Christof, she can damn well afford a damn Yamaha or something. Get a Nordiska, for fuck's sake."

"Jackson," from my mother.

"Her lessons are sponsored by her patron, Jack," Christof says patiently.

The girl lowers her head, her hair horseshoeing around her neck. This is a posture I know well: shame.

"Would someone like to explain to me just what the hell is going on around here?"

"Olivia lives in Elleber's Knob, Jack."

"Hickville ghett-*oh*," my brother whispers behind me, making a banjo gesture. "Snake handlers. Home brew. Kissing cousins."

"I know what Elleber's Knob is, Press. But no one is answering my question: what is she doing here?"

"She is Muriel's daughter," my mother says in her scissors voice.

"The stable hand," Press says.

"Jesus. I know who Muriel is. So what?"

"Jack," my mother says, "your father has arranged for her lessons with Christof since she was a little girl."

"He's arranged for them?" I say, processing. "What's the catch?"

My mother shrugs. As far as I know it is the first shrug of her life. On her shoulders the gesture looks infinitely vulgar.

"No catch."

"What?"

"Unless you count being able to listen to her play."

"He likes to listen to her play?"

"He never misses a lesson," Christof says.

"And he has arranged for all of this for her?" I try and fail to think of any time my father has done anything generous for someone else that did not have a puppetwork of strings attached. "Well," I say to myself, "I guess that explains why the Bösendorfer's in such good tune."

"You shouldn't be so shocked, Jack. He's told you about it."

"Who?"

"Your father."

"No, he hasn't. What is everyone talking about today?"

"In his letters. The letters I send you. There must be a hundred of them."

There are thirteen of them, I think. *Were* thirteen of them. What other revelations did they contain?

To Olivia I finally say, "And how do you like the lessons?" She still looks at me aghast. I see my reflection in the mirror and realize why. I am in my underwear and am clutching a tumbler like a weapon. I haven't showered in days; I smell of tomcat living and sour heartbreak. My black eye is draining sloe and raisin, my hands are crosshatched with cuts from the windows and other people's teeth, and dried brag lichens hem my mouth. I seem to be trembling.

Clearing my throat, I try to achieve a soothing tone. "I mean, do you find the lessons helpful?"

"Yes," she says timidly.

"Do you like Christof?"

"Yes."

"And it's my father—Guilford Tennant—who does this for you?"

"Mr. Tennant, yes."

"Don't you mean Colonel Tennant?"

The girl looks at me blankly: she is not required to call him Colonel.

"Do you understand what has happened to him?" I say. "Why he is in that wheelchair?"

She nods.

"But you're still here. Doesn't he frighten you?"

She shakes her head.

"Why not?"

"Jackson, really," my mother says. "Don't you think you should put something decent on and quit pestering Olivia?"

Ignoring my mother, I say, "Do you like the Bösendorfer? Yes? Why, then?" She sucks bodily inward, as if bracing for a blow. I do not care. "Why?"

"Easy, Jack," Press says.

"Why?"

"It's . . . big."

"What does that mean?"

"It sounds like the music is coming out of my body. Not the piano. I mean, it feels like the sound comes out of me."

I step back from the piano. The girl looks like she might cry. I feel stunned, epiphanically taxed and emptied, but falsely. I feel as if I must have just learned something important but I don't know what any of it means. What is the secret she's trying to tell me?

If the girl starts crying, I realize, there's a good chance that I will, too.

"Good answer," I say. Then, sniffing back tears, I say to my mother, "How long has this been going on?"

"Years."

"How many?"

"With Olivia, six. Before that there were Alice Marvar and Misty Ruka."

"For how long?"

"Five years, three years."

"So he's been paying for other people's lessons for almost . . ."

"Since you've been gone."

"I see." To Olivia I say, "Does he always listen when you play?"

She nods.

"Will you play something for us now?"

"What should I play?"

"Your favorite. No. Scratch that. Play *his* favorite."

She starts playing the first few bars of Beethoven's *Pathétique* Sonata.

"No. Not your favorite. My father's favorite."

"But that is his favorite," she says, making me swarm over with feeling.

When she resumes playing, Press whispers to me, "What's the matter with you? You look like you've heard a ghost."

"It's my favorite too," I say quietly. "It was my audition piece at Juilliard."

During the song I watch my father. Huddled in his wheelchair his eye knocks around in its socket, almost, it seems, in tune with the music. When the song hits the first movement in *allegro*—the same moment whose crossover I could not make after my finger was broken—a gemlike tear rappels down his cheek.

"Wait, stop." This is my mother interjecting. She is off her seat, kneeling at my father's side. Her government-issue smile, the only one I've ever seen, is gone. She is smiling an openmouthed, jaw-stretching, molar-showing smile. It is so unpremeditated it is almost horrible. "Stop for a moment, Olivia. Listen. Do you hear it?"

"What is it?" I say.

"Shush, Jackson."

My mother leans in toward my father, ear-first. His skin is mezzotinted in sweat and his eye is clenched shut, the bunched flesh around it a topography of strain. Outside an iodized sunset fills the branches of the trees. Olivia sits motionless, her fingers in her mouth. After a soundless interval we all hear it. It is weak but discernible. It is indisputably a quack.

"Quack," goes Ducky. My mother stares at him, gobstopped. "Quack," says the orange bill. "Quack quack."

I can see that it is so faint because my father is not squeezing with his whole hand but with just one finger. Only his right index finger is moving.

My mother discomposes. Her stony rectitude crumbles and her features form a disassembly of sheer joy. She hurls her arms around his neck and kisses him. Olivia shoots off the bench and runs to him, clutching his legs. Christof goes to him, too. Most of my father's body is claimed by celebrants so Christof just sort of sheepishly puts his hand on his shoulder, as if he were feeling a piano's vibrations.

Press emerges from behind me and approaches our father. He does not touch him but he stands before him, reaching out with his hand and then retracting it, pocketing and unpocketing it.

"Quack," he says, as if this explains everything. "Ha ha."

I can't get any traction. I send signals to my feet but they will not move. I feel like I did while standing uselessly on the dock that night at Lake George. Frozen with fear and awe.

There is a stinging sinus burn in my head as I remember Bess's word for this neural breakdown: apraxia. The failure of the body to do what it ought to.

Through her sobs my mother says, "This calls for a celebration. Who here wants to go to the steeplechase this weekend?"

From inside the huddle of bodies I hear a modest but emphatic "Quack!"

I say nothing.

Irony

My finger ruined my life. Now my father's finger is helping him reclaim his.

I am full of hatred.

Neuroplasticity 1.1: What My Father Wants

The next day Bess permits herself a formal pronouncement.

"This is an incredibly favorable factor. Nowhere in the documentation have I come across any improvement like this. Gil's brain is finding a way to remap itself. He is finding new neural pathways, new ways to communicate with his body and the world around him. He is changing his mind on a *cell*ular level, inventing a new self. We are privileged to be seeing a

totally legitimate neurological rebirth. Gil is changing himself "—
she can't hold back an emotional burble—"*lit*erally into a bio-
*log*ically new human being."

"Quack!" goes Ducky.

"That's right, Ducky," she says. "And now that Gil has such
good movement in his index finger I have installed a touch pad
communicator." Bess indicates a blue sensor underneath Ducky
on the wheelchair's armrest. "The Dynovox is a wonderful device that will dramatically increase his autonomy. Now Gil
won't have to blink to let us know what he needs. We won't
even have to be in the room. Just a few taps of the pad and Gil
can type out a message from the alphabet that appears on the
computer screen here. Then the message prints out below. Or,
if we are out of the room, Gil can select the audio feature here,
which will translate his message into a signal that feeds
through the portable speakers I have placed in all the rooms of
the house. We'll never be more than a sentence away from you
from now on, Gil."

My father's eye bobs happily in its socket.

"This Dynovox thing looks sort of expensive," Press says.

"Its usefulness is priceless," Bess says.

"Oh, I know," Press says. "I'm just saying."

"Who wants a demonstration?" she says brightly.

"We all do," my mother says, glaring at Press.

"O.K. then. Gil, will you show us how the emergency alert
call works?"

My father presses his fingertip on the pad. After he holds it
in place for a long moment, the speakers placed throughout
the house shriek to life, all rooms reverberating with an intense anvil-rupturing squeal.

"O.K., O.K., O.K. already," Press hollers, plugging his ears.
"Jesus. We get it."

"Phew," Bess says when my father removes his finger. "We might have to adjust the volume on that. All right. Now. To see how the verbalizer works. Gil, how are you feeling right now? Is there anything you want?"

His finger stabs awkwardly at the pad, selecting, finally, the first letter of his sentence. It flashes iridescent blue in enormous forty-eight-point font on the screen: L.

"Oh God," I say. "I can simplify this process. I know what he wants. I'll get him the damn Lagavulin. I'll be right back."

It takes me a second in the kitchen to find where Press has stashed the bottles. Under the sink and behind the garbage—one of the few places he knows my mother would never deign to look. It is when I am hunched over on my hands and knees, straining to reach around the fuming trash, that I hear my father's message broadcast from the speaker on the counter. It takes me a moment to process. When I realize what he is saying I drop the scotch. If the Dynovox did not have a repeat function I would not believe it. My finger throbs the way it does before a thunderstorm when I hear it.

"Liszt," the epicene voice intones. "Liszt Liszt Liszt."

My father doesn't want a drink. He wants to hear me play.

Neuroplasticity 1.2: Dirty Lullaby

Late that night I discover my mother downstairs with my father in his room, vigorously rubbing French vanilla–scented lotion on his hands. It is the first time in my life that I can remember seeing their hands make contact. At first she doesn't perceive my presence and I just watch them. Her massaging is firm but tender. My father appears to be asleep, a low dirge-like noise issuing from his throat, both eyes closed, and Ducky, cleansed of saliva, snuggling under his chin. On the speakers John Denver is singing about sunshine on his shoulder making him happy, on the water looking so lovely, almost all the time making him high. From here I can see the crepe-sag of my mother's underchin stretch gently as she sings quietly along, dabbing at his mouth. A lullaby, I realize. I am witnessing a lullaby.

My mother has never looked as vulnerable or as beautiful. I wait until the song is over before I enter.

"Up late?" I say.

"Oh. Jackson. You scared me."

"This music is scaring me," I say. "Don't tell me he asked for it."

"All right."

"Honest? Dad requested John Denver?"

"It's grown on him. Now he adores that John Denver. It makes him fall asleep."

"I see. How exactly do you know this?"

She shrugs—the second shrug my mother has ever committed. "I've been taking care of him, Jackson. You'd know this too if you came upstairs more often."

Outside, moonlight shatters into quicksilver on the moving surface of the pool. I wish I could understand something.

"I don't get it, Mom. You've never been like this before. As long as I can remember, nothing. And now, all of sudden, just like that, you start taking all this care of him? There is slobber all over your sleeve right now. Your fox towel is soaking with spit. You are touching his hands. You are touching his face. And don't think I didn't see you singing to him, Mom." This comes out like an accusation. "What is it? All of a sudden you, what, you love him?"

"I do love him."

"Why? It's never been like this. Why all of a sudden like this?"

She shrugs the third shrug of her life.

"He's never needed me like this before."

Neuroplasticity 1.3: Near-Death Experience

Bess declares my father fit for travel so that weekend we pack him up into a specially equipped Econoline and make for Middleburg, Virginia.

"Are you sure this is a good idea?" Press asks my mother when he discovers that the rental fee on the van is $450. "Won't it be a tad awkward to have Dad out there in public? I mean, among all those other people?"

I wait for her to say something like, The damage has already been done, and glare meaningfully at him, but she simply says, "Your father wants to go."

When the Middleburg people hear that Guilford Tennant is in the van they insist that we drive it up to the fences so that we can roll back the side door and give my father an unobstructed view of the steeplechase. During the race people approach the van and pay their respects to my father. A crowd develops. In his wheelchair, elevated above them, he looks like a monarch in his throne room, receiving court from supplicants.

No one seems to be paying much notice to the race. Although the horses are not visible yet, the ground starts shaking and I can feel the hoofbeats in my body the way I can feel it when I hit the Bösendorfer hard. Not many people turn away from my father as the horses thunder past in their jet-engine roar, spitting up turf. It is a photo finish but even then few seem to turn away from my father, such is his invalid celebrity.

My mother is unfazed by the attention. She presses a button inside the van and, with the sound of grinding gears and whining servos, the lift ramp lowers my father to the ground. Patiently she translates with the Ouija board when people ask him questions. One of the men in the crowd looks familiar—handsome, bespectacled, donnish, and straight-backed. After he has a few words with my father he approaches me and says, "Jack? That you, Jack?"

"Yes?"

"It's Franklin. Franklin Laindon."

"Hi."

"You don't remember me. You used to swim in my pond." When he sees this does not compute, he says, "Late at night. With your brother. In Brody's Gator."

"Mr. Laindon? Franklin Laindon? The Foxhall Farmer?"

"That's me." He seems to expand with pleasure at the recognition.

"No shit. Jesus. We thought . . . well, we thought you were dead."

"No kidding. How did I go?"

"Heard you got the boom coming about in a storm."

"They don't give my seaworthiness much credit, do they?"

"I guess not. But it's great. You're not dead."

"Working on it, though."

"And your wife? How's she?"

"Contrary."

"Thank God."

"How did they say she went?"

"Crushed by a chandelier at the Belvedere."

"Ouch."

"Seriously."

Franklin Laindon cranes his neck and looks affectionately at my father. "That's some dad you've got."

"You know, I'm not sure how you know him."

"We were classmates at Annapolis. We were friends. Good friends. But then we sort of drifted apart. I haven't seen him in years."

"Huhn. I assumed you were drinking buddies."

"We were what?"

"Drinking buddies."

"Your father doesn't drink."

"What?"

"He never touched the stuff. 'Makes your hands slow,' he said. 'Makes you a gashouse palooka.' "

"Are we talking about the same guy?"

"Your father?" he says. "Treetop?"

Franklin Laindon looks genuinely confused. His eyebrows caterpillar; his pupils pinpoint in dubious focus.

"Yeah . . . ," I say, trying to prompt Franklin Laindon to admit his sarcasm. But he won't.

"Your father never touched the stuff," he says. "Not in the years I knew him."

"Are you bullshitting me or what?"

Then I hear my mother scream. This is nearly a paranormal feat of identification, for I have never heard my mother scream in my life. Wheeling around, I see my father's wheelchair has gone haywire. His ascot kiting smartly behind him, he goes careening through people, overturning portable tables and inciting evasive high-stepping dance in those nearby. He nearly clips the bumper of a Land Rover and he flattens a stuffed pelican that a kid was pulling around on a leash of string. He repeatedly rams a post and a couple of nearby folding chairs get it. Then I see what the problem is. My father must have convinced my mother to let him take the controls. The joystick controller has been installed on his wheelchair and his one good finger is trying to manipulate it.

The Colonel wants to pilot his own chair.

A few drinks are spilled and some exclamations are heard, but they are expressions of benevolent surprise. No one is mocking my father. They are sympathetic. They admire his pluck. Press takes advantage of the diversion to raid a cooler behind a dualie. In one easy motion he extracts a bottle of clear liquid and brings it to his lips. He raises the bottle to me in a salute from afar. I am amused at this until I hear the character of the exclamations change: my father is heading toward the crest of the hill. Below is a trailer backing up. They are on a collision course and the driver can't see him.

It all happens so fast.

The wheelchair spurts ahead. A tweedy guy in red Wellies clutches at the chair but misses and falls. Franklin Laindon makes a move but derails on a mud slick. At first I don't understand why the terrain is blurring past me, but then I realize that I am running after my father. I am running as fast as I can, my lungs burning, my scalp constricting over my skull in terror, but it's hopeless. The wheelchair is outsprinting me; the figure of my father recedes from me steadily. I get close enough to see the chair approach, obtain, then go over the crest and start hurtling downhill toward the moving trailer. My father bobs up and down roughly in the seat. He looks like a novice rider trying to post. The trailer is reversing straight into his path. The wheels look massive. My mother shrieks.

No one else is close enough to do anything.

Then, at the edge of my field of vision, I see Press move. He drops the bottle and sprints over the edge of the hill, his long legs churning and his cowcatcher jaw clippering through the air. I see his muscles bunch up and he leaps wildly forward, moving gracefully through space, until a hand closes on the neck of my father's shirt. I hear my father make a shocked choking sound as he is plucked from the seat, his momentum suddenly reversed, the wheelchair spinning out from under him. Together my brother and father crumple into a human pile on the turf. There is a metallic crunching sound as the wheelchair is sucked under the tires of the trailer and crushed.

From the ground, his body spread out on the parking lot—as if making dirt angels—a ragged, wheezy noise comes rapidly out of my father's mouth. It sounds like laughter.

Press stands up and stares at the crowd, then at our father, then at me. He raises his hands before his face and stares at them for a long time, like a criminal, like a murderer, as if trying to understand what they have done.

Neuroplasticity 1.4: Pimp My Dynovox

That night, in the basement, Press doesn't want to talk about it. "I don't know, all right?" is all he says. "It just happened."

The next morning, though, he is up early, doing something private in my father's room with Bess. They won't let anyone past the door. When they emerge, late in the afternoon, Bess announces that congratulations are due Press for his blessed work on the Dynovox. Just look, she says. He has designed an improved, much-simplified command screen for the program. She lifts up above her head, trophylike, a printout of the new page display:

ACTIONS	I FEEL . . .	NAMES	THINGS
Bathroom	Hot	Adair	Wheelchair
TV on/off	Cold	Press	John Denver Hits
Move me	Hungry	Jack	Lotion
Bathe	Thirsty	Bess	Thick-It
Piano	Sleepy	Ducky	Pong

"It's just a start," Bess says. "Press and I have a whole smorgasbord of things to put down on this command page. Right, Pressman?"

"I guess," he says, embarrassed.

"I told him Ducky should go under 'things' but he wouldn't hear of it."

"Come on, Bess," he says, pained.

"And do you all notice the omission of a certain something? Anyone? Anyone? Islay. There is no Islay on the list."

"*Eye*-la," Pressman corrects, and blushes furiously.

Neuroplasticity 1.5: Down the Drain

Later that night Press and I do not convoy to the bar, as per usual. I am forced to venture upstairs, where I find him standing with Bess at the counter in the kitchen with a bottle of Lagavulin between them. The bottle looks ready, preparing itself. Is Bess going to share a glass with my brother? I take a half step backward and watch them from the shadows of the stairway.

"I don't want to," I hear him say pitifully. "I never did."

She nods and then, holding his hand in hers, helps him pour the Lagavulin down the drain. It takes a long time. I can see my brother's eyes yo-yo when he watches, full of wonderment and dread, as the copper liquid unspools into the sink. When it is over Bess removes her Swifties, takes his head in her hands, and kisses him on the forehead. She puts her arms around him and my brother buries his head in her hair. He makes wet whimpering noises as she strokes his head, murmuring reassuring words.

"Fucking fireflies," my brother sobs. "Fucking jigsaw puzzle." Then he says something I can't hear and clenches her tightly.

"I understand," Bess says. "God loves you anyway."

Mythology

My father turns out to be a pianist and the Tremain School joc-
ulacator. The neighborhood thinks he is the greatest. He is the
champion of little girl pianists. He is suddenly loved passion-
ately by my mother. His life is saved by my brother, his inveterate enemy and would-be assassin. He is recovering physically
in a way that defies all medical expectation. And he is suddenly
expressing himself in a way he never has.

I don't know what any of this means. It does not compute.
Everything I've ever counted on, believed in, struggled
against—it's all gone. I am stripped of my mythology. What do
I have left? I don't know. The sensory register oscillates. I feel
scarified, extracted from the only life I've ever known, reduced
only to my mistaken self.

There is one person left who can help me.

Importunity

I leave them to each other and retreat to the basement, where I
wrap myself in my brother's sheet, cower gnomishly in the
corner, and drink until I work up the courage to call a number

I haven't dialed in more than three years. As the tone pulses—it sounds like a digital warning, a recording letting me know this is the countdown to my last chance, to self-destruct—it occurs to me that he is still number one on my speed dial. Even after everything that happened, I have not been able to replace him.

I clutch my orange flip-flop—epoxied together with very mixed, nearly Frankensteinian results—in my free hand.

"Hello?" His wife's voice is turbid with sleep but also alert to danger—the voice of a mother. It is so late. She must be imagining emergency room doctors or local constables calling.

"Is Leon Flanders available, please?"

"Who's calling?"

"Blood Man."

"Who?"

"There's been a terrible mistake. Please, it's urgent. I need to speak to Leon."

Through the muffled sail-sounds of their sheets I hear baffled words of alarm exchanged.

"Hello?"

Oh Leon. All these years, your voice sounds the same. Tattered and Midwestern and worn by care—Leonine. How many syllables of kindness have you uttered today? Were you guiding an undergraduate through a thesis? Were you introducing a visiting writer with charm and wit? Encouraging a freshman not to transfer to the community college back home? Why couldn't your voice have said such things to me when I needed you?

"It's Jack."

"Who?"

"It wasn't me."

"Wasn't you what? Who is this?"

"Jack," I say, enunciating clearly.

"Jack who?"

"Jack *who*?"

"Do you know what time it is?"

"It's me, Leon. Jack Tennant. Jack."

"Jack Tennant?"

"Yeah. It's me!" I try to say this with game-show cheer but it just comes out desperate.

"Are you drunk?"

"I need to talk to you."

"It's one o'clock in the morning."

"I've been piecing my life together, Leon. I've been working as an adjunct in Georgia. It's tough. But I've been working hard. I got the highest student eval ranking the department has had in the last decade. Four point nine three. Out of five, that is. And that's not one semester either. That's accumulated. Three years. And that's teaching comp, too. Required, you know what I mean? Not an elective. No one wants to be there, you know?"

"That's great, Jack," he says. But I can tell that he doesn't mean it. He is trying to appease me. "I've got a first-period tomorrow, so . . ."

"I am trying to be just like you in the classroom. I keep every office hour. I'm always there for them. I even meet with them out of class to discuss Djuna Barnes or Paul Celan or whoever I've given them for extra credit." I pull up short here when I realize that meeting outside of class is not exactly what I mean, that it raises certain unfortunate parallels with Jordana Mochnik. "I mean, not *out* out of class. I just mean that I'm available all the time. To help. With school. Or with life. You know, like you."

Breathing is suddenly very difficult. When I exhale it feels like my lungs are awash in salt water. A nasally soblike noise comes out of my mouth.

"Fuck," I say. "This isn't coming out right."

"I think you'd better go, Jack."

"I work at this homeless shelter, too," I say brightly, trying to recover. "There's this kid, Rodney, and sometimes I give him the James Brown treatment. Well, Hahva mainly does that, but I sometimes help. And I let Miss D and Gail smoke in the morning. I know that's kind of bad but it seems sort of good too. I mean, smoking bad, yes, I know, sure: bad. But what pleasures do they have left? I can let them smoke, can't I? Isn't that something you would do? And I give them cab vouchers even when they've extended their limit. And this one time—"

"Go sleep it off, Jack."

"Leon," I say miserably. "Please tell me why. I have to know why."

"Why what?"

"You were like a father to me. I wanted to be a son to you. I wanted to be like an uncle to your kids. Hell, maybe I could babysit sometime again and—"

"You stay away from my family, Jack."

"I didn't do anything wrong!" I say, trying to swallow back the ignoble pigeon noises coming from my gullet. "Well, the fire extinguisher was wrong. Granted. I give you that. I was wrong there. Wrongo. But that was all I did. I never did anything else with her. Well, a kiss. O.K. Fine. A kiss. But *she* kissed *me*! And it was only one. One single abortive kiss. It didn't last, I don't know, five, six, seven seconds. Not even eight seconds. It wouldn't even count in rodeo."

"I'm hanging up now, Jack."

"Leon. I need some help right now. Things aren't so great. I don't know what to do. I've stupidly come back home and I'm back on the brag again and I lost the only woman I ever loved. I think it's final. I think I've ruined it. And God, there was the thing with Musser and then Robbie. It just happened. I was just so mixed up. But I can't stop thinking about it. And I think I've lost my adjunct job at the university. I'm not qualified to do anything but teach. I'm thirty-three and I don't have any other skills. What am I supposed to do, Leon? Learn a trade? I can't do anything else. Everything I've built since New York is gone. I don't know what to do. I feel like I might do something rash. I have this weird dangerous feeling in my gut. I need you to tell me what to do. You are the only person I've ever known who always knows what to do. Please, Leon. I'm begging you. Tell me what to do. I know everything will be O.K. again if you tell me what to do."

"Good night, Jack."

"Remember that night at the saloon? You found me in the Korean laundromat? You took me for a beer? You said fuck Manthia Diawara and screw Judith Butler and all those guys?" I am blurting all this out as fast as I can, nearly unintelligibly, in thirty-second notes. Mozart-style. I need him to hear it. "I was going to tell you something but I didn't. What I wanted to tell you was . . . I had a brother."

"I'm hanging up now, Jack."

I have no shame. I must make Leon understand. I need to tell him all of it, everything I've never said out loud—that I can't remember my brother, that every day I feel like I have this Lemon-shaped hole in me, that it is only getting worse, that I need help.

What I say instead is, "He was six years old."

Then I say, "All I have left is a fucking flip-flop!"

I also try: "I tore it by mistake!"

And: "It's orange!"

"Never contact me again," he says. "If you do, I'm calling the police."

The phone flatlines. In the cemeterian murk of my brother's corner I clutch what's left of Dex's flip-flop protectively to my chest and try to make my heart work.

Fortify

Inch, vein-laced and wary, evaluates me for a long bristling moment. His lobster eyes pinpoint into black focus; his jaw makes gristly chewing noises. The robust belly of his cheek is still draining blue with blood and his index finger is encased in a dull metal splint. I broke his pointer? I don't remember doing this. The chicken-neck pallor of his skin goes deep red as he considers me sitting across his bar, within range.

"You got a lot of nerve coming in here," he says at last.

"I just want to drink."

"If you breathe in the wrong direction I'm calling the cops."

"I get that a lot."

"It's almost closing time."

"I'll be fast."

Inch serves up a rank of tumblers full of rust-colored liquid as Robbie appears on the stool next to me. In the mirror I can see that the architecture of her makeup and banglery conjures the image of a wedding cake, a highly encrusted, gaudy, glitter-ridden, Vegas-issue wedding cake. The pink peel splits open as she speaks.

"Well well. It's my favorite source. Are you stalking me, dumpling? You have exquisite taste."

"Mmf," I say.

"What was that, you big galoot?"

I do not feel like a big galoot. I feel desperate and lonely and dangerous.

"Mmf."

"I see. And what are you trying to do with all that gas, baby?"

"Fortify."

"Hunh?"

In this light the salad-dressing tone of Robbie's skin looks ghoulish. Her knuckles are flaky like mica, the skin yellow and hardened with nicotine. With all the memories I've lost, why can't I forget this one?

"Prepare myself."

"For what?"

"Work."

"What kind of work? Fumigating apartments?"

"Inappropriate compensatory action."

"What, sugar?"

As I teeter on my stool and drink, I think about that night at the lake. All day it had been hot—adhesive New England hot—but in the evening it started cooling. But I still felt the heat in my collar and in my gut as I stood on the dock and watched my brother struggle in the water. His arms churned; it looked as if he were waving to me. How long did I stand there? Why couldn't I open the screen door? What took me so long to get help?

Why was my father already so drunk at five o'clock in the afternoon? He doesn't start until six.

However it happened in detail—despite what parts I may get wrong—the ugly, uneditable, unfictionable, relentless truth of it is: he is dead. I'm still alive.

My father is still alive, too.

"Hey Robbie," I try to pronounce. "Do you believe in for-giveness?"

Robbie utters some syllables but I do not hear them. I am not really interested in her answer. I know the answer. Instead I concentrate on the tumblers before me. Each time I finish one I upturn it and stack it on the table, making a glinting pyramid structure. With each shot I try to exhale my sadness. I let the brag transform it into a fever of hatred. I do this until the world around me tilts and drains of color.

I am ready.

Inappropriate Compensatory Action

I brady through the house. The lights are all off. Everyone else is asleep. There is only the quasar hum of the climate control system, the thready night quietude, the carpet pushing against my feet and filling the spaces between my toes. I am a part of it, at long last an agent of the silence, not its victim. From the doorway of my father's room comes the usual barium glow of the TV playing itself in Pong. The beavertail in my hand pulls heavily on the tendons in my shoulder.

My father is awake, on his back, his good eye tracking the white ball while his vitreous dead one looks balefully into the darkness of the ceiling. The Dynovox is attached to his hand with surgical tape and his chin is engummed with thick spittle, his skin a toilet gloss of—what? Alcohol withdrawal? Anxiety? Hate vinegar? It does not matter now.

I put the gun on the table beside us and pull my father into a sitting position. I am all fueled up, so it takes a few awkward tries. While my father's eye locks onto the movement of the bottle, I take a long pull of scotch and offer some to Ducky. Ducky declines; I accept his portion. Then, clumsily, I peel off the tape from my father's wrist and remove the Dynovox's touch pad, moving it a foot away from his hand.

"We won't be needing the emergency call feature, will we?" I ask him.

Then I sit beside him on the bed, the biosmog of fear and hatred rising around us. My father's eye pongs rapidly between me and the beavertail. For a long time we sit like this. Together we look out the window at the darkened doughy treeline, breathe the same sepulchral air of the room, listen to the same night silences. I don't know what my father is thinking about. Maybe regret. Maybe love. Maybe even Dex.

I touch my father's thick lustrous hair, the glistening concavity of his chest, the slack U-gape of his underlip. I put his fighter's hands on my head, my gut churning with a longing I do not understand. My heart, exhausted and sick with self, falls like a rotten fruit inside my chest.

I can feel it: death is in the room with us, a hunched froglike presence clogging the corners of the ceiling. I doublecheck the beavertail. It is fully loaded with hollowpoints, with one in the chamber. No margin for error this time.

After what seems like a long time: "I bet this is what Dex felt like, too."

And then, for the first time in my life, I work up the courage.

"Killer," I say.

Then I insert the barrel of the beavertail into my mouth and grind my molars together. I pull back the hammer on the gun and the room fills with polestars. This must be what birth is like. This must be why we aren't allowed to remember it. The mystery, the glory, the terror. I have a sensation of bees pricking my skin. My father's eye is on me. He is making desperate snorkeling noises that could indicate anything. This walrusy sound of desperation is identical, I realize, to the noises that Dex made when he went under the water. At least something runs in the family.

What else is left for me to do?

My finger nudges the trigger. I feel the inexorable undertow of gravity but also, at the same time, intensely buoyant. Dex's name rumbles in my throat. The last thing I hear is the mortifying click of the hammer and the deafening sound of atomic surf in my ears.

Part Three

Hell in Gasoline Bloomers 1.1

It is not like I imagined it. On cop shows dying people always report feeling cold, so cold. But not me. I have a pleasant feeling of immersion, a soothing warm-bath sensation. There is an encroaching shadow, but it isn't really dark; it doesn't envelop me. It's almost like mood lighting. It suffuses my body with a nerve-scrubbing hypnogogic heat. Being dead is almost . . . pleasurable. It seems like a luxurious and coveted secret possession.

When my surroundings materialize I see that I am barefoot on a dock looking out over the water. A boy in jeans cutoffs sits cross-legged on one of the pilings, totemlike, regarding me with his head cocked quizzically to the side. His eyes are brown. His mouth is round. His fingers are small and trinket-like. He smells like kid stuff: sweat and water and cut grass and suntan lotion. He smells, it occurs to me, like vacation.

On his feet are two orange flip-flops, which are—like his shirt, his shorts, his hair—perfectly dry.

He hasn't been in the water.

Grief and love aerosol through me.

For a while he just looks at me, head cocked, inquisitive, almost amused, as if listening for something he already knows is coming. I get the feeling he is trying to communicate something, but maybe I don't have the technique down, maybe my spirit self isn't skilled yet. It doesn't know what to do, how to receive.

You're dead, I want to say. Now I'm dead, too. Isn't that finally enough?

Can I understand now?

I feel just the same as I did as a five-year-old on the dock. I am thirty-three now but I am still the same Jack. I am still terrified and ashamed and completely frozen in place. Still praying for Press to leap out of nowhere and cry, "Ambush!" and do the saving for me. At thirty-three I have the same soul: craven and sad and useless.

"Is this my hell?" I say. "Do I have to live this over and over now? Is that how it works?"

Dex doesn't say anything. He just keeps looking at me curiously.

"Do I get another chance?"

Later, I say, "I know I can do better."

After a long time I say, "I want to try again. Let me try again." I know it doesn't make any sense as I say it—it's a little late now, Jack—but I can't help it. The words just come out. "I know I can save you."

Much later I try to explain how I knew nothing about him, how I tried to make it all up. I start to tell Dex about the *White Pages* but I stop before I get anything out. Suddenly it just sounds really stupid. It registers that maybe it *was* stupid.

Why did I love a phone book? Why did I crave the names of strangers? Why couldn't I just write about Dex? Jesus, why couldn't I even say his name?

"I just couldn't," I say, defeated. "I don't know why. I wasn't brave enough."

"I know," Dex says. "It's O.K."

"I've missed you for a long time," I say.

Then he smiles at me. Not a knowing smile. It doesn't have any afterlife-wisdom. It isn't communicating anything sage or mysterious. It is just a kid smile. And it's a big one, all thirty-two teeth. It is, in other words, perfect.

"Stop crying," he says.

The water around us swells and troughs in the silvery moonlight. It looks like an enormous field of undulant black glass.

Eventually Dex says, "You still want to know about that night, don't you?"

"Yes," I say, near tears.

"O.K.," he says.

But suddenly his smile breaks off. He looks a little sad. His eyes go downcast and his eyebrows apostrophe with worry. When he looks back up he appears suddenly to be far away, reduced and distorted, as if I'm viewing him through a flawed telescopic lens.

"There isn't time," he says sadly. "Here they come."

Behind Dexter the sky goes blotchy with wings. A thundercloud of screaming birds—orioles, thousands of them—swarm through the air toward us. Before I know it they have descended on us, carnivalian and phantasmic and violent. I hold up my arms over my head, fending them off, but it doesn't do any good. They are on me, forcing me down into the water. I am exiting, going under.

Through the teeming clot of orange and black I can make out Dex, sitting on his piling, looking so sad, waving at me.

"Go on, Jack," he says from far away. "You can't stay here."

Wings beat on my face.

Hell in Gasoline Bloomers 1.2: After Afterlife

From my vantage point spread-eagled on the floor, silky fibers pushing against my face, I can barely make out the looming figure of my brother. He is doing something vigorous and aerobic with my body that is sending blazing signals of pain to my brain. Eventually I understand it: not wings. It is my brother, slapping my face—chop chop, smack smack—bringing me around.

"Get up, get up," are the words hammering away on my anvils. "Get up, Jack. Incoming," is the message flaying my auditory cortex.

After quadrupeding disgracefully around for a few moments my brother rights me and I manage a semi-upright hominid stance by enlisting generously the assistance of the wall. It doesn't do the pictures any favors, but I can maintain at least temporary defiance of gravity. When my cones and rods sort it out I see that Pressman is standing before me—attired in a priestly white terry bathrobe I did not know he owned—and smoothing down his hair with one hand while hiding an obviously gun-shaped shape in his pocket with the other.

The sound of footsteps clatter down the staircase and then my mother appears in the doorway, a frightened apparition, with Bess standing behind her, Swiftyless, confused, wrapped in a robe that matches my brother's. I assay verticality, aware that it is not maintained entirely without some discernible shaking, and creak out a smile that my brother seconds with the aplomb of the sober. He indicates the Dynovox and shrugs.

"Sorry, Mom," he samaritans. "False alarm. My bad."

Lucky Me

"I didn't have to fool anyone with the story," my brother explains as I embrace the Everlast. "They didn't hear the gun fire. The gun didn't fire."

"I heard it go off," I say, still touching my head all over, searching for holes, amazed to be alive.

"What you heard—what we all heard—was the Dynovox going off."

"It couldn't have been the Dynovox. I untaped it from Dad's hand. It wasn't anywhere near his finger. He couldn't have touched it."

Press shrugs.

"It had to be the gun."

"It wasn't."

"But I know I pulled the trigger."

"Jammed," he says, demonstratively holding up a tiny spring. "Fouled primer."

"What?"

"Fouled primer. Spring's rusted. See?" He whistles. "Never seen a gun in this bad shape. Where were you storing it?"

"A hole in the ground."

"Buried in dirt?"

"In a box."

Press gives me a look. He knows very well what box I mean.

"Well, when the firing pin struck the rusted primer it didn't have enough force to ignite it. The secondary charge wouldn't fire. A dud. That's what happens you store a pistol in a filthy, humid, subterranean environment for twenty years without cleaning it."

"That explains that," I say. "Neat."

"Lucky thing you don't know anything about firearm maintenance and storage."

"Lucky me."

"So can I ask the question?" he says, regarding the beavertail in a Yorick's-skull sort of way. "Who were you aiming for? Dad or yourself?"

Wrong Wrong Wrong

When I don't respond to Press's interrogation he starts, incredibly, to lecture me about drinking. He tells me what Bess told him about the thick Tennant blood, the predisposition to "sludging," the heightened risk of becoming locked in ourselves, during which I try to act surprised.

"Oooh," I say. "Man alive."

"Are you listening? It's hereditary, Jack. The same thing could happen to us if we don't change. I didn't really think much of it, either, until that day at the steeplechase. I thought I wanted Dad's money more than I wanted Dad, but when it

actually happened . . ." When he sees me expressing insuffi-
cient awe, he iterates, "You are your father's son."

When I hear those words I nearly take a second swing at
my brother. Instead I just say, "Whatever, kettle."

"What?"

"You've been drinking since you were nine years old, you
fucking hypocrite."

He goes squinty with doubt.

"Um, no I haven't."

"Yes you have. You've been drinking since the day of Dex's
funeral. I was five. You are four years older than me. That
makes you nine when you had your first drink."

"I didn't drink at the funeral, Jack. My first drink was with
Coen, when I was thirteen, in the back room at the Handi-Mart."

"Press, you had your first drink at the funeral. 'Does that
hurt you?' I asked, and you said, 'Nothing hurts me.'"

"You asked me if it hurt when you were like ten years old.
In the basement. I had smuggled some of Dad's scotch downstairs. You were sitting right there on your Everlast."

"No. You drank out of Dad's flask at the funeral," I insist.

"Dad never had a flask, Jack," he says. "Honest. I'm not
kidding you."

"Press, we were out in back of the funeral home. You beaned
that oriole with a rock and then you drank out of Dad's flask."

"Oriole? I didn't throw any rock at any oriole at the funeral."

"Yes you did! Quit fucking around!"

"I'm not fucking around!" His hands shoot above his head
as if it were a stickup.

Suddenly I feel dizzy. The room dilates blackly. The tissue
in my chest ticks and hums.

"We were fucking viewing Dex in his coffin—well, you were
viewing Dex, really—and I saw these orioles out the window and

got totally mad and tore out of there and around back and tried to hit them with a rock but couldn't and you hit one for me."

"Jack," Press says cautiously, as if trying to talk down a rabid animal. "It was a closed casket."

"What?"

"Dex had been in the water for thirty-six hours."

"Wrong wrong wrong!" I blurt. "Shut the fuck up!"

A thrombus of despair and heartbreak forms in my throat. Something is leaking in my gut. I pull the resurrected flip-flop close to me and retreat into it turtleneckishly.

"What is that?" Press asks.

"What do you mean?" I say, beginning to feel suffocated.

"Why do you have some kid's torn-up flip-flop?"

"It's Dex's fucking old flip-flop, O.K.? I pulled both of them out of the water that night and I've kept them ever since. Is that all right with you?"

Even before he opens his mouth I know what he is going to say. It is terrible and inevitable; I have felt it coming.

Press's eyes flood with dolor and pity.

"Jack," he says, as gently as he can, "Dex drowned in his sneakers."

Farewell to the Suicide Palace

I can't feel anything. I don't think anything. My heart shuts down.

I tell my brother that I have to go. He doesn't want to take me—it's three a.m., he reasons, and he still wants to know what I was doing with the beavertail—but I remind him that I picked him up from BWI when he returned from California and never asked him one damn thing about it. He owes me.

In the airless, styrene space of the terminal, under the Arrivals/Departures sign, people shift around us with mindless herbivore benevolence. It's nearly five in the morning, so they are red-eyers and first-flighters, all dazed. At the counter, a woman with brittle corporate cheer informs me that there isn't a seat on any flight to my tiny town in Georgia until five p.m. and that one has two connections—through Chicago and Atlanta—and is priced at nearly seven hundred dollars.

"That's the one," I say.

"You don't have to do this, Jack," my brother says. "No one wants you to go."

Behind him I see an arrival shuffle by. He is a junior-executive type in a mediocre suit that's trying hard to look pricey. He has an overpolished tie clip and a newscaster haircut and he looks dejected and tired, dragging his carry-on behind him. Suddenly someone cries out from the automatic doors and the guy snaps to attention, drops his bag, and sprints toward a tall woman in a sailorish sweater with her hair up in a red UM cap.

"Please stay," Press says.

It is mesmerizing. I cannot take my eyes off them.

"Hey, maybe I was wrong," Press says. "Maybe Dex *was* wearing flip-flops."

They close in on each other in a beeline valence of pure joy.

"Stay for me," he says. "Come on, Bosco. Stay for me."

When they meet and embrace I feel it like a shock wave passing through my body.

· · ·

In my window seat, looking down on the terrain below, trying unsuccessfully to discern the plane's shadow and, somewhere toward the stern, melonlike, the dark outline of my own head bending protectively over another scotch, I try to ignore the growing resentment I feel over the impromptu shogunate of happy travelers forming around me: loved ones dispensing private divertissements or endearments to each other, strangers extending hands and embellished representative autobiographies. A woman dressed in a sweater of bright primary colors reticulate with tracery that suggests doilies ("She knows the softer side of Sears," Rodney would say) titters nervously at me.

"Are you all right?" she asks, using her body to shield her daughter from me, a gesture provoked, I realize, by my gnawing desperately on the knife-edge of my hand.

The daughter says something under her breath. It sounds a lot like "Tard."

"I must have done it myself," I tell the mother miserably.

The daughter starts reciting a singsongy chant under her breath. I am nearly positive it is "Retardation is sweeping the nation."

"What did you do?" says the mother. She is trying to be kind but I am making her uncomfortable. She hadn't counted on sitting next to a muttering, hand-chewing madman.

My fingers make a helpless crabbed gesture that is meant to indicate the act of writing. I feel my face contort with grief.

"I must have written 'Dexter' on the heel myself." I am almost pleading with her. "But I can't remember it. What the fuck is wrong with me?"

Suddenly the woman pantomimes a genteel expression of surprise: she misread her ticket. She is in the wrong seat. Silly me, she says. Oh dear. Please do excuse us. Hurriedly she gathers her things, keeping an eye on me the whole time, but smiling ingratiatingly as if she wants to make sure not to en-rage me. As they go, the daughter waves her hand flipperlike before her and enunciates quite clearly.

"Spaz," she says.

I bite the knife-edge of my hand until the pain almost makes me pass out.

Inventory

I was wrong about Press's first drink, the flask, the provenance of our oldest bragging ritual.

Dex's casket was never open. Press never peered into it courageously.

For nearly thirty years I have hated—have had nightmar-ish semi-near-death hallucinations about—the wrong bird. The oriole! The humble oriole! Who can hate the oriole, for God's sake?

And my prized possession, my most enduring talisman of love, of memory, is false. I've been loving some other kid's goddamn flip-flop. I had the worst argument I've ever had with Hahva over that flip-flop. I said the cruelest things I've ever said to her because of that flip-flop. And then I sent her away.

What is wrong with me? My idea of revenge is sabotaging a collectible car and killing innocent flowers. My role model for personal courage is a book about a guy and a lion. After two decades of dedicating myself to the Great Plan I started bragging again because no one has sat on a punching bag in years. I sent away the woman I love because of some meaningless footwear. And then I did what I did with Robbie.

It is all just hilarious and tragic and stupid.

Could I be any dumber?

Could it be any more pointless?

To my list of the unbearable subtractions of my life—my future as a pianist, I think, Leon Flanders, my career in academia, Hahva—I now must add everything I've ever thought I knew about Dexter. The truth is, I never had any real memories. They were all made up. They never belonged to me in the first place. But still I feel an eviscerating loss. It's like the past thirty years of my life never happened.

Correction: it's like they've been taken away from me.

What do I have left?

Hell in Gasoline Bloomers 2: Back in Georgia

Word is that the surface of the bar of the Manhattan is made of planks from old-time ships off which the condemned stepped into deadly waters. Seven vessels furnished them—seven ships, seven planks, innumerable mutineers, and me. I can feel their footsteps in my forearms and hear the sound of their splash in my tumbler. The drowned are speaking to me, and they are saying, *Drinking broke your father, Jackson, and you are your father's son. Drink it in.*

And I do.

I like this bar. It is punitive and unconcerned with you. It doesn't have the tumult and stench of glandular fervor that the Terrapin has. There is a routinized sadness to the drinkers here. People bring their tumblers to their mouths with panda slowness. They slug from stool to toilet. They disappear into the meady shadows of corner banquettes and bathroom stalls and the phone booth out back. The Manhattan has eternity on its side. It can outwait you. It knows you're not going anywhere.

I spend my days and nights here, counting the Saturnian rings I make on the planks with the spillage from my glasses, listening to the words of mutineers—*you are your father's son,* they say—until I slip under the waves.

.   .   .

My contracts for fall term are not in my stopped mail pile at the post office, nor do they appear in my box, and I do not bother calling the English department. When I don't pay the bill my cell phone dies. E-mail keeps arriving from my brother—incredibly, I receive three from Robbie—but I never get past the subject lines. I just delete them and block the sender. Letters in my mother's handwriting appear in my box; I write "Not at this address" and put them back. McGurk keeps stopping by the apartment but I refuse to open the door. "Come on, Jack. I know you're in there!" he cries, pounding on the door. "I see the phone books on the stairs!" I burrow deeper into the love seat and pick out new constellations in the nails overhead: lions, women, a piano, a gun, flip-flops, an infinitesimal engagement ring.

It's like the big Pain Box in the sky.

.   .   .

After only a handful of days—how many has it been?—my actions have acquired the authority of regular devotion. Here I am again today among the splintered, broken Manhattanites. Around me incurious off-shift busboys and on-call barbers bend scarecrow heads over their glasses. Hahva, I think, is less than a mile away right now, at the Ark, working with people who need her, helping them, helping Rodney, while simultaneously no doubt trying to keep it on the good foot.

"Hahva means love," I say to the mutineers.

My fellow drinkers are attuned and they sense it when my brother enters their space. So do I. He sits down next to me while outside a Harley cruises by, trailing crackling notes of brassy flatulence. Silently Chuck sets up another round of Bushmills.

"You're a hard man to reach," Press says. "Phone's out of service. You don't reply to e-mails. We've been searching for you like crazy."

I let the cloacal barroom fog rise up between us.

"Nice place," he tries again.

Press looks different in the mirror. He has been streamlined, rejuvenated. The skin of his face has been pulled taut, his larynx cutting the air in front of him. He is no longer the swollen wizard of the bottle. Was he like this during those last days in Maryland? I don't know, but what is clear is that I have taken on the bloat of his old features—a pallid, swollen, macerated quality—and that my hair has attained an electrified action-figure appearance.

"You look well," he says.

"Excellent fettle, yes," I reply.

"What happened to your hands?" He points to them. The knife-edges are chewed up and raw.

"Vampires."

"Vampires?"

"I mean rats."

"Rats?"

"Lawnmower, I said." I hold out my hands mummy-style and make spasms to illustrate.

Press regards the ziggurat of upturned tumblers in front of me.

"You've done it already. At three in the afternoon," he says. "You've gone full Seuss. Impressive, I must say."

"We aims to please." With my wrist I indicate his whisky. "Bottle down. Stuff doesn't grow on trees et cetera et cetera."

"I'm all right." He motions to Chuck. "Ginger ale."

My mouth waters with disgust.

"What's with the newspaper bag?"

Since the English department has declined to renew my contract for the fall term I have been reduced to delivering phone books door-to-door again. Since the Omni is gone I have had to deliver the phone books on foot, toting a spine-cracking load of shrink-wrapped *White Pages* in this newspaper bag I bought off a paperboy for ten bucks. I can carry about a dozen at a time before going back home for a refill. It's not a good time. Making rounds yesterday, for example, I encountered a band of students whose number included a frat guy to whom I once assigned a poor grade. Now he had his chance, six months later, to exact some payback, which he extracted with clever fraternity-style irony. "Nice work, Professor Tennant! I give you an A for delivery!" he cried with his cronies. Then, as they passed by me in a hulking German SUV painted university colors whose cost, I know very well, far exceeded the total pretax income of my entire three years of teaching, I was sprayed with all the saliva that three healthy, young, hydrated, sharpshooting mouths can produce. A drive-by spittling.

In a way, I have to admire the gesture. This ex-student had taken a commendable opportunity to evoke clearly for me just how academic my career in academia really is.

But that didn't hurt as bad as when one of my all-time favorite students—a shy Punjabi girl who cried over nearly every Chekhov story we read—opened her door right as I was ungently depositing a phone book on her doorstep. She looked at me, pleasantly startled at first, then baffled at the sight of her old prof so heavily laden and bending so low, then genuinely mortified. She pitied me but also looked betrayed and let down, as if she had spotted Santa Claus moonlighting as a mattress salesman.

"How could you?" her expression said. "What has happened to you?"

It's a good question.

"It looks sharp," I say finally to Press. "Chicks dig it."

A belch escapes me, filling the air with hot lactic particles.

"Dad wants you to have this," he says, placing a manila envelope on the bar. "He wanted to give it to you himself, but he's not ready for travel. Not yet, anyway."

"I don't want it," I say, pushing it back along the planks.

"He made me swear I'd make you read it."

"I'm not interested."

Press looks momentarily confused. He is trying to figure out how to say what is too hard to say.

"I want to tell you something," he says. "I lied to you that night we played Diceman. I didn't come back from California because of free brag."

Press fingers one of the tumblers. He picks it up and brings it eye level, handling it with papal solemnity.

"That night at Lake George," he says. "That night Dex and I were supposed to do a jigsaw puzzle together. I didn't want to.

I mean, we were at the lake, you know? I wanted to do something fun. Out the screen door I could see fireflies were just coming out. I thought they were so cool. Fucking fireflies, man," he says, suddenly unable to look at me in the barroom mirror. "When I think about it now it makes me sick. A jar of insects, Jack. Fucking bugs. I mean, *bugs* . . . Sorry. Wait. Hang on a sec."

Press takes a moment to pull back. He keeps staring down that tumbler.

"Dex wanted to do the puzzle but I taunted him. Told him he never wanted to do anything fun. That he was a sissy. I told him that I was sick of board games and indoor shit. I was going to have some fun, I said. Good for me. So I left him in the house and went outside with a jar and hunted around in the woods.

"I don't know how long it was. Half hour? Hour? I don't know. I was deep in the woods, counting all the fireflies I'd caught, admiring my collection, and all of a sudden the jar I'm looking at turns blue. Then it turns red. Blue and red, flashing. At first I don't get it. The sirens weren't on, just the lights. For a second it looked like a UFO landing through the trees. Then I saw the cars and vans. I thought it was cool. I had no idea they were for us. I just thought cop cars and ambulances were exciting. I ran after them. I wanted to see what was up. Even when they pulled in the driveway of our cabin I didn't really think anything was wrong. It just seemed like an adventure. It wasn't until I followed them down to the dock and saw Mom crying that I understood that something bad had happened. And I kept thinking: if I hadn't left Dex alone it wouldn't have happened."

Press brings the glass to his nose and inhales deeply, eyes closed.

"Ten years after that I went to California and I loved it. Man did I love it. It was so beautiful. The ocean was beautiful, the mountains were beautiful, the people were beautiful. The school was great. Everything was different there. It smelled different. The sunlight was different. I can't explain it. I saw things stretching out in front of me. I felt free. Then one night, maybe like the third week there, the dorm had a party for the freshmen. A mixer kind of thing. Cookout in the park. Volleyball. The RAs had us do these dumb drills. We all had to take off one shoe and throw it into a big pile. Everyone had to pick up a strange shoe and find its owner. An icebreaker thing. I wanted to talk to a girl. I picked up a pink Puma. I found her. She was really pretty. I was so excited. I mean, I was at a new school, sleeping in a dorm, three thousand miles from that fucking house in Huntfield. And I was talking to this beautiful California girl.

"I'll remember this moment forever. It felt like anything could happen for me. Then she says, 'Hey, you already have a friend.' She pointed to my shoulder. There was a firefly on my shirt, glowing at me. I felt something clamp down in my gut. I got this sickening taste in my mouth. I left the party and went back to the dorm. I packed up my stuff and the next morning I was on a flight back home. The whole way I was thinking about Dex, and about you. I kept thinking about what it was like back at this fucking house. And that you were alone there."

My brother's eyes zee frantically around the room as if searching for a useful tool, something that can save him. He grimaces as if he has just committed a galling disetiquette. The hand holding the tumbler shakes.

"I lost one brother because I didn't stay there with him," he finally says. "I wasn't going to lose you, too."

Press stiff-arms the tumbler across the bar. He embarks on another monologue about the perils of us Tennants drinking—he doesn't want to lose me now, either—but when he sees my expression, the speech trails away, *diluendo*.

After a long minute when I don't say anything he produces my forlorn, glued-up flip-flop out of his pocket and pushes it across the bar to me. It once looked wounded and ailing but now it just looks inert. Lifeless. It's over for that thing. The magic's gone.

It's just some kid's beat-up old flip-flop.

"You left this behind," he says tenderly. "I thought maybe you'd still want it."

I down the Bushmills and feel the gassy disassembly in my stomach. After hours of work my gut is shifting now, becoming tidal. I push the flip-flop back along the bar and stand up from my stool.

"Chuck," I say, "this is on my brother."

"Jack, hang on," he calls out after me, waving the envelope. "There's more!"

Tilting like a chloroformed tiger cub, I lurch out the door and into the unbearable light of the Georgia summertime afternoon.

· · ·

That night my brother finds me wandering around the halls of the English department. He trails me around from floor to floor, speaking words to me. It's useless to try to lose him. I have been reduced to a snowshoer's gait, taking one ponderous step at a time. I use the walls as a guide and take corners wide. My mouth is dehydrated and gessoed with dry spit; it hurts to open it, so I don't bother.

The index card that used to hang on 133B that read JACKSON TENNANT, ADJUNCT PROFESSOR OF ENGLISH AND LITERATURE has been removed. There is not even a shred of the Scotch tape that held it up. My mailbox now belongs to an H. Sawyers, better known as the Philosoraptor. And in my old classroom the chairs have been rearranged into rows. No more the egalitarian circle.

Who will take care of my students now?

Arrivals/Departures

The next morning my brother is still trying. He tracks me to the local airport and finds me in a seat looking out onto the eroded tarmac. The airport is a disappointment in ways other than merely being easily locatable for out-of-towners even when their brothers tiptoe over them sleeping in the hallway and walk the five miles to the terminal while staying low and zigzagging from groundcover to groundcover. The waiting area has a disconsolate Aeroflotian feel—plastic seating eroded to a shine by decades of shifting buttocks, a vending machine offering glossy sandwiches embalmed with undisclosed preservatives, exhausted indoor-outdoor carpeting—and it features a hand-updated analog Arrivals/Departures sign that indicates the next flight won't be due for four and a half hours.

I try to will an unfordable barrier of silence between my brother and me but it does not work.

"Ambush!" I hear whispered behind me. "Ha ha."

He makes a second effort.

"You know what?" he says, sitting down. "Things are different. I don't know how it happened. Maybe it was you. Maybe it was when Dad almost got hit by that truck. Maybe it was Bess."

"Bess?" I say, amazed. What has happened to my brother?

Press shrugs. "We've been talking a lot. I wasn't exactly right about her one hundred percent."

"Yeah?"

"Yeah. I'm beginning to think that I haven't been one hundred percent right about a lot of things."

"You serious about not drinking?"

"Ten days."

When I say nothing he starts talking again. Effervescing, really. He is agitated in a way I haven't seen before, not since he was a kid. Pre-brag. He is distracted, puckish, gesturing wildly with his hands. His legs pump back and forth on the seat like a pair of bellows, nudging to the floor an excavated Hot Pocket that had been rubberizing on the seat and which I had seriously contemplated scavenging.

"Want to hear something crazy?"

"Sure. There seems to be a real shortage of crazy lately. Why not."

"You won't believe it, but things have been changing with Dad. We talk now. It's not his voice, you know, it's the robot, but in a way that makes it easier. You have to be careful picking your words because it takes so long for him to respond. He has to pick out each letter. It makes you really have to listen to him."

"Neat," I say.

"I'm moving out of the basement. Yeah. I got an apartment in Fell's Point. It's not much. Just a one-bedroom, but it's nice. Hardwood floors, nice appliances, central A/C. And it's aboveground. That's refreshing. I have windows that don't open onto turf. Not to mention old Robbie doesn't know where it is. Know what else? I enrolled for a few classes this fall at State. Figure I might as well finish what I started in Cali. It'll just be part-time, though, because I'm starting to work nights at Cloudsplitter. Don't roll your eyes. It's true. I'll be a card-carrying member of the manual laboriat soon. I'll toil. How, you ask? We talked and Dad e-mailed on my behalf and presto, a job materializes. I know, I know. Why aren't I puking my brains out on this pukey carpeting right now telling you this? That I accepted a favor from Dad? I don't know, Jacko, I don't know. I should, I'll grant you that. But I'm not."

Press has the attitude of a thrilled Darwin making important, schema-shattering discoveries.

"You know what else? I still help out at the house, but I don't feel wumpy about anything. I douche up the joint real nice a couple of times a week. Give it the business with the old Swiffer and sponge. All while Mom is getting lax about cleaning. The woman who once connipted and spat acid if a mote of dust besmirched her floor is now up to her elbows in gook as she takes care of Dad. And it's manual care I'm talking, Jack. It's like she's a losing contestant on a Nickelodeon game show, she's so continually covered in stuff. And she just doesn't care!

"I tell you. Up is down, down is up. It's like the earth's magnetic core has reversed polarization, or my zodiac has gone crackers and flipped its atomic charge and started orbiting Pluto or something.

"Dad paid off Musser, so I'm in the clear. I'm on a schedule to pay him back with money out of my Cloudsplitter paycheck every week. So it's square. And Dad—Dad, it's crazy, Jack. Dad just keeps getting better. Bess says she's never seen anything like it. It's his motivation, she says. Changing his mind, making new neural pathways or whatever. Just by willing it. That's how the Dynovox alarm rang that night."

"How's that?"

"Motivation. You know when we hit him with the Jesus ball? It humiliated him and so made him want to move to catch it? Or when he squeezed Ducky for the first time when he was listening to Olivia playing your song? What was it?"

"*Pathétique* Sonata."

"Right. Same thing here. He was so moved by that song—your favorite—that he squeezed Ducky. That other night, he saw the gun and was intensely motivated to move his arm."

"The Dynovox was at least a foot away from his hand. I put it there on purpose."

"I know. And he moved his whole arm to get it. How's that for a feat?"

"There's no way he moved his whole arm all that way."

"He'll be saluting again in no time."

"No way."

"Yes way."

"He broke his paralysis? To . . ."

"Yeah," Press says, saving me the embarrassment of verbalizing my near-suicide.

"I find this hard to believe, Press."

"I know. That's why I brought this."

The Fourteenth Letter

The envelope is addressed in a scrawl that is chaotic and glyphic to the point of illegibility. Then I realize that I am witnessing the propinquity of the words "Dear" and "Jack" in my father's penmanship.

"Dad wrote me a letter?"

"It's sort of from all of us. But Dad insisted on writing it."

"This must be ten pages," I say to Press. "How did he type this?"

"On the Dynovox's word processor, one agonizing character at a time," my brother says, making a ponderous tapping gesture with his pointer.

As I unfold the pages, and my eyes skate over the lines that my father's highly motivated finger has keyed in, it all blizzards around me. It's too much. I just sit in my seat, inhaling the pepperonine odor of expired Hot Pocket, staring dumbly between my brother and the letter, stunned with Kafka-like disbelief at the very first page.

It can't be true.

"But Dad always drank."

"Not then. Not while Dex was alive," Press says. "He didn't start until after. I didn't totally believe it either until I heard it confirmed by that Laindon guy."

Franklin Laindon: he tried to tell me that day at the steeplechase.

"But I remember the smell of scotch on his breath."

"Not that night."

"But he drinks every damn day of his life. Six o'clock on the dot."

"Right. The same time of day that we lost Dex."

"What does that mean?"

"We didn't lose Dex because he was drunk, Jack. He started drinking because we lost Dex. Every day when the sun goes down he is reminded about it. Even though it wasn't his fault."

"But it was his fault. Even if he wasn't drunk. Dex was only six years old. Dad was supposed to be watching him. You can't just not watch a six-year-old when you are supposed to be watching him."

Press makes a pensive rubbing movement on his jaw like someone in a shaving cream commercial.

"That's not entirely true. See, the reason I never told you about why I came home from California is because I felt like it was *my* fault. 'If I had done the jigsaw puzzle Dex never would have gone down to the lake by himself in the first place.' God. I thought that for nearly thirty years. But I was wrong. And so are you."

"What do you mean?"

"You thought Dad was supposed to be watching Dex. The truth is that Dad was outside chopping up some wood for the fire." Press exhales hard. "*Mom* was supposed to be watching us. She was making dinner in the kitchen and we were playing in the dining room. She was having a glass of wine with dinner—"

"Mom doesn't drink."

"Not now she doesn't . . ."

"I can't believe it."

"Maybe," Press says, "maybe you should just read the rest of the letter."

* * *

Dad was out front chopping wood. Press was teasing Dex about the jigsaw puzzle and trying to convince him to come outside. I was playing with my *Battle of the Planets* action figures in the living room. Mom was making dinner in the kitchen and drinking some wine.

Not a lot, just a glass. Two tops. Two and a half, absolute max.

Press was driving her crazy. He wouldn't leave Dex alone. He wanted to go outside; couldn't Dex see the fireflies were coming out? But it was starting to rain, and Dex didn't want to. Dex lobbied for the puzzle. They were going on and on and on. Finally Mom made an executive decision: Press was to go outside and give her some peace. Dex was to stay indoors and do the puzzle.

But it wasn't long until Dex got lonely for Press. He wanted to do the puzzle together. He kept complaining to Mom about it. He started bugging her to do the puzzle with him. He was driving her nuts, and she might have had an extra glass of wine. Just to calm her nerves. Finally, though, she snapped. She told him to go play by himself in his room, more angrily than she meant. She was just so tired, and it came out more scolding than it was supposed to.

Dex went into his room, but came back out minutes later. He stood there in the living room, defiant and pouty. He just stared at Mom as she worked at the stove. He said something to her—some protest, she thought—but she couldn't hear it because the grease was popping so loudly in the skillet.

This is one of the greatest sadnesses of my mother's life, the letter says. She will never know what Dex said to her with his last words.

And she was so frazzled—maybe even slightly drunk—that she didn't ask what he had said.

She ignored him.

In fact, when she looked up next from the chicken sizzling in the pan she was relieved to see only me buzzing 7-Zark-7 with the Fiery Phoenix. A little while later she saw my father sprint past the window, around the back of the cabin, down the hill leading to the water, and out the length of the dock, pausing briefly at the end. She saw him cock his head to the side as if listening for something, strip off his shirt and pants, and leap into the water. Then she heard my father calling out Dex's name.

She called 911.

By then the rain had picked up. Visibility was poor and the water was getting dangerously choppy. But through the rain and the waves my father thought he could hear Dex's voice calling out from somewhere far away from shore. He was sure of it. He swam through the murky water toward the area where he had heard Dex and then dived down and struggled back up to the surface. He kept on casting about, calling and listening for the voice, diving down again.

But the lake was too wild, and my father hadn't treaded water in years. He was out of swim-shape. He kept swimming to where he had heard the voice last. But it seemed like it kept changing locations. He couldn't get there fast enough. When he did get to the spot where he had heard the voice it was suddenly coming from somewhere else. A hundred meters to the left. Fifty meters to the right. Just over that wave directly ahead. Right behind him, practically at his back. It kept moving on him, evading him. He tried to approximate Dex's location from the wind and the waves, but he couldn't get it right.

And he was exhausted. He no longer had the breath to dive. He was just churning his legs, trying to stay afloat. It began to occur to him that maybe he hadn't heard the voice at all. He had seen Dex struggling in the water—already pretty far out—while he was chopping firewood on the hill, but by the time he had run around the house and down the dock he had lost sight of his son. Maybe he never really heard Dex cry out in the first place, he began to think; maybe he had just wanted to.

My father started to feel weak and tired. It became tougher to keep his head up. Then, just as he was taking grim account of how much strength he had left and his distance from shore, he was plucked from the water by a rescue boat and returned shamefully to the dock.

I couldn't save Dex, my father says. I couldn't even save myself.

Neuroplasticity 2.1

My father tried to save Dex, I think. He tried to save me, too. He tried so hard that he broke his apraxia. He instantaneously created a new neural pathway to command his paralyzed arm to move. A direct order issued from his locked-in brain to his body.

In pitch-perfect, clarion tone I can hear Bess's Styrofoam squeak: to save his son he had to change, in an instant, *lite*rally into a bio*log*ically new human being.

In my own skull I feel a powerful, deep-sea atmospheric crush of love.

Neuroplasticity 2.2

"I never thought I'd say this," Press says. "But imagine what it has been like for Mom and Dad. Dad, the big Marine; he should be able to swim like a seal. But he couldn't swim far enough or fast enough to get to Dex. He was supposed to be so strong, but he couldn't get there. Couldn't even swim back home.

"And Mom. I never knew this—I have no memory of her drinking, either, Jack—but all these years Mom has never been able to forgive herself for having that wine. Maybe if she wasn't drinking she would have seen it. Maybe she would have recognized how upset Dex was. She wouldn't have ignored him when he said whatever he said. Imagine the guilt. For both of them."

Everyone has their What Ifs, I realize. Why hadn't this occurred to me before?

"Why did Dad let us blame him all this time?"

"Well, like all of us, he felt that it was his fault. He should have been able to find Dex. But also he didn't want us to blame Mom. He was trying to protect her."

Press shrugs.

"After that night Mom swore off alcohol entirely. And that's when she started to become so obsessive. She felt like Dex died because she was out of control. She never wanted to be out of control again. She wanted things to be safe. To be safe, everything had to be perfect."

"Why didn't Mom ever say anything about how it really happened?"

Press shrugs again.

"Guilt, I guess. Same as all of us. Maybe she just didn't want to think about it. Maybe she just couldn't. What would she say, anyway? 'Sorry I killed your brother, Jackie. I'll never drink again but your father will be driven to drink until it nearly kills him.' "

"But it wasn't really her fault either," I say.

"Bingo."

"This is crazy," I say. "It's too much."

"I know. But it's true."

It takes me a few minutes to process, but then I realize something. The night my father broke my finger, I was accusing him of killing a son he had nearly died trying to save. I was endangering my mother's secret, a burden that would, together with grief for Dex, cause my father eventually to drink himself into a coma. Suddenly that night seems dramatically different. It was awful, no doubt. Violent and ruinous, no question.

But not mysterious. Not anymore.

Not hateful.

And the years of silence make sense, too. Press never told me because he thought it was his fault. Dad never talked about it because he didn't want us to find out about Mom drinking. And Mom never said a word because she just couldn't.

It comes like a comet burning in me: All this time my father hasn't been loved the way he deserves, either.

Postscript

At the end of the letter my father's highly motivated hand has signed his own name. Underneath that he has written something else in the same nearly occult script. It takes me a long time to decipher it. The handwriting is wild and knotted with many intercrossing lines and tangles. It looks like a clot of inky blue hair. At first I think I must have it wrong. But I don't. It says what I think it says in all caps, like something written by one of my first-term comp students:

"FORGIVE?"

The hole starts to fill up.

Yes, But

To keep the tears from spilling out of my eyes in front of my brother I have to tilt my head up and act fascinated with the unchanging Arrivals/Departures sign hanging above us.

"Hey," my brother says. "You expecting someone? There's no one here but us, Jack."

Sniffle, sniffle, I go.

It doesn't make sense—Dex is still dead; I have still been denied a lifetime of knowledge—but I feel like my whole life has just been saved in an instant. I feel so different. Stripped down but exultant, scoured and energized, overcarbonated and delirious and pixillated and have you ever noticed how big your lungs can get—how hot-air-balloon huge they can feel—just by breathing?

But just as fast, the feeling is gone when Press says, "I wonder what Hahva will say about all this."

Pain ricochets through me. I want to tell her—all of a sudden I am wildly ready to talk about Dex and everything else; I feel like a punctured dam, building to bursting, I am so ready—but I can't. I've ruined it with her. I can't tell her about Dex. I can't even say syllable number one to her, not after what I have done.

"What's wrong?" Press says. "I thought this would make you . . . well, not so sad looking."

"I can't tell Hahva."

"Why not?"

"I just can't."

"Why?"

"I did something with Robbie. I didn't tell you. I couldn't. But . . ."

"Oh. That," he says, making a dismissive shoofly wave. "Never happened."

"What?"

"Never happened. Didn't do it."

"What do you mean, didn't do it? I know very fucking well I did it. I can't stop thinking about it."

"And what do you think of when you think about it? What is your memory of it, specifically?"

"I remember being in the basement with Robbie."

"Go on."

"You were passed out."

"Yep."

"Do I have to say this?"

"I'm interested. Keep going."

"Her clothes were off. My clothes were off. She kissed me. God."

"O.K."

"She was touching me."

"All right. Then what?"

"Then we had sex."

"Really? How?"

"What do you mean, how? The usual way."

"You fuck her proper Christian? Posteriorly? Plumber style?"

"Oh God. Don't say it like that."

"Well, which is it?"

"I don't remember. I just know it happened."

"Did you use a condom?"

"No . . ."

"Then where did the evidence go?"

"Press, what are you doing?"

"It never happened, little brother. Robbie made an attempt. No doubt about that. But nothing more happened. Robbie told me so after you left. She said you were so 'firsty' that you became 'infunctional.' You kept saying something about the 'veto power of the Ass President.' What the hell does that mean?"

"It didn't happen?"

"You could have spared yourself some grief if you'd read your e-mails from your big brother. I told Robbie to e-mail you, too. Did she ever do it?"

"Are you fucking with me?"

"Nope," my brother says happily. "Your maidenhead is safe. Your ass saved by the Ass President."

"Honest?"

"Maybe conscience helped," he concedes. "Maybe love. Who knows. Point is, you didn't go through with it. You were out of commission."

"I didn't have sex with Robbie?"

"Have you been following this conversation?"

"Are you telling the truth?"

"When have I ever lied to you?"

I eyeball Press. He exteriorizes all honesty.

"Well, I'm not lying now, O.K.?"

"Swear it."

"I swear," he says, looking around, injured and incredulous, as if appealing to an invisible jury of his peers.

"Swear it on the memory of your Toaster Tank."

"Jesus. I swear it on the memory of my Toaster Tank. Satisfied?"

"Holy shit," I say, seeing my future spreading before me like an opening fan. "I never fucked her."

"Nope," he says. "Not even close, apparently."

"I never fucked her."

"I believe we've been over this."

"There's no reason I can't go to Hahva. There's nothing in my way."

"Just seven miles of back roads."

I start rifling through my pockets.

"Shit shit shit."

"What is it now?"

"Do you have your cell?"

"Sure. What for?"

"I need to call for a cab."

"No you don't."

Press stands me up, faces me toward the glass, and makes an abracadabran gesture with his fingers. Out the window, crouching on the asphalt of the empty parking lot, its metal shining and pearlescent in the Georgia summertime sun, is the E-Type.

"Dad wants you to have this."

Joyride

Finally it is my turn under the Arrivals/Departures sign. Joyously I cling to my brother. My fingers dig into his shoulders. His hair gets in my eyes. I transfer some moisture to the skin of his neck. Over his shoulder the E-Type is barely visible. Hunkering in its space it is expectant, vitalized, race-ready. It looks as if it's been waiting for me all this time.

My heart unfists.

I keep thinking: I haven't done anything unforgivable. It's not too late for me. I still have a chance.

"The engine needed a little, ahem, tune-up," Press says into my scalp. "It seemed that some fertilizer had drifted in there somehow. Evil barn fairies, no doubt. But we trailered it over to Foxhall Farms and the trusty Franklin Laindon flushed it for us. Funny old coot. But I like him. He's always there for us, isn't he?"

When I take off through the doors running Press calls after me, "Hang on! You'll need a key!"

"Got one!" I yell back, feeling the metal blazing in my pocket.

I slide the key into the ignition but don't have the courage to turn it.

"It's an older car," Press says when he catches up and eases into the passenger seat. "You have to actually turn the key to start it. Like this. It's all in the wrist. See?"

I do.

For the first time in my life I use my hoarded key to start the E-Type. The engine roars to life. Even idling the vibrations are guttural and lionlike but when I put it in gear and gas it, the notes turn into a thrumming powerband that you can feel deep inside your stomach and spine. It produces the same feeling as the Bösendorfer. The sound doesn't seem to be coming from inside the engine. It seems to be coming from inside my own body.

Even with the top down, I feel encased by my father's history, but it doesn't hurt. At the next stoplight when I have to adjust the seat and mirror to accommodate my smaller frame and shorter reach it doesn't seem like an insult. The wind strafing my hair doesn't bother me, even though the front now looks like a bean-sprouty effusion. I am not afraid of taking corners hard on the antique bias-ply tires, either, nor am I reluctant to get on the gas. It's remarkable how supple and responsive this Jaguar is. It's as if it knows what I want to do before I do it. And driving it makes me feel like I'm someone else, too. Someone braver and smarter and capable—elect. I feel my father's ghost, his universe, moving through me.

I am my father's son.

Permission to Start Again?

When the E-Type pulls into the parking lot of the Ark some kids I've never seen before are chucking a basketball at the hoopless backboard. The kids stare as the E-Type growls past them and I back into a spot that is protected from poor rebounding by a U-Haul.

In the hallway, past the yellow line, I pull Press aside.

"I don't know how to do this. What do I say to her?"

While he thinks about it I can't help reading the Lost flyers taped to the concrete. PLEASE COME HOME, KITTER KITTY, reads one caption below a phone number and a Polaroid of a mangy Russian blue, WE MISS YOU. Another one says HAVE YOU SEEN MY POW-POW? and has scribbly tears drawn in under the name. BIG REWARD, it says, even though the handwriting makes clear that Pow-Pow's family's resources do not include big rewards. The signs make me want to find the lost pets, to save them all. I feel like I can.

Kitter Kitty, I want to say, your waiting is over! I'm taking you home!

Pow-Pow! I see you! Let me show you how to make a six-year-old happy!

"Beats me," he says at last. "What do I know about apologies?"

For some reason this makes me start laughing. It's not funny—I am not tickled—yet I giggle. Then it gives way to a cackle, then a guffaw, and when I try to stifle it I just make vacuum-cleaner noises. I feel charged and airy, walking in sponge cake shoes. I get a look at my reflection in the tinted glass and goggle owlishly at it. I am unshaven and my face is at once puffy and gouged with sleeplessness, but my eyes are alive.

"Yep," my brother assents. "You look like you've been shot out of the cannon once too often. But who cares? You've got work to do."

This produces more uproarious bronchial choking noises. I list badly to starboard and have to steady myself on my brother. My blowhole snorting has alerted some of the residents in the common area and a few curious heads bend around the corner.

"Jack!" says Fern.

"It's you!" exclaims Gail.

"He's back!" goes Miss D.

They rush to me, and just in time. I was momentarily thinking of Leon Flanders—I couldn't help it; with all this feeling of love he just popped in there—and I had started wobbling. A sensation of vertigo pulls at me and I feel dropped, and then, when they all come to me, I feel steadied and caught, like a trapeze artist clutched out of a midair tumble.

"Hey guys," I say happily, standing up on my own feet again. "Say hi to my brother, Press. Press, this is Gail, and Miss D, and Fern." My brother takes their hands and does a little caper. "Have any of you guys seen—"

Before I can finish my question I am interrupted by the sound of crashing boxes and familiar epithets. The only thing that is startling about this at the Ark is that the voice authoring the vitriol is baritone. It's a man, well past the yellow line, coming out of the women's quarters. When he shambles around the corner, dragging duct-taped garbage bags stuffed and punctured with folded clothes and hangers, Miss D runs to embrace him.

"Jack, this is Dukie, my son. He's helping me move out today. Dukie, this is Jack, the best night staff."

Miss D beams with pride. At first I am reluctant to shake Dukie's hand. He's done so much wrong to his mother, and the old indurate suspicion that the Ark has schooled into me surfaces again: he is only going to do it again. I've seen it a million times. They never change. Why is she setting herself up for heartbreak?

But when I see Miss D smiling so hard, and Dukie looking so happy, I believe.

"I told you he'd come back," she says.

"You sure did," I say, taking Dukie's hand. Then, as Gail and Fern and my brother start helping them with the garbage bags and boxes, I say, "Has anyone seen Hahva today?"

"She's in the office," says Gail. "Rodney's in there trying to get her to do James Brown again. But she won't. She hasn't done it in weeks, now that you mention it. What's been wrong with that girl?"

I push through the air toward the office. The tiles under my feet have never seemed more meaningful. Every step I take seems momentous. Through the door I can hear Rodney pleading. "Get up offa that thing!" he is singing. Then there is a long pause as he waits for Hahva to sing a line that never arrives. "And dance till you feel better!" he attempts. "Get up offa that thing . . . and try to relieve the pressure!"

Hahva says something but it is too quiet to make out.

I am about to knock on the door when I get an idea. Motioning Press, I weave through the peeling sofas and wade through the toy area to the spavined upright in the corner. Sitting down at the bench makes me nervous but when Press comes over behind me I feel the way I should have felt that day at Juilliard: hopeful and confident, as if I won't let anyone down.

I wait until I hear Rodney cry out another line—"I need some payback!"—and then I hit that riff hard on the keys. Everyone in the room—Press, Gail, Fern, Miss D, and Dukie—stops what they're doing and looks over.

There is momentary silence from the office and then Rodney tries another line. Again I jackhammer the riff that goes with it. Through the door comes another line and I play the chords to that one, too. There is another beat of silence, a re-orienting *lunga pausa*, into the mouth of which I start hammering out the rest of the song. The action on the upright is flaccid and the upweight is so flimsy it feels as if I'm rapping on balsa wood affixed to hamburger, but it's more or less in tune, and the concrete walls and drop ceiling throw the sound back at me hard, and I'm playing like I mean it.

It sounds good.

They all crowd around me—Gail, Fern, Miss D, Press too. Then other residents filter out of the computer room, the TV room, the kitchen. Rodney materializes from the cluster of bodies, his mouth gaping in astonishment. He looks small and quaint and kinetic, something you might find on the tongue of a cuckoo clock. He makes a move to hug me but then stops, afraid that it will screw up the song, then backs off.

I play the rest of "The Payback" flawlessly. My fingers are loose and articulate and unpremeditating. It is pure feeling. When I finish the song the room explodes in applause and laughter. Everyone mills around the piano. Rodney leaps onto the bench and hugs me.

It is possibly the best performance I've ever given.

"Superbad!" he says.

Then I see her. Hahva is standing in the middle of the room, under the air filter, arms crossed at her chest. For a long moment I say nothing. I want to make sure I encode this moment forever. I want to keep this memory of her perfect.

"Sorry if I interrupted your meeting," I say finally. "But it seemed like someone needed to turn on the funk motor."

It's a gamble, but a good one. I had to say *something*.

The silence as I wait is enormous and empty—interstellar—but my skin tingles with the mania of hope. I teeter a little on the bench, feeling a fireworky neural ignition in my head that makes my vision blur like a punch-drunk fighter. It produces three ghostlike Hahvas wavering before me, and I think one of them might be smiling.

The future fills up the air between us.

Epilogue: Neuroplasticity 3

Six months later: where to start?

There are still no overtures from the university. McGurk had told me of rumors that the department didn't have enough adjuncts to cover core—he had even heard my name mentioned favorably by the Philosoraptor—but the phone never rang. The Ark has upped my night staff schedule two shifts a week. That's not a lot of income, but now that Hahva and I are living together I can cover the rent.

Hahva and I still fight, but she has been bravely tidy around the apartment. She even cleaned out—excavated, with a rake and rubber gloves—her car about two months ago and so far the passenger seat has been more or less occupiable. And me, I never say a word about Hahva's Bo Dukey driving style. I spot her every time she does shoulder presses. I have dramatically reduced the frequency of sneering when we watch movies about loving and losing.

And I have told her everything about everything. I have told her about Dex. I have told her about the bragging, about where the quizzing came from, about cracking my tooth on the barrel of the beavertail. I even told her about Robbie. That wasn't easy.

Well, I did make one omission. Fine. I have technically lied to her about the Omni. She thinks the sale was in response to not getting any classes this fall. I couldn't tell her the truth yet because I couldn't bear to propose to her with the ring that I had. I pawned that thing for a fraction of what I paid for it—I will not reproduce the scoffing noise the guy made when he held the ring up to his eyepiece—and have started saving up for a new one. True, I'm out a car and a ring and have no real job and charcoal-grim professional prospects, but lately I've diagnosed myself as an Optimist with Enterprising subinfluences and I have a harebrained scheme to make the money I'll need to buy a worthwhile ring.

It's just crazy enough to work. More on that in a second.

Press doesn't especially like his job at Cloudsplitter, but he likes his classes at State, and he hasn't missed a day of work or an installment of repayment to Dad. As far as I know he hasn't had a single solitary brag even once in the last six months.

Mom has cut Bess's visits down to once a week. She handles almost all the therapy herself.

And Dad continues to get better, too. Bess took immense pleasure in wheeling him into Hopkins's neurology lab for a checkup recently. The doctor who gave him two weeks to live on the night of his stroke was there. He was dubious of my father's recovery and placed Ducky in Dad's hand to see if he could really squeeze out a quack.

The doc bent over him, inspector-close, and Dad hit him in the head with it. Hard.

The same doctor continues to put time frames on Dad's "end-of-life schedule" and he keeps living past them.

He is enjoying a semicelebrity, too. He has probably the most imaged brain stem on the eastern seaboard. Innumerable papers have been written on his unprecedented remapping. The docs and nurses and techs all hail him when he's rolling around neurology. "Hey Colonel," they say with a salute, which he is now fully able to return.

But not everything is great. I still have no future as a professor. Not even the local high schools want me. Not even as a sub. They want people who are younger, who have experience already with adolescents, who have degrees specifically geared to secondary schooling. And even though working two extra shifts a week as night staff doesn't endanger my spine and dramatically reduces my chances of being spat upon, it isn't exactly thrilling. Money is still tight. At one dark moment in December I nearly sold the E-Type because I couldn't afford insurance and gas. Hahva talked me out of it, though, so most of the time it just sits in the driveway, looking good.

My secret ring fund is only in the triple figures.

And still no one knows what happened exactly that night at Lake George. Was it an accident? Did Dex have some sadness in him that went unrecognized and unaided? Could it have been stopped? I don't know. We'll never know.

I'll never know what happened with Leon either. It's too late for me and Leon. It's too late for my career as a professor, too. It's too late for Dex.

But you know what?

It isn't too late for me and my father. I still have a chance with him. And I plan on making use of it. I plan on loving him exactly the way he deserves. Ditto Mom. And Press. And Rodney. And Hahva.

Sometimes it sneaks up on me, though. Sometimes I let myself start thinking about Leon. It's hard when someone you love thinks the worst possible thing about you.

On these days I try to delete Leon's phone number from my cell, but I never have the guts. A part of me still thinks he might call, and I want to be able to identify him. Pathetic but true.

I also can't help thinking about what could have been with Dex.

On these days I feel like an empty galaxy.

On these days I might—in private—have a little brag myself.

But I am still greedy to know about my brother. I am relentless, obsessed, voracious. I make Press talk about him all the time on the phone. Often I take notes.

Dex had the *Shazam!* theme on a looped tape that he played all day nonstop.

Dex could hold a grape in his mouth for hours without chewing it.

Dex thrilled at the smell of gasoline and Mom had to keep a sharp eye on him at the pump.

Dex would sit boddhisattva-like in front of the TV and when he heard a word he didn't know—if Honeycomb boasted that it had nine essential vitamins and minerals, for example—he would rock back and forth, holding his feet, and repeat it over and over: "Essential, essential, essential, essential."

Dex loved—I mean he went gaga for—oranges. This one is so perfect that a part of me is still unsure if he made it up, but Press alleges that I got the love of mandarins from him. In fact, Press says, that is where Dex's nickname originally came from. One day when Dex was peeling an orange, Press made up a joke.

"What did the orange say when he saw the lemon coming up the hill?"

"I don't know," said Dex.

"HELLO LEMON COMING UP THE HILL!" Press said. "What did the orange say when he saw the lemon going down the hill?"

"I give up."

"GOODBYE LEMON GOING DOWN THE HILL!" Press said. "What did the orange say when he saw the lemon going down the hill wearing sunglasses?"

"Goodbye lemon going down the hill wearing sunglasses?"

"No," Press said, acting disappointed in Dex's inability to grasp the obvious. "Sheesh. Orange said nothing. Lemon was wearing sunglasses—he couldn't recognize him."

Not that funny now, Press conceded to me, but when he told it Dex laughed and laughed and laughed. He laughed so much that Press started calling him Lemon. "Hello Lemon!" he would cry when he jumped on Dex's bed in the morning to wake him up. "Goodbye Lemon," he would say, waving mournfully when Mom dropped Dex off at kindergarten. Dex learned how to sign his name "Lemon." If you just said the word, he would roll around on the floor, clasping his feet in his hands, giggling with joy. A lot of the time he wouldn't even respond if you called him Dexter—he insisted on Lemon.

To Press, that's who he was. And when he died, Press couldn't bring himself to say the name. The name's secret was its power. Like my flip-flop.

It was after seeing me taking notes on the Lemon conversation that Hahva gave me the idea for the harebrained scheme.

"God," she said. "Look how much you've written down."

Casting about the apartment I realized she was right. There were Dex notes on napkins, printer paper, gum wrappers, title pages, magazine covers, ticket stubs, receipts, grocery bags, you name it.

It was nighttime when Hahva told me this. She was in bed. Wrapped up in our red blanket she looked like a bee in the petals of an Invincible.

"You've practically written a book."

Then, with an after-rain clarity, I saw it: write a book.

Is that what I've been doing?

It makes perfect sense. I have eaten of the tree of the knowledge of sad and stupid; what else can I do to atone?

Once I started it was hard to stop. Now I write nearly every day in the cramped apartment and every night at the noisy shelter. Hahva thinks it's great. It's a sign, she says, that the university didn't renew my contracts; fate is pushing me to write. How else would I have so much free time? She waxes semiclinical about the writing process, too. She thinks there is special meaning in the fact that I write with the *White Pages* sitting next to the laptop, but I don't think so. I don't flip through it. I don't invent stories from it. I don't need other names. I just like having it nearby. It helps make an empty room feel less empty. That's all.

On the other side of the laptop I put the injured orange flip-flop. Hahva has an incorrect theory about this, too. It's not there because it helps me access Dex memories. Or Dex imaginings. I just feel that even if it did belong to some other kid, it's not right to abandon it. Not after all we've been through together.

But Hahva *is* right about one thing.

About two weeks ago she shows up at the Ark looking guilty. Over the clatter of dominoes on the wintogreen table and a low-grade argument brewing in the kitchen over spatula rights, Hahva confesses that she read some of the manuscript. Not snooped, she maintains, as some pages were sitting out on the table in plain sight and she had mistaken them for a letter we were jointly writing to Mom and Dad, but just read. Scanned, more like. A few paragraphs. "Before I knew what I was doing." One page, two pages tops.

Something quantumish is going on in that book, she asserts. He's dead, sure. She knows that. And she knows that in a way the process of writing is a process of grieving, that I'm saying goodbye somehow, but it's also as if I am reviving him. It's like he's here, she says. In the room. It's like you're pulling Dexter out of the water with words.

And she's right. I am still trying to save his life.

I'm trying to save mine, too.

Acknowledgments

This book would not have been possible without the guidance and inspiration of Leena Sidhu.

Also due immeasurable gratitude and encomium are E. Beth Thomas, Patrick McCord, Bill Klein, Ron Sharp, The Glorious Kinklosity, R. Todd Giardinelli, Harry Houston Sawyers II, Jesse Sheidlower, Alexandria Morris, Kathleen Caldwell, Bill Augustin, CT Kriedel, Jay Young. The good people at Riverhead who boot glute on my behalf are Craig Burke, Rick Pascocello, Julia Fleischaker, David Moldawer, and Sheila Moody.

Special commendation to the Great and Inimitable Boz.

Perry and Myra Stevens spoke to me at length about locked-in syndrome, for which I will always be thankful, and honored.

Without the superheroics of my editors, Julie Grau and Megan Lynch, this book would still be in Hell in gasoline bloomers.

And profoundest thanks to my agents, Esther Newberg and Josie Freedman.